Complaint Letters

For Busy People

By

John Bear and Mariah Bear

1/2001

Career Pre

Copyright © 1999 by John Bear and Mariah Bear

COMPLAINT LETTERS FOR BUSY PEOPLE
Cover design by Foster & Foster
Typesetting by Eileen Munson
Printed in the U.S.A. by Book-mart Press

To order this title, please call toll-free 1-800-CAREER-1 (NJ and Canada: 201-848-0310) to order using VISA or MasterCard, or for further information on books from Career Press.

The Career Press, Inc., 3 Tice Road, PO Box 687, Franklin Lakes, NJ 07417

Library of Congress Cataloging-in-Publication Data

Bear, John, 1938-
    Complaint letters for busy people / John Bear, Mariah Bear.
        p.   cm.
    ISBN 1-56414-403-8
    1. Complaint letters.   2. Consumer complaints.   I. Bear, Mariah
P.   II. Title.
HF5415.52.B428   1999
381.3—dc21   99-21217
                                                       CIP

A couple of years ago, 18,000 feet up Tibet's holy Mt. Kailas, with a windchill factor of about four million below zero, somehow I lost my gloves. Fellow pilgrim Ted Hallstrom, far more prudent than I, loaned me a spare pair he had brought along. I told him that because I would now be able to type again, my next book would be dedicated to him. And here it is, and so it is. Thank you yet again, Ted.

John

Being unable to equal such a marvelous story, I'll not try. This book is dedicated to Joe. He's had every reason to complain any number of times, and has been remarkably restrained. Sorry about that latest concussion, dearest.

Mariah

Acknowledgments

❖

We would like to thank Dr. Marina Bear, wife of one author and mother of the other, who helped immeasurably in the processes of brainstorming, writing, rewriting, editing, and cooking wholesome dinners. We are most grateful to her, and to novelist Darryl Brock for introducing us to his agent Laurie Harper, and to her for introducing us to Career Press and Betsy Sheldon, the kind of editor that authors dream of, but rarely get to work with.

Thank you, all.

Contents

Preface

Your flight was overbooked. The dry cleaner ruined your best suit. The network canceled your favorite show. And your senator never votes the way you want. Do you shrug your shoulders and say, that's life? You shouldn't! It's surprisingly easy to get satisfaction, and overcome life's little—and not so little—inconveniences and setbacks. Sometimes all you need to do is to write the right letter to the right person, in the right way. This book will show you how.

I'm John Bear, and I don't like complaining. I want things to be done right the first time. But when they aren't, I don't want to have to make a second career out of trying to get satisfaction from some customer service department. I want to tell my story once, to the person with the power to correct the situation, and get on with my life. I have a Ph.D. in communications, and over the years I've learned a lot about how to find the right person to complain to and how to make that complaint clear and powerful enough to get results.

This book won't waste your time telling you things you already know about complaining. It will give you some ideas for attention-getting, creative solutions to dealing with those faceless consumer complaint departments, or that frustrating person behind the counter. It will reduce the amount of time and effort you need to put into complaining by making you a more effective complainer.

I started looking seriously at the art of writing complaint letters some years ago after the following saga: I had opened my gas credit card bill to find $400 worth of tires charged to me that I knew I hadn't bought. I did the usual stuff. I called the number on my bill to tell the company they'd made a mistake. "Write out your explanation and send it to us," they said. I did. I paid the bill, minus the tires, and hoped that was the end of it.

But the next month there were other service station charges on my bill that weren't mine. I wrote again. I telephoned. I kept getting different people telling me different things, and the charges kept piling up. Finally I lost patience. I went to the public library and found the name and home address of the president of the oil company and the next letter I wrote was addressed to his wife. The basic message was, "Your husband's company is driving me crazy. Please ask him to help me straighten this thing out."

Back came a letter from some presidential assistant. They discovered there were two John Bears in the same metropolitan area. They had given us both the same credit card number and their computer was randomly distributing our charges to either one of us. If he hadn't bought a set of tires on the card, we might have never noticed what was going on! But it took rattling the president's cage to get somebody with the brains and the authority to track the problem down.

And I'm Mariah Bear, co-author and eldest daughter of John Bear. Growing up with a world-famous (well, okay, semi-world-famous) complainer like my father, I learned early on that if you don't speak up, you don't get what you want. I also, thank heavens, learned that the best way to go about this sort of thing is by being pleasant, courteous, and businesslike.

My first big complaining coup came when I was a teenager, in my first year of college. Like any college student, my prime interest in life was upgrading my stereo system, and my parents were happy to indulge me, sending me a gift certificate from a major national electronics chain. Imagine my dismay when I went to cash in the certificate and was told by a man wearing a badge that said "I'm Bob and I mean Service" that because my parents had purchased it in Nashville and I was in Berkeley, it was invalid. "Surely there must be some mistake," I wailed. "The certificate says right here, 'Redeem at any Technology Hut'."

"At any Technology Hut in the area you purchased it in. How do I even know you didn't steal this?"

So, clearly, we were in the realm of silliness. I was being accused of stealing a gift certificate from a city 2,000 miles away, and driving across the country to try and buy a cheap pair of speakers. I tried to explain how silly this was to the clerk, and he started to get annoyed. I think that my blue hair and ripped jeans might have influenced his perception of me as a credit-card-toting potential repeat customer. I asked if I could speak to the manager. He told me he was the assistant manager, and that there was no manager. Things weren't getting any less silly.

I went home, researched the Hut's parent company and the name of that company's president, and wrote a letter saying, in part . . .

> "I am a college student in Berkeley, California. Recently, my parents sent me a gift certificate from Technology Hut as a birthday gift. I have been buying electronics from the Hut since high school, and have always been happy with your products and service. Today, however, I experienced something that makes me question whether I ever want to enter one of your stores again."

I went on to describe the situation. A week later, I received a very nice note from a customer service representative saying that of course Technology Hut will honor its own gift certificates, and sending me an additional certificate to compensate me for my troubles. I put on my very best Doc Martens, marched proudly in to assistant manager Bob's store, slapped down the letter and certificates, and left with a much better pair of speakers than I'd initially tried to purchase, partially paid for by Bob's company. He never said a word. I felt good.

I like to think that Bob saw the error of his ways, and started treating teenagers, even scruffy-looking ones in ripped jeans, like valued consumers. I also, of course, like to think about him herding penguins in Antarctica.

This early experience with consumer power has stayed with me. In the years since then, I've taken on a landlord who wouldn't fix my apartment (it's fixed), a towing company that caused $300 in damage to my car and then tried to blame me for it (I won), and a host of other daily indignities. You can do it, too—it's empowering, it's fun, and it's a lot easier than you probably think. Read on!

Who's Complaining?

Nancy and her husband bought a fairly expensive living room suite from a local outlet. Eighteen months later, when the usual warranties had expired, they began noticing little piles of sawdust on the floor and tiny holes in the wooden parts of the furniture. Their lovely furniture was infested with termites. The store denied any responsibility and because of the length of time they'd had the furniture, they were advised by a few people to give up hoping for satisfaction.

Nancy refused to give up. From the local university entomology department she leaned that the bugs in her table legs were well-known to be the kind that would have been in the wood for at least two years before they started boring their way out. In other words, they were stowaways from the Philippines, where the wood came from.

Armed with this information, and in a moment of inspired creativity, Nancy wrote to the U.S. Customs Service. Customs took the case on (The government doesn't like illegal insect aliens) and ended up nailing the furniture company for importing animals without a license! The furniture was declared illegal and the manufacturer had to make a full refund.

We keep hearing that we're living in a service economy, and in many ways that's true. But when you're not getting the service you need, it doesn't do you much good. Consumer attorneys point out that the so-called "consumer revolution" has made people aware of problems that have been around for a long time, but that much of the time, people still don't get satisfaction. "Very often consumers accept bad treatment as one of the inevitable frustrations of modern life," says Steven A. Newman, author of *Getting What you Deserve: A Handbook for the Assertive Consumer.* Very often, yes. But it doesn't have to be that way.

Attitude adjustment

You may feel uncomfortable complaining. You may wonder if you're being a jerk. Or you may think it's useless. That's just not true. If you aren't getting the service or product you purchased, you have a right to complain. The people who can make things right, whether it's the president of the appliance company or the clerk at your neighborhood hardware store, are not "doing you a favor" by listening to your complaint. They have an obligation to make things right, because in a very real way, they work for you.

The dry cleaner, the airline, the car dealership, the supermarket, even the politician and the TV network—they all work for you. Wherever and whenever people are doing things that make it necessary for you to complain, keep saying to yourself, "These people all work for me. They would be out of work if it were not for me. I will not let them push me around."

The people who run businesses and organizations are not stupid. They don't want trouble and they don't enjoy it, because they know trouble costs time and money. So in a rational world, they will avoid trouble by dealing responsibly with your complaint. Why don't they, then? Because ignoring people is so easy, especially if they don't squawk. So squawk, if necessary, to convince them that you're not going to go away until you are satisfied.

Your rights as a consumer

"People don't realize that being heard and expecting results are fundamental consumer rights." says Polly Baca, director of the U.S. Office of Consumer Affairs.

If George Washington had bought a non-functioning musket from a mail order house, or Ben Franklin had been forced to stand in line endlessly at his bank, we might well have found basic consumers' rights embedded in the Constitution along with bearing arms and pursuing happiness. Rights like these:

1. The right to complain and get satisfaction. A complaint is the organization's chance to make things right.

2. The right, after complaining, to hear "Yes," not, "We can't do that," or "I'll have to ask my manager." People who deal with the public need the power to solve problems now.

3. The right not to wait too long, whether the issue is getting a reply to a letter, being noticed in a store, standing on line, or being treated well on the telephone.

4. The right to have everyone and anyone in the business serve you. Sometimes presidents, vice presidents, and supervisors need to be reminded that without customers, there are no presidents, vice presidents, or supervisors.

Why people don't complain

The sad fact is that most people don't complain. Ever. In every study and survey on complaining, the findings in one key area are essentially the same: A great many people have something to complain about, and a very small percentage of them actually do anything about it.

Many of the organizations that compile and release complaint statistics report rising numbers as the public becomes more aware of consumer issues. Scott Paper received 1,000 complaint letters the year they established a consumer relations department. Ten years later, it was up to 70,000. General Foods gets more than 100,000 letters a year, and nearly 40 percent are complaints. Best Foods has several dozen people handling more than 60,000 letters each year, two thirds of them complaints. Scott lawn care received 200,000 letters one year, 30,000 of them complaints.

But the Federal Trade Commission has estimated that buyers in the U.S. are unhappy with 75 million purchases every year, from chewing gum to luxury cars and "as few as 4 percent ever complain."

One researcher asked consumers how they felt about various products they had purchased from a television shopping channel. The dissatisfaction levels were remarkably high for such items as "miracle" stain remover (48 percent were unhappy), a "permanently sharp" kitchen knife set (33 percent unhappy), and a treadmill exercise device (35 percent unhappy). Yet only 15 percent of the dissatisfied people took any action: 5 percent returned the goods for a refund, and 10 percent wrote a complaint letter but did not follow up. Another 10 percent of the unhappy people complained only to family or friends, and the vast majority, 75 percent, did nothing whatsoever.

When a state office of consumer affairs asked a large number of people about their complaining behavior, 95 percent said they had something to complain about, but fewer than 10 percent had actually complained.

Another university researcher discovered that 23 percent of the people in his survey had a complaint about their medical doctor. Of the people who were not satisfied or had a problem, only 11 percent complained to anyone, although many more than that either switched physicians or planned to do so.

In one large survey of the reasons people don't complain, nearly half said it was just too time-consuming, a quarter felt that nothing would ever come of it anyway, while the remaining quarter found the act of complaining personally unpleasant; they didn't know how or where to complain, they believed they had only themselves to blame for the problem, or they believed the dollar amount was too small or the problem was otherwise too trivial to bother about.

The cost-benefit model of complaining

"If my time is worth $12 an hour, and it will take two hours to complain about this defective $9 clock..."

Complaining can be a costly activity in terms of time, money, and other factors. A full-fledged complaint effort might involve time off from work, travel, telephone calls, postage, and paying for third-party advice and professional help. If the main reason for complaining is reimbursement, not revenge, personal satisfaction, or other factors, then it makes sense for some people to sit down for a few minutes with calculator in hand, and treat the launching of a complaint as a small business venture. What is it likely to cost, and what am I likely to get.

Janna bought a small tape player for $30 from a store near her workplace. It was one of those shops with a window crammed with electronic gadgets. Everything in the window had a sign claiming the price was 20 percent, or 30 percent, or 70 percent less than "list price." After a week, the "pause" button on Janna's tape player stopped working. Janna took it back, complained to the clerk, and got a replacement. The replacement lasted two weeks before the "play" button got stuck. The player was useless. Janna took it back again, but this time she got a clerk who wouldn't do anything.

Because it was on the way to her job, she stopped in a few times over the next week, hoping to get the same clerk who replaced the first machine, but he never reappeared. She asked to speak to the manager, but he was never there. She did get his name and wrote a letter to the store, but it was never acknowledged. She had thrown out the box it came in (and never even noticed if there was a warranty in the box). She went back and asked to see a tape player like hers, so she could at least copy the manufacturer's address, but was told that they no longer carried that brand. By this time, Janna figured she'd spent more time than it was worth on the problem. She threw the defective tape player away and resolved to buy from what she hoped would be a more reliable store in the future.

Another person in Janna's situation might have decided to teach the store owner a lesson, and turn a simple problem with defective machinery into a moral cause, writing letters to the Better Business Bureau, to the owner of the building where the store was located, to consumer fraud agencies. When you feel that twinge of righteousness and you find yourself thinking, "Somebody needs to teach these turkeys a lesson!" be sure you want to spend your time on the crusade.

For some people, a consumer complaint escalates easily into a personal insult that has to be avenged, or a wrong to be righted in the universe. All the timid types who wouldn't dream of taking on an electronics store, let alone a major manufacturer should give thanks in their hearts for the occasional crusader. But if you're the crusader, give yourself time to consider if the satisfaction of a check for $30 in your mailbox after six months of annoyance would be worth it.

Sometimes the benefit of complaining is psychological, and not monetary. For example, therapists know that many patients are helped just by having somebody really listen to them. Paddy Calistro, a reporter for *The Los Angeles Times* captures the spirit, describing what happens when you have been wronged: "Your fury knows no bounds. You resolve to take action. You're going to write a letter. In a very few minutes, pen in hand, you reconstruct the crime, get mad all over again, shout a few deletable expletives and vent your frustrations as you demand satisfactory reparation. You seal the envelope, apply the stamp and feel better as you drop it in the mailbox. But does that letter get results? Or was your 33-cent exercise merely an economical substitute for a visit to the psychiatrist?"

Even the least sophisticated or the most unrealistic complainer takes into account, at some level, whether the complaint has a snowball's chance of succeeding. That is, of course, a matter of opinion. Many people explain their non-complaining behavior by saying, "You can't fight city hall." And others have fought city hall very successfully.

Be a good consumer

There are dozens of fine books and hundreds of magazine articles that tell you how to be a wiser shopper and buyer. Smart buying makes for fewer complaints. And we don't need to tell you to follow instructions, although we may make an exception for the woman who complained to the shampoo company that her hair was ruined when she washed it with a combination of shampoo and mayonnaise.

We do not need to tell you to comparison shop, to buy from known sellers, and to be very clear about the refund and exchange policy. But if you feel you could benefit from a good "Shopping Wisely 101" course, we have a suggestion:

In what may have been one of the best uses of taxpayers dollars since the purchase of Alaska, our government has produced a fine 142-page book, that puts more valuable and specific consumer information in one place than anything else we have seen. It is called the *Consumer's Resource Handbook.* You can get the current edition absolutely free by downloading it from the Internet (www.pueblo.gas.gov), or by sending $2 for shipping costs to CRH, Consumer Information Center, Pueblo, CO 81009.

How to use this book

Most people won't buy this book because they're looking for something to do with their evenings and they think they'll try complaining by mail for fun. If you live in the modern world, you've been the victim of an unfortunate trend in shoddy merchandise and indifferent service. You want something to change. How about starting with fewer unasked-for catalogs in your mailbox or a refund on that jacket that started coming apart at the seams after the first dry cleaning?

If you've got a complaint you have to deal with right now, go straight to Chapter 5 for step-by-step advice for writing a letter. Then review Chapter 6. You'll find more than 50 letters covering a wide range of problems and tactics to deal with them, along with ideas for adapting those letters to your particular situation.

The appendices at the end of the book are packed with helpful, practical information for the complainer.

- *Appendix A* lists state places to complain: the consumer protection offices.
- *Appendix B* includes federal agencies that accept complaints.
- *Appendix C* lists trade and professional organizations that handle complaints against companies in their fields.
- *Appendix D* provides the consumer affairs department of many major companies.

As you get into it the complaint process, you might find yourself wondering exactly how you find the right person to write to, or where you find the names of those consumer defense groups you can mention as back-up ammunition. Or you might begin to lose heart and wonder why you're wasting time doing this. Don't give up. Go back and start from the beginning.

Unfortunately, it's a given that you'll have occasion to complain about something more than once in your adult life. This book is the perfect resource for those times when you need to speak up or lose out.

With this book you stand a better chance of correcting those annoying, dangerous, expensive, stupid, and unfair things that happen to all of us. And if more of us do complain, and complain well, we have a better chance of changing that unfortunate trend toward the shoddy and the indifferent. Go forth and complain!

Chapter 1

Gripe
Session

"I'm sorry, but we have no record of your purchase. I'm afraid we can't let you board. The flight's full." The check-in agent was all smiles, but Maryanne fumed. "This can't be happening," she thought to herself. After all, she'd purchased her plane ticket according to the directions, and even confirmed it online. Her Aunt Claudia would be waiting for her at the Boston airport, but it was clear Maryanne was going nowhere.

Bob nervously eyed the ceiling above his couch. What had started as a little damp spot was now, three weeks of rainy weather later, a giant, discolored patch that was starting to sag ominously. Bob had left more than four messages with his landlord—without a single return call. He'd postponed calling in a repair person, because the last time he'd made an emergency repair without notifying the landlord first, he refused to pay. Looks like Bob was going to have to shell out the bucks again—or risk having his bedroom collapse on him.

Jenna tapped her foot in frustration as, once again, the department store clerk assisted another customer before her. She was starting to see a pattern after several trips to this particular section—it was not her imagination that the clerk ignored customers of color, to the point of downright rudeness. But what could she do, other than shop elsewhere?

✳✳✳

His third trip to the new restaurant that everyone raved about—and the third time his order of steamed clams was delivered 15 minutes after everyone else's meals. Andrew was steamed, but wondered what he could do about it. After all, it probably wasn't the waiter's fault, and he didn't want to ruin everyone else's dinner by throwing a fit, and, besides, it wouldn't bring him his dinner any quicker. So he sat in his chair and sulked through dessert.

✳✳✳

Kim looked at the report card and shook her head. How had Lee's grades fallen so quickly? An A student last semester, and now he was barely passing. She was sure that this new teacher he complained about had something to do with it, but what can one parent do?

✳✳✳

Raj put the phone down and fumed silently. His car had been towed to the garage following a breakdown, but the first time he drove it, he heard a funny scraping sound. He took it back to the garage, and was told that a vital part of the undercarriage was damaged, and would cost $500 to fix.

The tow company said their driver couldn't have done it, he must have damaged the car himself. Or maybe the garage had. The garage said it had to be the tow company. Meanwhile, he was stuck with an undriveable car or a big repair bill.

✳✳✳

Carla sat down on the bathroom floor and burst into tears. The "perfect" wedding dress she'd ordered—and paid for—was coming apart at the seams. How could they have done such a shoddy job? And with the wedding only a week away, how could she ever get a dress in time?

♯★♣♚

The Ng family opened the door to their vacation rental, and recoiled in horror. The beds were sagging, the sheets dingy, and roaches ran from the light of the single flickering bulb. This was the "charming little getaway" their travel agent had promised them?

♯★♣♚

Lars took a big bite of his candy bar, and spit it out in disgust. Whatever he'd tasted wasn't hazelnut chocolate. He was afraid to look.

♯★♣♚

Sabine hurried home in time to watch her favorite show. She popped a bag of microwave popcorn, kicked off her shoes and settled down to...a weight-loss infomercial? It became abundantly clear that the network had canceled the show, with no warning. But what about the fans? Surely other people wanted to see this show continue. What could she, one viewer do?

♯★♣♚

From genuine crises to little annoyances, we consumers are constantly faced with situations that challenge us. Too frequently, we just shake our heads, chalk it up to the stresses of modern life, and move on.

Well, we're here to tell you that you don't have to resign yourself to "putting up with it." There is a way to get satisfaction (repair work, refunds, apologies, free merchandise, replacement airline tickets, and more), and this book will show you how. Remember, you do have to right to complain.

That said, it's important to complain correctly. Just because you have the right to resolution doesn't mean you have the right to be a jerk about it. With a few exceptions (and I think we've all met our fair share of them), few of us set out to be jerks. But rile us up a little, and we just may rant, rave, scream, yell, and swear. Well, that's actually not okay—partly because the world doesn't need any more jerks but, more importantly, because it's not the best way to get what you want.

This book shows you the best ways—a number of them, in fact. While it is focused on writing, and features dozens and dozens of letters showing how to get what you want by writing the right letter in the right way to the right person, it does more than that. Some-times, the best way to get satisfaction is not by letter, but with a phone call or an in-person complaint.

Let's look at a few examples of successful and less successful com-plaining strategies.

Nicole and Susan both took blouses to be dry-cleaned, and both discovered damage when they picked up the cleaned gar-ment. Nicole pointed out the spot, and was told that the cleaner couldn't have caused it. She must have done it herself. She argued, was told she'd need to speak to manager, and left feeling annoyed. She tried to reach the manager later in the day, was told he wasn't there, and let the matter drop. She resolved to start going to a dif-ferent cleaner, and to buy a new blouse.

Susan had the same initial experience. However, she asked the manager's name and, when she couldn't get him on the phone, wrote a polite but firm letter stating the day the damage occurred, the name of the employee she'd spoken to, and the cost of the blouse. She made it very clear what she wanted—an apology, re-imbursement for both the blouse and the cleaning costs, and a reply to her letter within one week. She got it all. Susan felt com-fortable returning to the same cleaners, because she felt they'd made an honest mistake, owned up to it, and reimbursed her.

This example illustrates several points: Sometimes you can't get satisfaction with the first complaint, and you need to write a letter. That letter needs to be directed to the right person, to be clear, to state what you want, and to indicate when you expect to receive it. However, this example also concerns a very clear-cut case of a con-sumer who has been harmed, and wants that harm made right. Some-times the issues aren't quite as clear.

When James picked up his rental car at the off-airport-cheaper-rates company, it was late and dark and he didn't do the thorough walk-around he usually did to make sure the car was okay. The next morning he found a large scrape along the top of the trunk lid, which he knew he couldn't have caused. The rental company assured him that it couldn't have been there when he picked up the car (he did sign that rental contract with 50 lines of tiny type).

After considering the time he'd need to spend getting repair estimates during a jam-packed business trip, he decided to back off. Eventually he and the rental company split the cost of the repair and James vowed never to get caught that way again. It was an expensive lesson.

Win back the power!

Okay, now that we've fired you up with several annoying complaint stories, it's time for a little reality check. Yes, you can fight big business (or city hall, for that matter). And you can win.

The bigger the issue you're addressing, the harder you're likely to have to fight for it. For example, if you write to a restaurant chain complaining that you had a bad meal or an incompetent waiter, you're likely to get an apology, a refund, maybe some coupons for a free meal or two. Problem solved. If you're writing to complain that the restaurant should be serving healthier meals or shouldn't serve beer and wine, you're in for a much bigger battle.

That doesn't mean that you shouldn't address more global issues, of course, but you should prepare yourself accordingly. A big battle may involve writing more than just one letter—it may require a series, to various different people, or just a series of reminders to the key person who's very busy and easily distracted. You may need to get others involved (start a petition drive or a letter-writing campaign), or to find out the proper authorities, and get them involved. Is it worth the effort? Only you can decide that. But if you feel strongly, or if there's something important at stake, there are ways to effectively complain and get what you want!

A few success stories

A good complaint letter has a few key characteristics, which we'll get into in greater depth in Chapter 5. But basically, it's direct, to the point, and asks for resolution.

Some years ago, Pillsbury introduced "Funny Face" powdered drink mixes. Each drink packet had a supposed-to-be-funny cartoon drawing of a smiling fruit. These included "Injun Orange," complete with war bonnet, and "Chinese Cherry," with protruding front teeth and slanting eyes. Most Americans either didn't notice, or didn't bother to write, but a handful of concerned consumers *did* write letters, and Pillsbury repackaged the offensive products as "Choo Choo Cherry" and "Jolly Olly Orange."

And what about the distressed folks we met at the beginning of the chapter? How did they address their problems? Let's take a look at just some of the situations:

Maryanne, the unhappy airline passenger, managed to maintain her cool. Rather than yelling at the ticket staff—and she was tempted—she calmly reiterated her story, and asked to see a manager. She offered to call the credit card company and have them verify the purchase. She noted that there was another shuttle flight leaving soon that would satisfy her needs, and told the staff she'd be willing to accept a flight on that plane.

Eventually, the ticket agents realized that her story was legitimate and the evidence she supported confirmed the facts; she was clearly a good customer who'd been done in by a computer problem. They got her on the next flight for no extra charge. Once she got home, Maryanne wrote to the airline, detailing the situation and the anxiety it had caused her. She asked only for an apology, but the airline decided to award her some bonus frequent flier miles.

Bob, the nervous renter, realized that his landlord just didn't care, or was too lazy to respond. So, he copied his next letter to the Renter's Rights Union, and the city Rent Equalization Board. He also got an estimate for what it would cost to have the roof repaired, and volunteered (in writing, with copies to the aforementioned authorities) to pay for the repairs and deduct the full amount from his rent over the next two months.

That letter got a response from the landlord, and he's now living mildew-free.

Jenna wrote a thoughtful letter to the human resources department of the store alerting them to the discriminatory treatment.

When it wasn't answered, she followed up with another, offering to help the HR manager find sensitivity training in the area, and hinting that perhaps a story in the local paper would help focus attention on the problem. She then got a call from the HR person, who expressed embarrassment about the problem, and assured her that sensitivity training would be implemented, and the behavior of the particular clerk would be monitored. Jenna also received some generous discount coupons for use at the store.

As the dinner bills were passed out, Andrew quietly asked to see the manager. In short order, a concerned manager appeared at the table. Andrew expressed his disappointment, and suggested that the restaurant add a notice to the menu that diners should expect a longer wait for the steamed clams. He also suggested that the clams be deducted from his bill. The manager went one step further—and gave him his entire meal, drinks and dessert, free. Andrew left the restaurant pleased, and resolved in the future to speak up immediately when he was unhappy.

Kim wrote to the school's principal, detailing her concerns, and asking for a conference. At that conference, she presented her prepared notes, and brought the documentation to prove her point. It became clear that other parents had complained about this teacher as well. She asked that her son be moved to another class, and the principal agreed. She wrote a follow-up letter, asking that the incident report be placed in the teacher's personnel file, and was pleased to hear that he was not invited back after the summer break.

Raj, the carless fumer, decided not to accept the runaround. He had his car fixed, and asked the mechanic to save the damaged part and to write up his observations, supporting the contention that the tow driver had cause the damage. Raj marched into the tow company's office with the note and a big, greasy piece of damaged metal, and demanded that someone look at it and acknowledge that it was the company's fault. Eventually, he found the right person, who looked at the damaged piece, read the note, and said, "Well, I guess we owe you $500." The check was cut immediately.

Carla took the wedding dress back to the store and demanded a replacement. When they said they didn't have that dress available in her size, she picked out an even better (and more expensive) dress, and demanded that she be allowed to substitute it, given the urgency of the situation (and the fact that her bridesmaids and other attendants had already given the store a rather vast amount of business). The manager eventually agreed, and Carla looked absolutely gorgeous on her big day.

The Ngs moved to a better but much more expensive hotel rather than ruin their holiday. When the family returned, they presented their travel agent with photos showing the conditions, and received an apology, a promise that no more vacationers would be sent to that resort, and a refund of the difference between the price they'd agreed to and that they'd ended up paying.

Lars wrote a letter to the candy company immediately, and included what was left of the tainted confectionery. Within a week, he'd received a letter of apology, complete with coupons for purchasing $20 worth of treats.

Sabine wrote a letter to the network about her canceled show, and got no response. Annoyed, she organized a petition drive over the Internet, and got hundreds of people demanding their show be reinstated. While the network never acquiesced, their campaign did generate a lot of publicity and, as a result, one of the cable channels picked the show up or renewal.

In each of these cases, the wronged person could have just accepted the situation. What makes some people fight, and other just give up and go on a little poorer, wetter, later, unhappier, or otherwise downtrodden? Are some of us just born with the complaining gene and, if so, are the rest just destined to be wronged?

We say no. Complaining may come more easily to some than others, but anyone can learn to be an effective complainer.

Read on to find out why you or someone you love has been a door-mat in the past, and how you can change all that. As we've seen, there are a number of approaches to take when you need to complain. What approach is best? We'll soon find out.

Chapter 2

The Fine Art of Complaining

Lydia was furious. Once again, her grandmother had been taken advantage of—this time, a carpet-cleaning outfit had taken a rather large down payment, but had canceled three appointments to clean her grandmother's carpets. It had been two months and the woman was stressed to tears. "For heavens sakes, Gramma," she pleaded, "Do something! Call the office, write a letter, file an official complaint!" But, like always, her grandmother just shook her head, threw up her hands, and discouraged further conversation. Why wouldn't her grandmother complain? And what could Lydia do to get her some satisfaction?

Some people just *don't* complain. But they can, and often should. Understanding the whys and wherefores of this decision process can help you to help yourself and others get results. Whether the issue at hand is a one-dollar error on your bank statement or a horrendous cruise trip that ruined your honeymoon, a bad bottle of wine at a restaurant or a luxury car that caught fire and burned down your garage, the choice to complain is yours.

Choosing to complain—and doing so effectively—is influenced by background, culture, gender, and other factors. No two people will handle a problem in exactly the same way. It will depend on the nature of the problem, on personalities, and on available time and money. But everyone begins with the same question: Is it worth it to me to complain?

The answer should almost always be, "Heck, yes!" Sure, complaining involves an investment: our time, our emotions, and sometimes our money, if only in the certified letters we send. But, as with any investment, there is a payoff—a refund, an apology, a sense of accomplishment. Some people seem to have an easier time than others understanding this relationship. They are the gifted complainers, the naturals. Others have obstacles to overcome. But everyone can be an effective complainer, with just a little practice.

Who complains?

Let's start with a room full of 10 people, every one of whom has had exactly the same problem. University research (at Penn State) suggests that there will be several responses represented in that room.

Somewhere between one and three of those 10 are very likely to complain. They believe in securing justice and righting wrongs. They often blame businesses and government agencies for having an impersonal, uncaring view of people. They may not know the best or most effective ways to complain (which is why some of them will be reading this book). But it is safe to predict that they enjoyed the movie *Network* with its rallying cry of "I'm mad as hell and I'm not going to take it any more."

Another one or two of those 10 people are quite familiar with the notion of complaining. They like Ralph Nader. They read *Consumer Reports.* They're informed consumers who seek out good value. But when it comes to complaining—they're just not comfortable with it.

The remaining six or seven people in the room fall into a category that the academics politely call "uninformed unconcerned non-complainers." These are the people who take whatever life dishes out—the surly waiter at the restaurant, the rejected insurance claim, the mover who broke a dozen dishes—without a clue that it doesn't have to be that way. We don't worry about insulting these people by calling them dopes, since none of them would ever read a book like this anyway. And if they do, we know they won't complain about it.

Coping styles

So we have a room full of three kinds of people: the complainers, the informed non-complainers, and the dopes. The researchers and the psychologists have been let loose in this room, and they love it. "Let's give people tests," they say, "and let's learn about their complaining behaviors, and let's find out what kinds of people complain, and why."

It turns out that there are some major factors that seem to have an effect on coping styles: demographic factors (nationality or ethnic background, age, wealth, etc.), and personality type. Let's take a look at some of these:

Nationality and complaining

Of course you can't characterize an entire population by its complaining behavior. But when researchers analyzed questionnaires on complaining from more than 100,000 people in 53 different countries, they found significant national similarities (and differences) in these five categories:

Individualism. In some countries, such as the United States, people are much more likely to act on their own, while in other places, in many Asian countries, for example, complaining behavior would only be done as a group effort, or with group approval. Researchers noted that many Asians have a certain sense of fatalism. "Because others have more control over my destiny than I do, complaining is often inappropriate." Another study found that many dissatisfied Asian buyers don't complain, because of "losing face" when required to criticize another.

Gender. There are cultures (many in Latin America, not very many in Scandinavia) where men are more likely to be assertive, aggressive, competitive, self-reliant, and oriented to things and money. In these same cultures, females are likely to manifest fewer of these qualities, and tend to be less likely to complain.

Power and prestige. In some cultures, especially but not limited to African communities, consumers tend to feel that they are in a weak position when treated badly by those whom they see as having more prestige and power, especially businesses and government officials. So when there is a problem in faulty goods and services, they often shrug their shoulders, and accept the circumstances.

Fear of change and risk. There are places where it is felt to be much more comfortable keeping the status quo, even if there are problems, rather than taking the risk of changing something, perhaps for the worse. "If I complain, I will create a conflict, and that is not good for me or for society." Some cultures in the Middle East and Asia manifest these behaviors.

Guilt. In some cultures, including Scandinavia and Russia, it is not uncommon for people who are unhappy with products or services to blame themselves for having gotten into that situation. When a home shopping channel came to Norway, there was a fair amount of unhappiness with the quality of the products, the prices, and the delivery time. But the vast majority of dissatisfied Norwegians didn't complain. Why? Some said it was just too much bother. Some felt that nothing would happen anyway. Some said they were brought up not to complain. But most blamed themselves for being stupid, or felt that they had taken a risk in buying, and if it wasn't satisfactory, well that's life. When asked if they would use the television shopping channel again, 90 percent of the satisfied customers said yes and, strangely enough, more than half of the dissatisfied ones *also* said yes. (Something to do during those long dark winters in Norway, maybe.)

Economic status and complaining

Economically disadvantaged people tend to complain less. Researchers speculate this is due in part to the same sense of fatalism or lack of power that is seen in certain cultures outside the United States. On top of that, there may be the assumption that "you get what you pay for." In other words, because the poorer consumer is probably paying less for products and services, he or she assumes that the quality will be inferior.

And finally, complaining takes time—and, frequently, money. Resources that may be in short supply to the individual struggling to make ends meet.

Age and complaining

People over 60 complain much less than individuals of younger ages, even though they are victimized at least as much as younger people if not a great deal more. Older people typically have less money, and have grown more willing to suffer. But older people *can* be very effective complainers, and their very age can be a factor in their success—because who wants to offend someone's grandmother?

Social reformer Saul Alinsky, himself a "senior citizen" when he was active in the 1960s, had considerable success training older people to be more effective complainers by focusing on their immediate needs and problems. Instead of writing to Washington to help prevent Medicare cuts, he said, "The important complaining is right here in the neighborhood: meals on wheels for the elderly, stop signs installed at dangerous intersections, enhanced funding for senior drop-in centers, and so forth."

Personality and complaining

Psychologists have known for years that people with different personalities will behave very differently in identical situations. Consider the classic case of coming upon a thug beating up someone in a public place. Some people will plunge into the fight to try to save the victim. Some people will rush off to try to find or call for help. Some people will attempt to reason the bully into stopping his actions. Some will panic and shriek, cover their eyes, or even faint. And some will ignore the situation entirely, and just walk on.

And so it is in the world of complaining. Faced with an identical situation—getting poor service in a restaurant—the way in which any given person deals with it may depend in part on the nationality and demographic factors (an elderly Swede may respond very differently from a young Mexican), and in part on one of these five coping styles:

1. The passive acceptor. Some people take whatever life (or the waiter) dishes out. Whether through fatalism or a mother who taught them that it is improper to "make a scene," they simply do nothing about that waiter.

2. The saint in the making. Forgive and forget. Turn the other cheek. Let sleeping dogs lie. Look for the silver lining. Whatever their fortune cookie message, they are able to rise above most occasions, perhaps shedding a tear for the state of the world (or some of its occupants).

3. The bully. It really doesn't matter who is right and who is wrong, because, by golly, he (or she) is unhappy and is going to make sure that everyone knows it. When they were younger, they might have thrown a full-fledged tantrum. Now they do the adult equivalent—yelling, blustering, or making threats to "close this place down."

4. The avenging angel. Some people simply thrive on getting even. Many of us feel that such behaviors are neither productive nor ethical, but these folks feel a certain buzz, a satisfaction that they can achieve in no other way. Faced with the surly waiter, they might do something only moderately dreadful (like unscrewing but not removing the tops of the salt and pepper shakers) or something truly awful (you won't get any ideas from us).

5. The practical problem-solver. If everyone were in this category, there would be little need for this book. Some people are just naturally, well, *sensible,* and they behave that way when things go wrong. Sensible, but firm. They have a healthy sense of self and justice, and are quite comfortable demanding their due.

Of course, not everyone fits neatly in one of these categories all the time. There is the shy and reclusive woman, who would never, ever engage in a face-to-face argument with someone, but who may be the terror of the postal system, firing off one angry and vigorous complaint after another. There is the power-seeking, hard-driving executive who may avoid complaining entirely, because he knows he might not end up winning, and his ego doesn't take on fights it can't win.

There is the quiet scholar, who might resort only to gentle, reasoned arguments, until some threshold is passed, whereupon he registers his complaint by launching an ingenious and diabolical sort of revenge.

And there are people whose style or personality leads them to consider doing something other than writing a basic complaint letter, no matter how persuasive that might be. This is mainly a book about letter-writing, but some of the stories about other complaining methods are so lovely, we had to share.

The garage that overcharged

Writer Alan Abel tells about the time a local garage advertised "$49.95 for a complete tune-up. Any foreign car. No kidding." Abel brought in his old Mark II Jaguar for a tune-up and a few minor (he thought) repairs. He said to do what was necessary, but not to exceed $200 for the tune-up plus any necessary repairs. A bit later, he got a phone call: "Your baby is purring nicely and you can pick her up."

At the garage he was presented with a bill for $1,700—$49.95 for the tune-up and $1,650 for various "minor" repairs. He was told that he must pay at once by certified check, or the garage would secure a mechanics lien and sell the car to recover their costs. Abel phoned his attorney, who scolded him for not having a written agreement.

Abel rented a wheelchair from a hospital supply company, put on an old army uniform, and had a Polaroid photo taken, sitting in the chair looking ill and forlorn. The photo was reproduced on 100 circulars that read: "Army Veteran Victimized," and went on to tell his story. Circulars were posted at neighborhood gas stations, auto supply stores, and bars. Needless to say, Abel received an angry call from the garage's lawyer threatening a libel suit. He pointed out that everything said was true and, by the way, he would be sending out thousands more fliers, and would soon be picketing the garage in his wheelchair, wearing his uniform. The lawyer said, "Don't do anything; I'll call you back in an hour." When he did call, he attempted to negotiate a price, but Abel said that he'd pay the garage $200, but that was his bottom line. The lawyer agreed.

The iron that no got hot

When her out-of-warranty steam iron failed to heat up, a housewife wrote to General Electric, to see if they might have suggestions before she sent it to a repair center. A GE engineer wrote back, offering some thoughts and suggestions. The woman tried them, they didn't work, so she wrote again.

Once again, a prompt and thoughtful reply from GE. This exchange went on for a while, until it occurred to this woman that she didn't need a pen pal, she needed an iron. So she put the defective iron in a paper bag and, holding her broad tip marker in the opposite hand, scrawled "Iron she no get hot" on the bag, and mailed it off to General Electric. Within a few days, she received a brand-new steam iron.

So now you know who complains and why. Now, how do you apply this to your everyday life? We're glad you asked. The next chapter focuses on how to assess your ideal reaction strategy, and put yourself in the best position possible for getting what you want.

Don't know what you want, exactly, just that you're mad as hell and you aren't going to take it anymore? No problem—we tell you how to figure out what you want, as well.

Chapter 3

The Goal of Complaining Is Getting What You Want

The Fox family arrived at Kennedy airport in New York after midnight. When they claimed their luggage, they discovered one of the suitcases was covered with oil. The airline representative insisted that something must have spilled from inside the suitcase. They opened the suitcase, finding only personal clothes and belongings, all saturated with oil. Still the representative denied responsibility for the damage, and advised the family to go home and wash the clothes.

By this time it was 2 a.m., and the Foxes, exhausted from their journey and tired of arguing, left.

In the morning, Mr. Fox called airline headquarters, working his way up the chain of command until he reached an executive who asked, "What do you want us to do?" Without hesitation, Mr. Fox replied, "I want you to pay me $600 to replace the suitcase and all the clothes in it. And to repay me for having to stay at the airport until 2 a.m. with my family and for suffering abuse from your personnel, I want three round-trip tickets from New York to California."

The airline executive promised to be in touch within a week. A few days later came a letter that stated "as a customer relations gesture," the airline was issuing a check for the full refund requested, and enclosing three round-trip ticket vouchers—unaccountably not to California, but Florida instead.

The family, who had been planning a trip to Disney World anyway, thought that was just fine.

For most people in most situations, complaining is (or should be) a business transaction, pure and simple. Something has happened that has dissatisfied you. Now you need to decide what, if anything, will resolve that dissatisfaction. If you do anything at all, it will involve some amount of time, probably some emotional energy, and quite possibly some out-of-pocket expense. Is it worth complaining? You may or may not get satisfactory results. What should you do—or not do?

Start with a simple plan. Exactly what would it take to make you completely satisfied? This can range from a simple apology to $1 million. And what would you be willing to settle for? How much time, effort, and money are you willing to expend to gain satisfaction? This might range from a couple of minutes to communicate your dissatisfaction with the store manager to months—even longer—of writing, phoning, visiting, consulting third parties, and fretting.

What is your best-case return on investment? If that five-minute chat with the maitre d' results in a complimentary $20 bottle of wine, you're earning at the rate of $240 an hour! If it takes 10 hours of writing letters, making photocopies, and waiting on line or on hold to get a $10 bank statement error corrected, your earning rate is now $1 an hour. Even if this is your result, however, you still may feel that it's important to pursue the complaint to receive satisfaction. (Although if it requires 10 hours and countless photocopies to correct a bank error, *that's* something else to complain about!)

8 strategies that will get you what you want

Once you've determined that it is indeed worth your while to seek resolution to your problem, there are many ways to get there.

Following are several strategies that will help you get what you want when you complain. Some of these will be discussed in more detail in Chapter 7. And, because sometimes it is awfully important to know which paths *not* to take, we also list some strategies that are well worth avoiding.

1. Act immediately

Often, your most effective option is to complain immediately, especially when there is a time-sensitive issue at stake, such as the hotel room without the promised view or the overcooked steak. In a business that is seriously committed to customer service, there will be procedures in place to handle complaints. Most businesses want to resolve complaints as quickly as possible.

In a well-run business, front-line employees or their immediate supervisors should have the authority to offer a replacement or a cash refund without admitting guilt or pleading lack of authority to do so. If you don't get satisfaction at the time, then you may have to resort to a phone call or letter.

There are some situations in which it may be prudent *not* to complain immediately. If you know yourself to be quick-tempered, you'll want to hold off before pursuing your complaint, rather than let loose a string of expletives, quite possibly directed at a person who not only *didn't* cause the problem, but now may be less eager to help resolve it.

2. Assess the damage

Just what, exactly, is the harm done? Your burger was overcooked? Then it is likely that a fresh medium-rare hamburger with an apology is all the recourse you're looking for. But what if you picked up the burger at the drive-through for your *boss*, got back to work, got chewed out by said boss when he bit into his overdone patty, and you had to drive all the way back, lost another hour of work, and missed an important meeting?

In addition to the sincere apology, you may wish to ask for your money back (your boss decided to dine on leftover cookies he found in his desk), free coupons for a modest number of burgers in the future, even compensation for the hour of work you lost.

When assessing the damages resulting from a poor customer experience, consider whether you had to make extra trips to return a defective product, whether its failure forced you to spend money on repairs or replacements. You very well may be justified in asking for reimbursements or compensation for these costs as well.

3. Be reasonable

We've all heard about the fast-food customer who won millions over a cup of spilled hot coffee. Another individual sued a public transit company—and won—because she claimed a fall in one of the vehicles caused a case of nymphomania. But these situations are rare indeed. It is in your best interest to be reasonable about the restitution you are asking for. Why? Because if you demand absurd compensation, your complaint may not be taken seriously and you won't get *any* compensation.

You may be mad as heck that your Sunday newspaper is soaking wet and unreadable. But suing the publisher for mental anguish because you couldn't complete the crossword puzzle with your morning coffee is not reasonable. Asking for another paper to be delivered within the hour and the cost taken off your bill is.

You are always justified in asking for full or reasonable compensation for money you had to spend. A little more problematic is lost time (you had to drive an extra hour to return a defective product) or opportunity (because the film was faulty, you have no pictures of your son's first steps). And the hardest to defend, but by no means indefensible, is psychological injury or trauma caused by the event. One good benchmark is to try out your complaint or demand on a trusted friend or relative. If they giggle or roll their eyes, it may be time to rethink your plan.

4. Be clear about what you really want

Lynn's favorite string of pearls broke two weeks before a big party, so she took them to her local jeweler, who assured her that he would repair the necklace in plenty of time. Lynn returned the day of the special event to discover that the pearls had not been restrung. Lynn's first impulse was to throw a tantrum, but she realized that would not get the necklace repaired in time for the party.

What did Lynn really want? To walk into that party in three hours wearing her stunning new red silk dress, with a string of real pearls. So even if the jeweler offered to string them for free by tomorrow afternoon, and give her a year of free watch repairs, that simply would not do.

Lynn was smart. She worked backward from her real need, saw an even nicer string of pearls in the window, and negotiated a 24-hour loan.

Often, monetary compensation isn't what we really want when we've had a bad customer experience, although that is typically what we ask for. Instead, think about the final outcome, and work backward from that in making your demands.

5. Don't be afraid to ask for more

When you've had a bad experience with a business, you need reassurances on two levels. First, you want the specific situation resolved. And then you want to know that this company will do right by you in the future. Therefore, it is often reasonable to ask for and expect a little more.

For example, your new set of thermal underwear from that famous mail-order clothing supplier has come apart at the seams after one washing. You call the toll-free number. A friendly phone rep assures you that another set will be on its way, as soon as you mail back the defective pair.

Well fine...but, you wonder aloud, "Why should I have to go to the trouble of packaging it up, waiting on line at the post office, buying postage, and then waiting all that time until the next pair arrives? It's cold here. And besides, how can I be sure that the next pair is going to be any more durable?"

You might insist on having the replacement sent first, by overnight service, along with postage or a shipping-service pick-up slip for the return shipment. And ask for a coupon good for a nice discount on a future order. Why not? If the company has half a service brain, when you get your new thermals tomorrow, there will be an unexpected little gift enclosed, along with the note of apology.

6. Communicate with the person in power

In organizations with good customer service policies, this might be the front-line employee—whether the phone representative, the counter clerk, or the delivery truck driver. At one enlightened manufacturer of expensive baby buggies, for instance, every employee is empowered, without seeking permission, to spend up to $300 in refunds, replacements, overnight shipping, and anything else it takes to make a customer happy.

Sadly, it is generally the very organizations that generate consumer complaints with frequency that are reluctant to empower their employees to make things right. So as soon as you hear the words, "I'm not authorized to…," move on. Get the name of the person who *is* authorized to resolve your complaint—and proceed to introduce yourself.

This may well mean that you won't be able to resolve the complaint immediately. Follow-up phone calls or letters may be necessary. So this is the time to gather all pertinent information: the name of everyone you spoke to, receipts, documentation of facts and conversations. In this way, you will be on solid ground when you make your claim.

Even if you're given the name of a next-in-line supervisor, it can do no harm to ask for the name of and contact information for the president. If your difficulties continue, you may need to go to the top, and the very fact that you asked shows the underlings that you mean business.

7. Make friends, not enemies

For many people, it is human nature to want to make things as difficult as possible for those who have made them difficult for us. Some people are inclined to yell at, insult, intimidate, even humiliate the individual who seems to be the source of the complaint.

But often, not only are such people *not* personally responsible, they may react to your harsh treatment by making things for difficult for *you.* If you chew out a counter clerk in front of a growing line of customers, she may just decide to "lose" your claim form, or "accidentally" transpose a couple numbers in the manager's phone number.

It is often healthy to start out by assuming that the first company representative you talk to, whether in person, by phone, or by mail, is your ally. He or she may be more than eager to see that you are satisfied, and to resolve the matter as quickly as possible.

John once arrived at a major chain hotel at 3 in the morning after some airplane horrors, to find that his confirmed reservation could not be honored. The hotel was full, and so was every other one within 20 miles. It was all too clear that the young night clerk was genuinely distressed, and that she had nothing whatever to do with the problem. When John behaved relatively calmly, she went out of her way to be helpful, finding a luxury accommodation an hour's drive away, offering to pay for a taxi, and, perhaps inadvertently revealing much about this chain's overbooking policy, which stood John in good stead when he later wrote to the chain present demanding compensation.

8. Keep two secret weapons in your arsenal

When preliminary efforts fail to resolve your complaint, you may have to take further action. When communicating with the appropriate management, department, and even the president of the company doesn't work, you can take your story to others in the firm. Here are two communications strategies that may result in action:

The "hardball" strategy. Send your complaint letter to the corporate counsel or chief lawyer for the company. Or send it to the head of the company's advertising or public relations agency, where they may better appreciate the value of keeping a competent complainer like you happy.

The "shotgun" strategy. Send complaint letters to three or five or 10 different people in the company, and perhaps to the accountants, the lawyers, and the ad agency to boot. Some people send a slightly different and personal letter to each of 10 or more people in a large organization. This may get more than one person working on their behalf. If you shoot 100 shotgun pellets, it only takes one to score a bullseye.

4 strategies destined to fail

Sometimes it's as important to know what *not* to do as it is to learn what to do when launching a complaint. Here are some "don'ts" to avoid as you consider how best to approach your own situation:

1. Do nothing

Regrettably, this is the most common response of all. Out of every 100 people who have reason to complain, fewer than 20 will actually do anything. Whether for lack of knowledge about what to do, fear of retaliation, mistrust of the system, indecision, difficulty in writing letters, lack of time, or simply the feeling that it was "no big deal," most people just walk away and forget it. It is safe to suggest that the president of General Motors is not going to phone you and say, "Hi. How's everything going with your new Buick?"

2. Do nothing now, but "badmouth" later

This is a very common response. Many dissatisfied people say nothing at all to the source of the complaint, but tell their family, friends, co-workers, and anyone who will hold still about the unsatisfactory experience. This strategy may bring you some degree of satisfaction, and it will likely even hurt the business that you are complaining about—but it is not going to get you your refund or replacement.

3. Humiliate or publicly embarrass an employee

When you feel wronged, you may have the urge to take out your frustration on *someone.* But don't resort to chewing out the cashier, waitress, or clerk in a way that's personal or demeaning. When one irritated customer blew his top after waiting for 20 minutes in a "fast-food" line, he lit into the 16-year-old server, calling her names and bringing her to tears. The man had a legitimate complaint, but humiliating an individual who didn't cause the problem did nothing to resolve the situation—and it just wasn't nice.

4. Make a "generic" written complaint

Some unhappy people address their letter "to whom it may concern," or "to the consumer affairs department." This is never recommended; it is the business equivalent of all those "Dear Friend" or "Occupant" junk-mail letters you get—and you know how memorable those are.

You need *never* address your letter to a generic department—if you didn't get the name of the proper contact person in your initial contact with company representatives, it's easy enough to get that information from a number of sources, many which will be discussed in the next section of this chapter.

To whom should you complain?

Complaining is clearly an art, not a science, and that is nowhere more apparent than in the simple-sounding matter of deciding who should be the first recipient of your complaint letter.

The experts in this field, both the academics and the people who write books and magazine articles, are very much divided. And with good reason, because there clearly is no one approach that is best for all situations.

Some advise you to start at the very top—complain to the top officer of the company. Write directly to the president first. You may as well go straight to the top, and he or she will certainly pass it along to the right person, and probably follow up to make sure something is done.

But how do you find names of the president and other corporate officers of major corporations, let alone their addresses? Do you have Internet access? Many corporations maintain a Web site with corporate officers' names and headquarters addresses. And your public library is a great source of this kind of information. It's a reference librarian's job to help you find what you need. There are business directories such as, *Standard & Poor's, Barron's*, and *Dun & Bradstreet,* as well as personal listings in *Who's Who in Business* to try. Your librarian will know what to point you towards on the shelves and, increasingly, online.

Other experts suggest going back to the very clerk or employee who sold you the complaint-producing item or delivered the unsatisfactory service. They say, in effect, that by going over the heads of the people who are empowered to resolve your complaint, you'll cause resentment and perhaps jeopardize your chances of resolution. They advise you to start at the bottom, and go to the top only if necessary.

Our best advice is as follows:

- Whenever possible, act immediately and complain to the highest-level person who is on the spot at the time.
- In other cases, get the name of the appropriate person, whether department manager, owner, or president—and the correct contact information (address, phone, e-mail address).
- Write a letter—don't phone.
- Whatever you do, do *something.* Doing nothing will never resolve a complaint.
- Keep copies of everything.

When determining whom you should take your complaint to, remember that your objective is to *get what you want.* If you want your money back and a discount on the replacement item you were forced to buy—then by all means go to the refund desk if they can do this for you quickly and easily. No need to write letters to the president of the national headquarters or hire an attorney to take the case to court. By keeping in mind your main goal—getting what you want—you'll waste less energy on productive activities such as getting mad and getting even.

Chapter 4

Complaining On The Spot

Carolyn was tired and hungry, and just wanted to have a quick dinner before heading back to her hotel room to catch some sleep before the morning conference. She sat down in the hotel restaurant, and ordered the enchilada plate. What a disappointment! Soggy and clearly from a package, the enchilada was frozen in the middle. Should she complain, or would it be easier to just stay hungry, or dine on honey-roasted peanuts from her mini-bar? Should she save documentation and write a nasty letter, or should she just have it out with the waiter right there? And what could she really expect to accomplish in such a confrontation? Her stomach growled.

Yes, this book is titled *Complaint Letters for Busy People*. And we hope to arm you with strategies, tips, and tactics that will enable you to combat any unsatisfactory situation with a well-aimed complaint letter. And, yes, in most cases, we recommend letter-writing as the most effective way to complain and get results. Often, stepping away from the annoying situation gives you a chance to regain your composure and react rationally.

It also gives you a chance to collect your thoughts and gather supportive documentation so you can build a strong justification for resolution. A letter is also more likely to reach the person you want to reach—the person who has the power to resolve your complaint. And, finally, a letter performs as documentation if your complaint is ignored and you want to take the issue to the next step.

But there are plenty of circumstances that call for immediate, on-the-spot action. You're seated in the smoker's section at a restaurant? Sure, you could cough your way through lunch and wait until you get home to write a complaint letter to the president of the restaurant chain. But it'd be a lot simpler to simply ask to be moved. (Of course, if the maitre d' is unable or unwilling to move you, writing that letter may be the next reasonable course of action.)

So, when do you write a letter and when do you demand immediate action? Are there cases in which you might do both? What do you do in the heat of the moment to get the result you want?

Something needs to happen right away

There are complaint situations that are so immediate, if you don't complain right now, you may as well forget it. Why? Well, think of it as a quality-of-life issue. It's true that with a properly worded complaint letter, you may well eventually get a reimbursement for your expenses and troubles. But is that the outcome that would make you the happiest? After all, you'll still have to experience the discomfort, and you might lose something more valuable by not re-acting: your time. Not only will your honeymoon be ruined and years of good memories and happy photographs be wiped out, but instead you'll replace those positive experiences with follow-up letters, phone calls, and frustrated attempts to get compensated. On the other hand, if you complain immediately and effectively, you may avert the problem entirely.

Many situations call for immediate, on-the-spot complaints—followed, of course, by letters and other sorts of action if you don't get satisfaction. Here are a few examples:

- You arrive at the resort for your honeymoon, and discover it is ugly, dirty, far from the beach, and full of bugs.
- Your important dinner guests are being treated badly by an incompetent waiter.

- The plane leaves in 20 minutes, you've got to be in Omaha, and they tell you that your "confirmed" seat is not available.
- You get out on the slopes and realize that the skis you rented are old and cracked, and not nearly as good as those that others have rented.
- You go to the emergency room with severe symptoms and are shuttled to the side and made to wait for hours in a cold, drafty, not entirely clean room.

In almost all cases, the first thing you should do when you have a complaint is to ask politely for the error to be corrected, or the problem addressed. Seems simple enough, but it's all too common to either overreact ("How could you overcharge me, you incompetent jerk? I'll sue this place and everyone who's ever worked here!") or under-react. ("Gee, she overcharged me, but it was a simple mistake, and, anyway, I probably read the price wrong, and I hate to cause a fuss, so maybe I'll just never shop here again.")

Neither one of these is a useful reaction. Instead, state firmly and clearly the problem, and what you'd like to have done. In a face-to-face situation, that means addressing the person who's wronged you, or the front-counter person with whom you have contact.

Often, however, you have a complaint that can't be dealt with in a face-to-face situation—an incorrect billing on your credit card, for example, or a problem with your car after you've already brought it home from the shop. It's still a good idea to respond to the situation immediately, by making a telephone call.

In the best case, these tactics will get the problem fixed, and you won't need to write a letter. And best-case scenarios do sometimes happen. In a less-than-best-case situation, you can at least use these initial conversations, whether in person or by phone, to gather information that will help make your letter more effective. Here's some data you should try to gather:

To whom are you speaking?

If you're face-to-face, check to see if the individual is wearing a name tag. In this case you don't have to ask, but there's a certain power in pausing and asking, "And what is your name?" especially if you're sensing resistance. This communicates that you're documenting the situation for future follow-up. Most employees will want to avoid reports of belligerence or less-than-stellar customer service performance to management. This may very likely result in immediate resolution.

Whether your exchange is in person or over the phone, make sure to get the person's last name. There may be more than one "Cindy" who works the front desk. In the case that you do have to follow up with a letter, it's always better to start a letter with, "I've spoken to Cindy Jones, a service specialist in your customer service department" than "I spoke to someone at your office."

Who has the power to help you?

If Cindy tells you that the manager is the only one who can authorize a refund, ask to see that manager immediately. Often, a difficult employee in a conflict situation may use stonewalling tactics—or even offer misinformation—to avoid trouble. You may be told that the manager won't be in today, or that "I'll have the manager call you when he gets in at 1."

Don't settle for that. Insist that there ought to be someone on site who can resolve the problem; ask to see the highest-level supervisor currently on duty—*or* that manager's manager. If that's not possible, get as much detail about the manager as possible. Ask the manager's name, exact title, work hours, and direct phone number. And make a point of getting Cindy's full name and title as well. This will communicate to her that you're not going to let the matter drop.

If you're confronted with this situation over the phone, make sure that you gather all contact information—manager's name, number, extension—*before* the employee offers to transfer you right then. Often, whether on purpose or accidentally, the transfer fails and you're left with no idea of the manager's name or number.

What is the company policy?

You may well wish to ask for an outcome that's not covered by company policy, but it helps to know the playing field, so that you can address possible reactions in an informed manner. ("Ms. Jones tells me that it is your policy not to refund money spent for package tours. However, I feel that the severity of the problems we encountered, due to the unsanitary conditions at the resort, warrants an exception to this policy.")

Ask for details about policies in writing. If the policies aren't in writing, then pull out a pad and pen and write them down.

What would you do in my situation?

You've been trying to get a positive response, using all the tools you have, but you're getting nowhere. Whether on the telephone or in person, if you are being stonewalled it may help to try to get the person involved by asking what he or she would do in your situation.

Say, for instance, "I'm in business, too, and I would be upset to learn that one of my customers was being treated as poorly as your company is treating me. The repairman has been out to the house three times and the heating system you installed still doesn't work right. If this was your house, what would you do?"

Albert had had a long tiring day on the road, and when his twice-delayed flight finally got him to Chicago near midnight, he made his weary way to the hotel where he was told, "Sorry, we only held your room until 6 p.m. It has been rented to someone else, and the hotel is completely full."

Albert pointed out that he had guaranteed the room with his credit card. But the number the hotel had was one digit off, and they couldn't get approval from Visa. Because of a major convention in town, there were no vacancies at any nearby facilities. The hotel did find a vacancy way out in the suburbs, but the prospect of another hour on the road was unacceptable to Albert.

Eyeing the large, soft sofas in the lobby, Albert had an idea. Without a word to the night clerk, he repaired to the men's room, and emerged a few minutes later in his pajamas. He padded over to a large sofa and settled in, using his overcoat as a blanket. Within minutes, a security guard tapped him on the shoulder and told him he would have to leave.

Albert said he would be delighted to leave, as soon as they found a room for him; otherwise, they would have to carry him bodily from the hotel, and if they did that, please carry him to a phone booth, so he could phone his lawyer, the two local newspapers, and the hotel headquarters.

It was now 1 a.m., and the hotel somehow managed to find a room for Albert—more than likely, one guaranteed to some other traveler, whom they prayed would never show up.

Albert may have had to resort to some drastic tactics to resolve his problem, but he had few options, other than to pay for a cab to drive him to some distant community that might have a vacancy—or stay up all night. And he could have written or called the hotel head-quarters the next day—but nothing would ever gain him back a good night's sleep.

This sort of gung-ho tactic won't always work—and not many people will feel comfortable asserting their consumer rights in their pajamas. But drama can be very effective. Albert might have achieved his desired outcome simply by telling the desk clerk that he planned to sleep on the couch if they didn't find him a room.

The point is, it pays to be persistent *and* insistent when complaints need to be resolved immediately.

There are two common customer environments in which immediacy is almost always crucial in resolving a complaint satisfactorily—these are restaurants and travel.

Complaints about restaurants

Because the stakes are relatively small, it makes sense to resolve complaints with restaurant service or food on the spot. (If the steaks are small at the restaurant, well, that's something to complain about, too.)

Do patrons really have the right to complain? Should restaurants really provide a new waiter, another dish, a table farther from the cigarette smokers who are annoying you? Well, of course they should and of course they do. You were not forced to go there, and surely there are other places in town. So you're in charge and have every right to complain and to have your complaint dealt with.

But more than half the people don't complain on the spot. A survey by MasterCard International found that only 48 percent of diners thought it was all right to request or demand a different waiter, no matter how unhappy they were.

The National Restaurant Association reports that customer satisfaction in table-service restaurants has risen substantially in recent years, and stands at 69 percent. But this means that 31 percent of the people are not satisfied, and yet more than half of them fail to complain. Most restaurants would much rather have you complain than silently suffer. They'd rather hear from you there and then, rather than have you leave, never to return (or, worse still, leave and tell everyone what a dismal time you had).

Alison Arnett of the *Boston Globe* put these four questions to an executive of the prestigious Culinary Institute of America, and got these answers:

1. Is it ungracious to complain in a restaurant?
   No.
2. Should you complain when you are unhappy or pick at the food and mention it later?
   Diners have the obligation to speak up at the time, so things can be fixed.
3. Should you suffer in silence, and simply never go back to that restaurant?
   No! And if you decide not to leave a tip, be sure to tell your waiter or the maitre d' why you are not leaving a tip; otherwise they will just assume you are a cheapskate.
4. If you don't like the dish, should you be required to pay?
   No, but only within reason. If you eat it all and then say you didn't like it, you might be expected to pay at least part of the bill.

What sorts of complaints might you have at a restaurant? You should speak up if:

- You're seated at a bad table (too near the kitchen, near a drafty door, where you can smell garbage, etc.).
- Nearby diners are smoking (not that likely these days, but it does happen).
- The food is overdone, underdone, too spicy, lukewarm—or otherwise not as you expected.
- More than one item listed on the menu is not available to order.
- Utensils, table, or dishes appear dirty.
- The service is excessively slow.
- All diners in the same party are not served at the same time.

There are probably dozens of other problems that could occur. But in any case, when you complain, be sure to clarify the problem. If, for example, you're upset because you're seated near the kitchen and waiters keep bumping into you as they rush in and out, don't say to the waiter, "We hate this table." Instead, explain why the table is unsatisfactory and indicate where you would prefer to sit.

As in Carolyn's case at the chapter's beginning, it is one thing to complain—"I don't like my enchilada."—but it's important to state what you want in a clear, concise manner. The waiter may simply heat up the enchilada in the microwave oven and return it to you, but what you were really unhappy about is that the enchilada was obviously not fresh. If that's so, then you're better off saying, "This enchilada is frozen in the middle. I thought you made them fresh. In this case, please bring me a taco salad as fast as you can—as long as it's fresh and not pre-made—and I also want the enchilada taken off my bill."

In most cases, your restaurant-related complaints ought to be reasonably resolved on the spot. But if the waiter, or manager dismisses your complaints, you may find yourself writing to the owner or headquarters of the restaurant chain.

Trouble with airlines

Every month, the Department of Transportation publishes figures on the volume of complaints received about airlines and their service. The complaints are not categorized, either by their content or their severity, so complaints such as, "They didn't have my favorite brand of beer" counts just the same as, "I was stuck in the bathroom for two hours." In a typical month, several thousand complaints are received.

Needless to say, as in every other area, most people don't voice their complaints about their airline experiences—at least they don't complain to the D.O.T. Still, it seems clear that people vote with their checkbooks. After all, two of the airlines that garnered the most complaints over the past decade have gone out of business. Perhaps if Eastern and Pan American had heeded more of those complaints, they'd still be around.

With airline problems, you should probably do a quick assessment to determine how truly vital your problem is to you, and what you absolutely must have done immediately.

If, say, you're annoyed at being delayed, that's worth a letter to the airline, and you may receive at least an apology, and perhaps some miles on your frequent-flyer account. If, however, you absolutely have to get somewhere, and the airline staff is not cooperating, you'll need to be more forceful. Ask very specifically for what you want, explaining why.

("I see that you have a shuttle leaving in 15 minutes for Reno. Please put me on that rather than making me wait the two hours for my delayed flight to Reno. I must make a business appointment this morning.")

If they cannot or will not help you, however, all you can really do is gather all the information you can—names and titles, as well as documented events—and write a detailed letter to the airline (see Chapter 6 for examples). You may find that the very act of gathering this data suddenly causes a seat on the shuttle to become available.

Other travel complaints

A "ruined" trip produces a level of complaint involving much more disappointment than a faulty appliance. It is much easier to complain to a local company than to a motel in Fiji, so travel agents bear the brunt of complaints, deserved or not. Courts and arbitrators commonly hold travel agents responsible on matters of interpretation (Was it really an "ocean view" hotel if you could only see the ocean by leaning out the window?), but less often on matters clearly outside their influence, such as weather, strikes, etc.

Ask clearly and calmly for what you want at the time the situation occurs. If you can't get satisfaction (most hotels and resorts want happy repeat customers, and will accommodate you, as it were, within reason), document everything. You brought that camera on vacation, right? Well, use it to snap shots of the sagging bedsprings, lousy view of a garbage-strewn alleyway, and the bugs in your bathtub. These will come in handy when you have to write your formal complaint letter.

Timing, timing, and timing

In her article "The fine art of complaining," Betsy Wade, columnist for *The New York Times,* says that with travel problems, "The three most important aspects of complaining are timing, timing, and timing." Complain immediately, since money can never buy back lost time, and at a later time it may be impossible to find the culprit who caused your problem.

Wade says that if something is not right, don't eat it, sleep in it, or get on it. Separate emotion from reality, call your travel agent, tour operator, or the travel provider at once, and collect. Prepare your words carefully, say exactly what resolution you require, and be firm.

One travel article suggests that airline travelers carry a slip of paper in their wallets, to use as necessary: "Since the flight has been delayed/canceled, under CAB Tariff #142, Rule 380, I am entitled to meals, hotel room, transportation from the airport to the hotel or home, and a three-minute, long-distance telephone call."

When posed with an unsatisfactory travel situation, act as if there is going to be a lawsuit eventually, even if the chances are small. To summarize:

- Stay cool. Don't get angry or insulting or burn any bridges. Treat the offending parties pleasantly and professionally.
- State exactly what the problem is and what you'd like done about it. ("This hotel room is absolutely unacceptable. The shower doesn't work and there are insects living in the bed sheets. Please move us to a room in proper repair.")
- Speak immediately to a person who has the power to resolve your problem. Don't waste time with those who can't.
- Document everything! Collect and save everything (including people's names), to be used later, as necessary.

Whether it's a bad restaurant meal, a delayed flight, or some other situation that's bound to spoil what should be a positive and costly experience, your best plan of action is to act immediately rather than delay resolution. Most often, these problems can be resolved on the spot. You should always assess whether a little assertiveness now might save a lot of time and effort down the road. Speak up, be clear, and ask for what you want. But also, be aware that even when you do all of this, and do it well, you may not get satisfaction. That's when the need for a letter comes in, as we'll see in the chapters that follow.

Chapter 5

Writing a Letter That Gets Results

As a single guy living in his first apartment, Ben had little interest in the mail-order catalog that advertised fashions for adolescent girls. Yet they seemed to be mailing to him on a near-weekly basis. Each time he received a catalog, he called the toll-free order line, the phone rep brought up his name in the company's database, and assured him it would be removed and the catalogs would stop coming.

But more than six months—and a stack of catalogs—later, Ben was frustrated, not to mention fearful that his neighbors would think he was weird. Ben decided to write. He did a little research and got the name of the president of the company, as well as those of other corporate officers. He mailed each a letter that documented the number of catalogs he received and the dates he had called. He included a snapshot of himself sitting on a stack of the catalogs that he'd collected over the six-month period. He concluded his letter with a plea to stop the mailings. While Ben had little in the way of leverage (after all, he couldn't threaten them with the loss of his business), he reasoned that the company *was* wasting paper, postage, effort—while creating a great deal of ill will.

The catalogs stopped coming. While Ben never got a phone call, or even a letter of apology, he achieved the most important result—no more catalogs!

When is writing a letter the most effective strategy for resolving a complaint? When you can't get a problem solved over the phone, as Ben experienced with the mail-order company. When you can't even get *through* to a live person on the phone. Or when your face-to-face efforts with a frontline clerk at a store or business go sour. Or maybe even as a first-step strategy when the problem is so serious, you feel it needs to be brought to the attention of someone at a higher level.

While you may often be able to resolve your complaints in person or over the phone, it's almost *never* a bad strategy to write a letter. It gives you the opportunity to clearly think about the complaint, document the details and chronology of events, build your strongest case, and, yes, give yourself time to get over the *emotional* reaction and approach the situation rationally. You can take your time to say it just right. And, finally, your letter serves as documentation of the situation—which may be valuable later if you're not able to achieve resolution through your letter-writing efforts.

How to write a winning complaint letter

Each complaint situation is so unique, that it is virtually impossible to create a "prototype" letter. Nevertheless, we've attempted to provide a number of sample letters in this book, appearing in the following chapter, in the hopes that you might find some application from these to your own situations.

Having said that, however, all complaint letters share the same basic components. We identify those for you in this chapter.

1. A complaint letter should be businesslike.

First of all, your letter should look serious. You expect your complaint to be taken seriously, so put in a little effort to make it look as if what you're writing about is important. Make sure your letter has a letterhead. Use business stationery, or create a letterhead look on your computer.

Create your letter on a computer, even if you have to go to a library or rent time at an office shop. Not only is the professional appearance of a computer-generated letter important in terms of getting the attention you deserve, but by creating it on computer, you can then save the file and use the letter for future reference, as well as a prototype for future letters if your complaint is not resolved initially.

2. The letter should include contact information.

Name, address, phone, fax, e-mail address—all this information should be included in your letterhead. (If your letter is separated from the envelope, which it likely will be, you want to make sure that the recipient has a way to get in touch with you.)

Be sure to date your letter, so you can keep track of the timing of the response. If you need to write a second time, it's better to be able to say, "As I wrote to you on March 1," rather than "You must have had my letter from a couple of weeks ago by now...."

3. Address your letter to a *real* person.

If you send your letter to "to whom it may concern," you may just discover that your situation doesn't appear to concern anyone. Although a company with a good understanding of the importance of its customers wouldn't ignore such a letter, it's awfully easy to dismiss a "generic" letter like this to the recycle pile.

Do the homework necessary to direct the letter to the appropriate person—or several people.

Here's another hint for catalyzing a response—send a *copy* of the correspondence to the individual's manager or department head. It's difficult to ignore a situation when you know your *boss* may be asking you about it.

4. Begin your letter with a good reason to read it.

A good way to start your letter is to begin with a paragraph explaining why the reader should listen to you: You are a regular customer—been one for years. Or you work for a company that could send more business their way. Or (most basic), you're a customer, and if it weren't for people like you, they wouldn't have a business!

Another way to add clout to the introduction is to refer to a person or agency that the reader may know, respect, or even fear. For example:

> Dear Mr. Robbins:
>
> Sheila Aronson, your colleague in the Elite Professionals of Metropolis, assured me that if I brought my problem to you, you'd address it quickly and satisfactorily..."

> Dear Ms. Lapidus:
>
> The editor at the *Consumer Advocate Newsletter* suggested I contact *you,* before they ran my letter about my dissatisfaction with the way my recent wedding was catered....

However you choose to introduce your letter, the lead-in should be brief. You simply want to launch your letter with a good reason for the reader to continue.

5. State the problem.

As clearly as you can, in just a couple of sentences, explain the problem. Sometimes you're so upset, or the problem seems so obvious, that describing it in a clear, complete fashion doesn't seem necessary. But compare the following two excerpts:

> Dear Mr. Smith:
>
> When I picked up my blue silk blouse from your Potrero Hill location (EZ Cleaner #37) yesterday morning, I noticed a large brownish stain or discoloration on the right sleeve. This stain was definitely new, and appeared to be the result of some sort of chemical damage to the fabric...

> Dear Mr. Smith:
>
> Your company totally ruined my blouse!

Clearly, the first excerpt explains the situation—in a much more neutral and non-threatening tone—much better than the second excerpt.

6. Back it up with documentation.

Once you've established the problem, move into the documentation, background, and chronological detail that supports your problem.

Your "evidence" may include a recap of the events, an accounting of all the phone calls you made, a list of the people at the company you've talked to. Your letter may include copies of receipts and credit card statements (never send originals of anything—receipts, statements, estimates, invoices, whatever). You may enclose photographs that show product damage or deficiencies.

You also might want to document all dates on which contact occurred.

> Dear Bugg-Off Exterminating Service:
>
> On your January 7 and 28 visits, you supposedly sprayed my home against fleas and other insects. On January 11, my grandson was playing on my living room carpet and complained of "bad itches." I contacted you that day, and you promised to send out a representative on the 12th. It wasn't until February 1 that anyone....

The important thing is, provide as much detail as possible in as clear and organized a fashion as you can. This documentation will be helpful in resolving your problem—and if it doesn't, then it will be essential if you end up in small claims court, or worse.

7. Ask for what you want.

Don't let your complaint dangle without clarifying what sort of response you expect. You want a full refund? Say so! You want a written apology from the president? Ask for it. You want a million dollars and free products for life? Tell them (but don't expect to get it). Too often, we're so busy *complaining* that we forget to focus on what it is we want. Make sure you know what you want and that you ask for it. If not, you're liable to get a less-than-satisfactory response.

8. Set a deadline for response.

Finally, give a reasonable deadline for a response. You tell them when you expect to hear from them (and make certain you've given them your name, address, and telephone number, so they can get in touch with you).

You should also include the "consequences" if the recipient should *not* get back to you within the specified time frame. Let the person know what your next step will be. You'll go to the national headquarters, or to the newspaper, or to the Better Business Bureau, or to small claims court, and so forth.

A note about tone

Your letter can take a variety of tones and still be effective. You can be stern, angry, factual, friendly, or even humorous, as represented in the examples of letters in Chapter 6. The tone of the letter is one way of indicating how important the issue is to you, how close to boiling you are about the situation.

Remember that sometimes a slightly humorous letter might get you what you want even faster than an angry one. For a sense of different tones, look at letters 2 through 6 in Chapter 6. We've taken one incident and written five different letters, from five different kinds of people who react differently to the same incident.

Sometimes when pleasant, courteous, firm letters have failed to do the trick, it might be necessary to take a stronger tone. Being firm, even angry, does not mean you should *attack* or insult the recipient.

> Hey You Idiot:
> What kind of crummy operation are you running? You totally ruined my vacation and you're lucky I don't sue you for everything you're worth, you jerk. (etc.)

Now, what's the likelihood the reader is going to want to rush to solve this guy's complain?

Finally, never use profanity. It doesn't matter what you yell at your car when it doesn't start in the morning, or what you call the chain that keeps slipping on your mountain bike. When you sit down to write your complaint letter, the easiest way to get your letter shoved to the bottom of the pile is by swearing at the company and its employees.

And here, a note of reality. Most of the people who read complaint letters are not the top executives. Sorry, even if you write to the vice president in charge of sales, chances are your letter will be opened by a secretary and passed back to customer service. And you know who works in customer service? Nice young kids trying to earn money for college textbooks. Older ladies who can't keep up the pace in the secretarial pool any more. You don't want to curse at them. In fact, you want them to slip an extra coupon into your envelope because you wrote an understanding letter, or better yet, to pass your letter onto that supervisor who takes the serious cases.

So stay civil, even if you let them know you're mad as hell and they aren't going to get rid of you until you're satisfied.

Chapter 6

Sample Complaint Letters

In this chapter, you'll find a collection of effective complaint letters reflecting a variety of situations and tones. Included are letters to airlines, dry cleaners, government officials, and best friends. Obviously, each complaint situation is one-of-a-kind—and no "generic" letter or format will be applicable. But it is our hope that you'll find these letters helpful as you write your own letters, adapting their format or components of them to your own unique situation, and using them to inspire effective ways to present your own complaints.

1. Frequent flyer dumps on airline dinner

This letter would be on company letterhead for greatest impact—it communicates that the writer may influence more than his own travel plans. By copying the letter to the presidents of his own company as well as the airline, Mr. Wellington is increasing the odds that his complaint will be addressed quickly and to his satisfaction. More than likely, he'll be reimbursed for his meal, and he might even get some bonus miles or an upgrade to first class on his next flight!

Peter Scott-Wellington, Vice President
Ashcroft Industries
2000 Beltway
Philadelphia, PA 19102

April 28

Ms. Gladys Pipp, Vice President, Public Relations
Fly-By-Knight Airlines
1422 Wilbur Avenue
Cleveland, OH 44115

Dear Ms. Pipp:

Your records will show that my colleagues and I have been flying on FBK Airlines for quite a few years now. Although the service has been generally satisfactory, we have noticed that the quality of meals served has been going downhill. A new low was reached when I flew on your Flight 214 between Houston and Atlanta on April 17.

Problem #1: Even though I was sitting in the middle of the plane, by the time the flight attendants reached me, there was no choice of entree available.

Problem #2: I accepted the fish entree. It was a blessing that the portion was so small, because the fish was so overcooked it was actually mushy, quite tasteless, and stone cold, as were the mashed potatoes. The salad was okay, but the dessert consisted of one rather stale cookie.

As a result, when we arrived in Atlanta, my partner and I headed straight for The Abbey, in order to get a decent meal.

A good restaurant pays attention to the uneaten food that is left on customers' plates. A good airline should do no different. Before I ask my company's travel to book me on FBK Airline again, I would hope for reassurance that you are addressing the food problem on your flights.

It would not be inappropriate for you to reimburse me for the cost of the meal that we had to buy, since yours was so inadequate. Accordingly, I enclose a copy of my receipt from The Abbey for your attention.

I look forward to your response by May 15.

Yours sincerely,

Peter Scott-Wellington

2. The case of the crispy cockroach

The following five letters all relate to the same problem, but each one is written in a different tone. Read through them to get a sense of how you might respond to the same situation.

This letter is well-reasoned, clear, and specific. The writer lists in detail exactly what he wants and why he believes he deserves it. Note that he does not include his telephone number. This may be fine—after all, he is asking for a check, which isn't going to come over the phone!

———

James Hill
2 Ivytangle Path
Nathan, NH 03030

May 1

Mr. Miles T. Andersen, President
Golden Flake Cereals
1422 Henley Avenue
Madison, WI 53834

Dear Mr. Andersen:

As a lifelong consumer of your cereals, I am very disappointed to find myself writing this letter. This is my request for payment of $49.65, for injuries and damages caused to me by a recent incident involving my family and your Golden Crispies product.

This morning, I opened a brand-new box of Golden Crispies, purchased yesterday at the local Spend 'N Pay Market. As I poured the cereal into my wife's bowl, she shrieked, and dropped her glass of orange juice, when she saw what appeared to be a small, dead cockroach in the cereal.

I am well aware that this cannot be a regular occurrence, or your company would have gone out of business long ago. On the other hand, it did happen to us, and we feel very strongly that you have certain obligations to us as a result.

Specifically, we are asking you for $4.65 to replace the tainted box, and $2 for the juice glass that broke when my wife dropped it. Further, it will cost us $35 to have the rug under the dining table professionally cleaned, and $8 to have my blazer jacket cleaned where the juice splashed on it.

If you see fit to reimburse us, we will let the matter rest there, and take no further action. I am certainly prepared to take legal action, but before I do, I wanted to give you a chance to respond and act fairly and ethically.

We would appreciate a response, preferably with check enclosed, by May 17.

Yours sincerely,

James Hill

3. The case of the crispy cockroach, part two

Every complaint letter doesn't have to read like a threat. Although this letter has a "meeker" tone, the writer isn't exactly a pussycat. Note that she still sent it to the president. While she didn't demand her money back, you can bet that she'll get it—plus an apology.

Mrs. John T. Banning
2774 Underhill Lane
Salt Lake City, UT 84104

December 10

Mr. Miles T. Andersen, President
Golden Flake Cereals
1422 Henley Avenue
Madison, WI 53834

Dear Mr. Andersen:

I'm sorry to bother you at this busy time, Mr. Anderson, but my husband thinks that you would want to know what happened when I opened a brand-new box of Golden Crispies at the breakfast table this morning.

What happened was that along with the cereal, there was some sort of little cockroach in the box. Dead, of course, but still pretty revolting.

Is it safe to use the rest of the cereal? What would you recommend? And how could this sort of thing have happened, anyway?

Thank you very much for letting me know. I look forward to receiving your reply soon. In the meantime I'll be eating eggs for breakfast.

Sincerely yours,

Amanda Banning

4. The case of the crispy cockroach, part three

It's yucky to find something in a food product that clearly doesn't belong there, but a lighter approach can be effective in achieving the results you want—whether reimbursement for the product or free coupons.

———

Ronald S. Dillingham
21 Renata Crescent
Miami, FL 33137
(305) 555-0298

June 1

Mr. Miles T. Andersen, President
Golden Flake Cereals
1422 Henley Avenue
Madison, WI 53834

Dear Mr. Andersen:

I know you people are always trying to come up with new additives for your products, but this time, I suggest that you've gone a little too far.

This morning, I opened a brand-new box of Golden Crispies, purchased yesterday at the local Spend 'N Pay Market, and, with my usual anticipation, poured your tasty flakes into my bowl. And what should some cascading out of the box, along with said flakes, but an ugly small black object that looks for all the world as if it were a cockroach in its earlier days.

The little creature certainly was dead, thank goodness, and the good news is that it was found in time to avert a hideous culinary disaster.

So things were not utterly ruined, but you must admit, this was a rather unsettling way to begin one's day.

I've been using your excellent products for years, and doubtless I shall continue to do so, if you can assure me that you have no plans to make this unwelcome additive a regular one. You might wish to send me a case of your product, so that I can assure myself, in the weeks to come, that all is well at Golden Flake.

Yours sincerely,

Ronald S. Dillingham

5. The case of the crispy cockcroach, part four

Although this writer is definitely angry, notice that he still manages to get all the facts out and make it clear that he's not going to let the company ignore him. He conveys very clearly just exactly what the consequences will be if his letter is not answered.

Albert Tanner
75 Stockbridge Dr.
Wayne, NJ 07470
(201) 555-3421

June 1

Mr. Miles T. Andersen, President
Golden Flake Cereals
1422 Henley Avenue
Madison, WI 53834

Dear Mr. Andersen:

My wife and I were so upset at what happened at our breakfast table this morning, we hardly know what to do next. So I'm starting with you, since you're in charge, but I can assure you that I am quite prepared to go to the Department of Health, the Attorney General's Office of Consumer Affairs, the Daily News Help Line, Channel Seven on Your Side, and anyone else who will listen. I mean this.

This morning, we opened a brand-new box of Golden Crispies purchased yesterday at the local Spend 'N Pay Market, and we found at the top of the box a dead cockroach. We were so disgusted, we couldn't eat any breakfast at all, and I've canceled lunch with the guys because right now the thought of any food turns my stomach. My wife says she is probably going to have nightmares thinking about this situation.

Because we are fair people, we will wait to hear from you before we take any further action. We expect a refund for the cost of the cereal ($4.50) and an apology. But that better be before the 18th of this month.

Sincerely,

Al Tanner

6. The case of the crispy cockroach, part five

A clever and catchy way to get the reader's attention and convey the facts clearly. Saying that you're not going to the authorities is a nice touch—it reminds the reader how difficult things could be...if you were a difficult customer.

Noah Archer
Sunnyside Acres Farm
RR #2 Box 5
Iola, KS 67208
(316) 765-8394

October 1

Mr. Miles T. Andersen, President
Golden Flake Cereals
1422 Henley Avenue
Madison, WI 53834

Dear Mr. Andersen:

The setting
Breakfast table, this morning. Four of our family at the table, preparing to eat cereal.

The event
My wife opens a new box of Golden Crispies, purchased yesterday at the local Spend 'N Pay Market. As she pours the cereal into my bowl, a small, black, dead cockroach also pours into the bowl. It clearly had been in the box.

The consequences
Our daughter cried and said she will never eat cereal again. My wife said she felt nauseated all day. My son said he'll probably have bad dreams. And I find myself wondering about the standards of cleanliness and hygiene at your factory, and what should be done about it.

The desired outcome
While we have no wish to take this matter any further, with local or state agencies or the media, we do feel that we deserve a certain recompense for the alarm and anguish caused to members of our family. We feel that a carton of eight boxes of family-sized Golden Crispies (or coupons good for this many) would be fair payment for the distress we all suffered.

Timing
May I please hear from you on this matter by October 14?

Yours sincerely,

Noah Archer

7. Exercise product reduces wallet, not waistline

There's very little risk in returning a bad product with your letter—after all, you can't use it, and the fact that you no longer have the product strengthens your case for getting a refund. And a letter, arriving on the desk with the product—whether it's the "exercise system" referred to in the following letter or a box of cereal with the cockroach—makes a bigger impact on the recipient.

Lisa Boran
2958 Sutter Street
San Francisco, CA 94508

March 7

Joel Spellman, Director Customer Service
ActionFlex Products
7039 Green Street
Palm Springs, CA 92262

Dear Mr. Spellman:

Enclosed please find the "Ab Toner System" I ordered from you on February 4. I received the "system" two weeks later, on February 18. I have to say, I was envisioning that such a highly touted system would involved more than a couple of rubber bands and a photocopied booklet, especially for the $189.95 price.

Having now tried the system, I am not impressed. I didn't really expect that for two hundred bucks I'd end up looking like your surgically altered spokesmodel, but I was hoping for some sort of effect. In fact, I think plain old sit-ups work better for me, and cost a whole lot less!

As your ad states, "If you are not satisfied for any reason, we'll offer you a full refund." I am returning the product, and expect to see the $189.95 credit to my MasterCard at the next billing cycle.

Thank you,

Lisa Boran

8. The robe that faded too soon

Large-ticket items like cars and washing machines have warranties (the company's estimate of how long you can expect trouble-free use). But what about products like shirts, blouses, sweaters? It's reasonable to expect to wear an item for more than a few weeks before you notice wear. You can adapt this letter to any of those instances where something just didn't give you the length of service you'd expected.

Joan MacIntye
399 Brandywine St.
Las Vegas, NV 89119

April 15

Samantha Childers, President
Intimate Pleasures
Box 33445
Seattle, WA 98789

Dear Ms. Childers:

The enclosed robe was bought from your Spring 1999 catalog. It was a lovely color and felt really luxurious. You can imagine how disappointed I was to find that after only two washings on the gentle cycle of my machine and in cold water, the color has begun to fade in streaks, and the soft, raised pile of the collar and cuffs is already showing signs of flattening and wear.

This is unacceptable. I have had the robe for only two months, and have done nothing unusual to it. I would expect to be able to wear a robe for several years before feeling it was time to replace it.

Please refund my full purchase price of $69 plus shipping costs. I do not wish a replacement, and there are no other items in your catalogue I need at present.

Joan MacIntyre

9. Playing hardball with a used car salesman

After you've failed to resolve the complaint by telephone or in person, you may have to get tough. And creating negative publicity, delivered right to the doorstep, is one way to get tough. This kind of action, however, might not be advisable in every neighborhood. If the writer is at all unsure, he might let Sparky know that he's also contacted local authorities, and his cousin's patrol car will be cruising the neighborhood that Saturday, too. Chances are, though, that Sparky will be quick to give the writer what he's asked for.

Chuck W. Kim
4020 Prairie Street
Tulsa, OK 74136
(918) 555-8392

April 22

Sparky Wilson
Sparky's Quality Used Car Emporium
1422 Elmont Ave.
Tulsa, OK 74136

Dear Sparky,

You're playing hardball with me, so now I'm going to play hardball with you.

The facts so far:
I purchased what was identified as a 1991 Incontinenta at your used car lot on April 5th. I was assured by your salesman, Eddie Atkinson, that this was a one-owner car, in excellent condition.

In the course of having the transmission repaired two weeks after the purchase, I learned that this is a 1991 chassis with a 1988 engine installed, and papers found in the filthy glove compartment suggest there have been at least four owners.

When I came in to explore the notion of either a price adjustment or an exchange, I was told that Eddie does not work there any more, and no one was available to help. My subsequent telephone calls to you have been ignored.

What I am going to do next:
I am told that Saturday afternoon is your busiest time of the week. I have made two large signs for the side of my car, urging potential customers to talk to me before they visit you. And I have prepared a one-page handout to give people, explaining what you did to me, and your unwillingness to make things right. A copy of this handout and a Polaroid photo of my signs are enclosed.

I plan to park outside your place and to give my handout to your potential customers. If parking is not available, I shall drive slowly back and forth, and my wife will be handing out the fliers. I plan to do this every Saturday until you make things right with me.

What I want you to do:
I want you to give me a $500 refund on this so-called 1991 car, which I purchased because of misleading statements made in your literature and by your salesman. If this is received by noon on Friday, I will call off my Saturday activities, which, I think, will be no fun for either you or me. Please let me hear from you, or I'll see you on Saturday afternoon.

Sincerely,

Chuck Kim

10. Child safety issues anger concerned parent

Anger isn't always the best response when dealing with complaints. But when the complaint involves issues of child safety, it's generally understandable. Although the writer of this letter expresses his anger, he does a thorough job of offering the facts, documenting events, and explaining the response he expects.

Jay Byrd
732 Holmes Way
Arlen, TX 78965

February 6

Felix Katz, President
Acme Safety Company
666 Harwood Street
Oklahoma City, OK 73116

Dear Mr. Katz:

I am returning the enclosed child safety gate for a full refund. I believe it is not only a bad product, but a dangerous one. I am shocked that a company supposedly dedicated to home safety would carry such a thing, and demand not only my refund, but an explanation.

When I ordered the enclosed Model 679 Child-Gard Gate after seeing it advertised in Parenting magazine, I asked the salesperson whether it was, indeed, designed to keep children up to the age of 2 safely contained, and she assured me that it was.

I followed the instructions exactly in assembling it, and assumed my 22-month-old would be safe. Instead, I found that she could easily work the "adults only" release, when I found her wandering in the front yard. I thought maybe I had left it open, but then I watched in horror as she opened it a second time.

This is absolutely unacceptable. Thank God my child was uninjured, but others may not have been so lucky. If that gate had been the top of a staircase (as pictured on the box), my baby could have been seriously injured, or worse, and it would have been your fault.

I want my money back, but more importantly, I want a letter from you, assuring me that this dangerous product has been taken off of the market. If I don't hear back from you, I will be forced to take further action to ensure that no children are hurt or killed as a result of your negligence.

Awaiting a reply,

Jay Byrd

11. Car expires—two weeks after the warranty

If your investment was significant and your loss sizeable, don't hesitate to pursue a complaint—even if the product is no longer covered under warranty. You'll definitely want to seek the ear of the highest-level representative possible.

H. B. Zindermann
Acton/Zindermann Distribution
2 Industrial Parkway
Detroit MI 48303

June 1

Mr. Vernon C. Haas, President
United Motors
1422 Sparkplug Avenue
Detroit, MI 48303

Dear Mr. Haas:

I read in a book on consumer complaining that complaints about automobiles are among the most common ones that people make. But when I bought my brand new Corsair Turboglide 10 months ago, I never believed that I would be joining the ranks of those who write to complain.

As a sales representative covering nine states, I drive a good deal. I want both comfort and reliability, which is why I bought a Corsair in the first place. Your 24-month, 24,000-mile warranty seemed adequate at the time. But now, after only 267 days, the warranty has expired, and so has the car!

I reached 24,000 miles on May 9. Less than two weeks later, I was halfway between Nashville and St. Louis when the engine self-destructed. Evidently, a cylinder head flew apart, destroying the cylinder and half the engine. I had the car towed back to the place I bought it, Spurgeon Motors, where the message was, in effect, "Gee, it's too bad it isn't under warranty." Your zone office gave me essentially the same message.

Mr. Haas, before I go to the BBB's dispute resolution program, or the National Automobile Dealer's Consumer Action Program, or the Center for Auto Safety, I thought it would be only fair to give you a chance to solve the entire problem with a simple nod of your head and stroke of your pen.

My car is sitting at Spurgeon Motors. Will you please have someone give them a call at (615) 555-3475 and tell them to go ahead and fix it, under warranty? It will save both of us so much time and effort, and you'll have a friend and customer for life.

Please let me hear from you by June 10.

Yours sincerely,

Helen Zindermann

12. Hey, lady, is your carpet running?

Even if a product defect isn't specifically covered by warranty—sometimes even if you've been told that it is not the company's problem—the right letter can make a difference. A reputable company wants to keep its good reputation, it wants more customers, it would even like you to come back next time you want another one of whatever the expensive item is that it sells. Explain the benefits of doing the right thing. You'd be surprised how often this approach works.

———

Sue Tuttle
712 Evergreen Terrace
Portland, OR 97219

June 4

Bob Scarsdale, President
Bob's Carpet World
546 Oak Street
Portland, OR 97219

Dear Mr. Scarsdale:

I have a problem with some recently installed carpeting, and would like to request your assistance in making things right.

Here's the situation: Two months ago, I decided to have my entire house recarpeted. Your salesperson Mary showed me the Bargain King brand, and assured me that it is as good as the more expensive name brand, and that it was guaranteed against excessive wear and tear for one year. I bought the carpeting, and paid for installation at a price of $3,500.

Soon after the carpet was installed, it became clear that it is not colorfast, as the deep red color ("Evening Burgundy") has rubbed off on clothing. When I spoke to Sheila in your customer service department, she told me that the warranty covers wear only, and suggested that I not sit on or otherwise touch the floor in light-colored clothes until it had been steam-cleaned several times. This is not an acceptable solution.

Your store has a good reputation, and I trust that you will want to keep a customer happy. I would like to offer you two options:
1. Replace the carpet with a colorfast option, at no extra charge to me.
2. Pay for several steam cleanings. If this does, in fact, resolve the problem without leaving the carpet discolored, I will be satisfied.

Clearly, the second option is the simplest and most cost-effective. For approximately $90 (the cost of three steam cleanings according to a local service), you will have made a $3,500 customer happy, and proven that you understand the value of creative problem-solving.

If I haven't heard from you by next Monday, I'll give a call to follow up, but this really is rather important, and it is affecting my quality of life.

Sincerely,

Sue Tuttle

13. When your jewelry turns you green

You really, really wanted the necklace—if only it didn't corrode on your neck! When there's a possibility that the particular item you purchased is defective, leave open the option of getting a replacement, rather than demanding a refund. The writer of this letter used a sense of humor—which also underscores her openness to alternative solutions.

———

Lucy Kyle
546 Gardenview Parkway
Elton, IN 46601
(657) 555-4356

April 6

Carol Glassman, Director Customer Service
Jewelry Madness
456 Silver Avenue
San Francisco, CA 94116

Dear Ms. Glassman:

Enclosed please find a necklace that I purchased from your catalog two months ago. You will note that the silver plating is already wearing off—when I wear the necklace, it turns my neck a most unappealing greenish color.

Now, here's the situation: I really like this necklace, but I don't really like the green-skin look. If this one item just happens to be defective, or if you have something similar that doesn't have this little side effect, please just exchange the necklace.

If, on the other hand, this is a basic flaw in the product, please refund my $17.95 to the address above.

Thank you for your prompt attention to this, and I look forward to receiving a new necklace, or a refund check, in the mail soon.

Sincerely,

Lucy "Green Neck" Kyle

14. Time out for a cheap watch

People often neglect to complain because, "It's just not a big deal" or, "It's only $20. It's not worth the fuss." Well, you don't have to make a fuss. You can simply state the problem and ask for your money back. Even if there's no warranty or other guarantee, a company will generally give a refund for a faulty product—without argument.

Melissa Combs
444 Calistoga Way
Burlington, VT 08765
(456) 555-0132

June 3

Amar Markhan
Customer Service Dept.
Time Co.
1 TimeCo Plaza
New York, NY 10021

Re: Faulty watch

Dear Mr. Markhan:

This January, I purchased one of your illuminated-dial watches at a local department store, for about $20.

As you will note, the button that causes the watch dial to light up no longer functions. I took it to a local watch-repair shop, and they told me that repairing it would likely cost as much as the watch did originally.

Now, it seems to me that even a $20 product should last longer than four months. I know that you have built your reputation on reasonably priced, durable products, so I'm assuming you will agree with this assessment.

Please repair the watch and return it to me at the address above, or send me a new watch that will last longer than a few months. I would appreciate hearing from you within the week.

Thank you,

Melissa Combs

15. A service bureau that's all "bureau," no "service"

The writer documents the chronology of events well. And she makes a good case for her future as a valuable client. She appeals to the reader as a business person, and although she does imply the company might lose her business if they don't respond, her emphasis on rational business justification for her needs is something the reader will understand immediately.

Sandy Beach
Beach Office Services
572 Broadway
Elk View, MT 56789

February 7

Woody Glen, Customer Service Manager
Computer Galaxy
5582 Interstate Parkway
Ormond Beach, FL 32174

Dear Mr. Glen:

This is my second letter to you, following three telephone calls, and I am quite frankly at the end of my patience. What could have been a relatively simple problem has, through your company's negligence, grown into something that is costing me a substantial amount in lost work time.

To reiterate the facts: Four weeks ago, on January 8, I ordered a 266 series Pentium 2 laptop from your company, specifying the 64 mg hard drive upgrade. I spoke to Mark in your order department, who assured me the machine would be delivered by the 10th. The computer did arrive, but it was a Macintosh machine, incompatible with everything in my office.

When I called Mark back, he acknowledged the error and told me to return the machine for exchange. I did return it, COD, as evidenced by the attached UPS receipt, and have been waiting for my replacement machine ever since.

Mr. Glen, I am the owner of a small business that relies on computers for our day-to-day income. Every day that I don't have the machine I need, I am losing money. I've always been pleased with my service from Computer Galaxy before, and don't want to find a new vendor. Still, if I don't receive my new computer within two days of your receiving this fax, I will be forced to buy one at another vendor. I will, of course, expect a full refund from you. I will also be telling all of my customer of the treatment I've received from you, and alerting the Better Business Bureau. I may also be forced to look into asking recompense for the lost income.

Please help me avoid this unpleasantness, by sending me the computer, as promised a month ago. I await your call.

Sincerely,

Sandy Beach

16. Hitting a brick wall with a car insurance company

Often, when you telephone a customer service department repeatedly, you find yourself talking to different people, not all of whom are successful in finding your file, or in understanding the history of your complaint. Taking down names for your records still makes sense, but it's frustrating. Going to the top when you hit the kind of brick wall is a way to short-circuit the run-around.

Joseph J. Holland
24 Marple Street
Louisville, KY 40205
(502) 556-2324

July 3

Mr. Lloyd R. Bingham, President
New Haven Automobile Insurance Company
Cranston Towers
New Haven, CT 06525

Dear Mr. Bingham

My wife and I have been buying our car insurance from your company for more than 10 years, and we have been very satisfied customers—until now. Permit me to explain briefly what your company did to us this summer, because I know you will want to make things right, to keep us as your customers.

Our policy (number PHD3546564) expired last June 15. As always, your people sent us a questionnaire asking for our current odometer mileage, which we promptly returned. A few weeks later, we received an invoice for $1,054 for one year of coverage. As always, I got bids from several other companies, and determined that yours was once again the lowest. Accordingly, I sent you my check for $1,054 on June 1.

On July 2, I received a revised bill from your company for $1,462. When I telephoned your consumer service line, I was told by Marge that the increase was because of the fact that I drove more miles than your underwriter had expected. When I pointed out that I had supplied my mileage well in advance of the expiration date, I was told that someone must have screwed up, but that I still needed to pay the surcharge.

Mr. Bingham, I can assure you that if I had been supplied with the correct figure, I would have bought my insurance from either of the two competitors of yours (Central and Fidelity) whose prices were higher than my original bill, but significantly lower than the revised amount of $1,462.

When I told the polite woman on your consumer hotline that I had no intention of paying the surcharge, she informed me that your company would simply cut off my car insurance three months earlier.

Is this any way to treat a long-time faithful customer? You have every right to raise my rates next year, based on mileage, but not, I submit, to expect me to pay a retroactive bill for this year, because you "screwed up" in your mileage calculations.

Please let me hear from you by August 1, assuring me that I am, in fact, paid in full until next June 15.

Sincerely yours,

Joseph Holland

17. Crying over spoiled milk

Sometimes it's not the money, it the principle. In this letter, the writer reasonably requests a refund for the moldy cheese, but he might have considered asking for more to compensate for the return trip he had to make with the spoiled milk. If the company is customer-savvy, Mr. Wolfe will receive something more than his $6.99 refund.

Leo Wolfe
3445 Argent Road
Argusville, ID 87906
(398) 555-2054

May 6

Duane Tallman
Argusville Dairy
4567 Louis Lane
Argusville Heights, ID 87910

Dear Mr. Tallman:

I am quite displeased and concerned with the quality of product coming from your plant recently.

- Last week, I purchased a gallon of low-fat milk at my local Food Mart. When I got home and opened it, I discovered that the milk was spoiled, despite being well within the "sell-by" date stamped on it. I returned the milk to the store and received a refund. This is a major inconvenience, as the store is a 30-minute drive from my house, and I am a disabled veteran.
- Today, I brought home a pound of cheddar cheese from the Food Mart, only to discover that it was completely moldy. I am simply not going to drive to that store again.

I enclose the receipt for the cheese, $6.99. I expect to be reimbursed, and would also like some assurance of your commitment to quality control. If it is the case that the Food Mart is not storing your products properly, you need to know this. You are both local companies. It is simply not acceptable to sell spoiled products, and I trust that you will remedy this distressing state of affairs.

Sincerely,

Leo Wolfe

18. Thread makes consumer fall apart at the seams

Sometimes the negative repercussions of a defective product are far greater than the cost of the product. In this case, thread that disintegrated poses a threat to a girl's teenage dreams. The writer of this letter effectively spells out the consequences of the product failure, and requests compensation beyond the cost of the thread.

Mary Coweles
17 Flat Bridge Road
Oveland, NE 68506

May 5

Maxine Ashcroft, Vice President, Customer Relations
Yarn and Thread Division
Meadowland Industries
1422 Betsy Ross Place
Boise, ID 82323

Dear Ms. Ashcroft:

I'm sure you can remember how important it was to look and feel your best at the high school senior prom.

My daughter's prom is only three weeks away, and I'm afraid that your company is going to be the cause of a really major problem for her—one that could affect her life for years to some. Here's the situation:

Our large family operates on a very tight budget. My daughter Melanie has been sewing her own prom dress for the past two months, and it was a lovely creation. I say it <u>was</u>, because when she put her finished creation in the washer-dryer, it literally came apart at the seams. I don't know if it was the tumble action, or the water, or the heat of the dryer, but for whatever reason, your thread came loose, and now her beautiful dress is in pieces.

We've never seen anything like this before. I enclose a couple of separated pieces for your comment.

Of course we want to know how to prevent this from happening again. But the situation right now, this May 5, is that there is neither time for Melanie to make a new dress (she has her final exams, you know), nor funds readily available to buy her a new one.

Because it was your product that caused this situation, I wonder if you might find it in your hearts to help out. There is a dress at Connelly's in town that is her size, and costs only $70. We can contribute $20 from the sugar jar for this. Can you help out with the rest? Please contact me as soon as possible at the phone number below.

Yours sincerely,

Mary Coweles
(308) 555-0678

19. Who ordered the hatpin-chip ice cream?

The first sentence establishes the writer as a valuable customer. The potential that did exist for a much more serious complaint makes the idea of communicating both by letter and e-mail highly reasonable. Although the writer did not request a refund, he will probably need much more than that to restore good feelings about the company. And he hinted broadly at an opportunity to restore those feelings in mentioning his upcoming ice cream needs. We hope the company has the sense to respond appropriately.

Including the package number of the ice cream is an excellent idea. The company may never figure out how the hat pin got into the ice cream, but it can certainly pinpoint (sorry) the place, date, and packer of that particular container through the number. In any event, it marks the reader as a helpful consumer—and one whom the company will want to keep happy.

Marvin Dawson
11 Donkey's Path
Springtown, TN 37205
615-555-9876

9 July

Mr. Allen Ezelton, President
Alpenrose Ice Cream Company
1422 Benjamin Court
Knoxville, TN 37919

Dear Mr. Ezelton:

Our family has been consuming your ice cream products for years, and have never before had reason to complain. Earlier today, however, something occurred that we found alarming and I strongly suspect you will, too. The reason I am sending you this letter by e-mail, as well as through the postal service, is so that you may be alerted to the situation at once.

At dinner today, while I was scooping your Golden Vanilla ice cream from a one-pint container purchased at Haroldson's Market here in Springtown, I found a two-inch-long hat pin in the ice cream.

I'm sure I do not need to tell you how distressed and alarmed we became at this incident. We're thankful no one was injured, but our confidence in your company and your product is badly shaken.

We may be willing to give you another chance. In fact, we had anticipated buying three gallons of Alpenrose Chocolate Delight for our lodge picnic next month.

But meanwhile, I hope and trust you will take all necessary action to make sure this situation does not happen again.

Yours sincerely,

Marvin Dawson

PS: The small numbers on the bottom of the carton read: 398549473.

20. Poor floral service nipped in the bud

A complaint can be urgent because of timing. The following letter begins with exactly what the customer wants and then explains why it's the right thing to do. The writer concludes with the course of action he expects.

———

David Bonnington
2 Zinfandel Ct.
Napa, CA 97654
(707) 555-3856

September 2

Ms. Amelia Levinger
National Flower Delivery Service
1422 Burbank Blvd.
Cincinnati, OH 45242

Dear Ms. Levinger,

I am faxing my urgent request that you:

1. Deliver your Springtime Joy floral assortment (or something very similar) within the next 24 hours to Miss Jeannie Callison, 375 "M" Street, Freestone, California 95123.
2. Express your apology for the quality of product that was delivered yesterday to Ms. Callison.
3. Do this efficiently, without any charge to me.

Permit me to explain:

I telephoned your toll-free number on Tuesday morning, and consulted with your helpful customer service person regarding the proper gift to send to my favorite niece on the occasion of her engagement. Springtime Joy seemed just right, and so I placed the order for guaranteed delivery yesterday.

Well, the delivery was as promised, but the quality of the flowers was embarrassingly dreadful. I had occasion to see them when I visited Jeannie yesterday evening. She was too polite to say anything, but I was not. When she told me that the eccentric and partly wilted array of blooms was, in fact, my gift to her, I assured her that I would make things right. Or, rather, that I would see that you did.

Please give this matter your personal attention, Ms. Levinger, and make sure that the flowers are delivered promptly. Jeannie returns to college next week, and I want to be sure she has the benefit of several days of cheerful flowers before she leaves.

Thank you for your assistance.

Sincerely,

David Bonnington

21. Cola, store service leave customer flat

"It's only $1.59. Why complain for that amount?" Why not, when it's relatively quick and easy to write a letter and send it to a company representative who has the power and interest in resolving your complaint? In the following letter, the customer lets the Zippy Cola folks know that she is also writing to SpeedoMart. This two-pronged effort ought to bring quick results.

Deonora Davies
354 Colliewood
Appleton, WI 54667
(404) 555-2567

Mr. Michael Finley, Vice President, Customer Relations
Zippy Cola Company
1422 Peppercorn Road
Grand Rapids, Michigan 49503

Dear Mr. Finley,

I have just had a rather annoying experience with a bottle of Diet Zippy Cola, made even more annoying by the uncaring treatment I received when I attempted to return the soda to the SpeedoMart where I bought it.

I purchased two two-liter bottles of my favorite soft drink at the SpeedoMart on Graceland Street last week. The price was $1.59 per bottle. I put one in the fridge and one on the shelf. When I opened the one in the fridge a couple of days ago, I found it to be absolutely flat. No fizz whatsoever. The second bottle, from the shelf, was quite satisfactory.

I stopped by the SpeedoMart, where Scotty, a junior assistant manager listened to my story, and suggested that maybe I had left the bottle open on the shelf. He told me that he was not authorized to make a refund.

SpeedoMart will be hearing from me, as well. But I thought you should know, and I request that either you or SpeedoMart promptly replace the defective product, sending me a refund, or a bottle of Diet Zippy Cola within the week.

Yours sincerely,

Deonora Davies

22. A fight for your life with an HMO

In a time of decreasing personal service, one of the most difficult areas to cope with is health care. Too frequently, people who are seriously ill, find themselves not only fighting for their lives, but fighting for essential medical help to save their lives. In these situations, it really pays to document everything, to keep records of everyone you speak to with, to record the times and topics covered in conversations, and to keep copies of everything sent you and everything you send.

This letter would probably be just one in a series, but it's a good place to start. Notice the details.

———

Julia Carson
235 Hearst Street
Berkeley, CA 94709
(510) 528-3984

May 23

Jennifer Reyes, Patient Services
HealthCom
3 Juniper Parkway
Palo Alto, CA 94778

Re: Follow-up biopsy for breast cancer, policy number: 32000-H 403

This letter follows a telephone conversation with Stacy, in your Patient Services Department, this morning, May 23, at about 10 am.

I am requesting a tissue biopsy of a lump I found in my right breast earlier this month. On May 19, I was given a needle biopsy, as an outpatient by Dr. David Harper at Good Samaritan Hospital. At the time, Dr. Harper said that the technician who prepared the results pointed out to him a few cells that were not normal, but not definitively cancerous. I asked Dr. Harper, if I were his wife what would he do? He told me that he would have a lumpectomy performed and would examine very closely the surrounding tissue. This is what I want.

When I called to schedule this procedure through my primary care physician, his office manager told me that the procedure was not covered by my policy since the results were not definitively cancer and I would have to wait at least six months before they could authorize another test.

This is totally unacceptable.

I spoke to my primary care physician, Dr. Martin Cohen (510) 555-7155, and he said that he would be contacting you later today to support my request. I understand that in cases where family history shows a number of cases of breast cancer in close relatives, a different set of testing protocols may be used. Dr. Cohen has agreed to mention this to you when he calls.

I cannot emphasize to you how terrifying I find this. It has made it almost impossible for me to function normally in my job and I have simply stopped trying to have a social life.

I will be telephoning your Patient Services Department in three days to see if you have managed to get the necessary authorization cleared. If there is anything else I can do to further this process, please do not hesitate to telephone or fax me. My home phone, above, is also connected to a fax machine and instructions for faxing are on my answering machine, should you call during normal business hours. At those times, I am reachable at my work number: (415) 555-2005, ext. 545. I expect to receive a phone call from you no later than Friday, confirming that the lumpectomy procedure will be covered.

Thank you for your help.

Julia Carson

23. Dentist drills carpet company

Writing the manufacturer is the next step when a product doesn't live up to its name, and the store you bought it from refuses to help. The writer does several things effectively: He uses his professional letterhead (implying that his dissatisfaction will reach all those he works with), he expresses anger but directs it at the situation, which allows the reader to be sympathetic rather than defensive. He explains what action he wants, and clarifies the consequences—Dr. Soronson is not going to chalk this one up to experience!

Joel Soronson, D.D.S.
Warren Professional Building, Suite 5
223 Evans Street
Charlotte, NC 28226

March 14

Mr. Jason T. Donovan, Chairman of the Board
Schuyler Carpet Mills
1422 Youngstown Road
Charlotte, NC 28226

Dear Mr. Donovan:

Every day, I grow angrier at your company. This has been going on for more than six months. Each morning, I go to work at my dental practice, at the address on this letterhead. Each morning, I open the front door leading to the waiting room, and I grow angry all over again.

Each morning, what I see is my not-inexpensive carpet, a product of Schuyler Mills, and installed less than two years ago, and it looks awful. There are clear paths worn in the carpet, where people regularly walk between the door and the chairs, and between the chairs and the door into the back offices. This is a commercial grade carpet. This should not have happened in 10 years, much less two.

I have telephoned and written the Carpet Barn, from whom I purchased your carpet. All they did was remind me that there was no warranty on carpet. They didn't even send someone out!

You are in a position to help me, Mr. Donovan. Before I grow angrier still, and decide it is time to talk to my lawyer, I ask you to send someone out to look at my carpet, and then to replace it, without cost to me, with something that is new and long-lasting. I expect to hear from you within 10 days.

Sincerely,

Joel Soronson, D.D.S.

24. Bank customer has limited time assets

When your time is at a premium, a letter may be the most efficient way to resolve a problem. In this case, the writer copied the branch manager, as well. Chances are, the recipient of the copy will resolve the complaint before the Big Guy Downtown even lifts up the phone receiver.

Kent Coranis
2443 Everett Street
Pittsfield, MA 01201
(978) 555-0895

July 10

Mr. Clovis Morgenstern, President and CEO
First Bank and Trust Company
1422 Albemarle Street
Boston, MA 02110

Dear Mr. Morgenstern:

I work hard for a living, and I'll bet you do, too. I have a very limited amount of time to deal with personal financial matters, and I need to tell you that First Bank is making it harder and harder for me to do what I need to do. I have two problems, one specific and one general, and I am writing to you because I can't seem to get help on either one.

The specific problem is a small but annoying error on my June statement. I am being charged for use of the ATM at the very branch where I do business.

The more annoying problem is that I have been unable to speak to a human being about this situation. On three occasions, I have come to the bank during my lunch hour, only to find the lines so long there seemed no hope of reaching either a teller or an officer during the limited time available. And by telephone, I just get lost in your complicated voice mail.

My local branch manager never seems to be at his desk, so I'm sending a copy of this letter to him, as well.

Will you please have someone credit the incorrect charges on my statement and mail me a corrected version. Because I figure this should take about four minutes, I would like to hear from someone within one week.

Sincerely,

Kent Coranis

cc: Michael Rumbrano
    First Bank, Windsor Branch

25. When your broker sells you short

Once you've registered your complaint in writing, it's important to know what your next step is if you don't receive satisfaction. You don't have to threaten to go to the authorities with your first letter, but be prepared to know what you will do. The mere suggestion that you're prepared and knowledgeable is enough to trigger the company into action.

Geoffrey Leowerk
24 Swan Trotting Lane
Sarasota, FL 34232

November 15

Mr. Guthrie F. Flanders, President
Merton Lyman Prentice
25 Wall Street
New York, NY 10002

Dear Mr. Flanders:

Attached is the letter that I shall be sending by certified mail to the Securities
and Exchange Commission in Washington D.C. on December 3 unless I have a
satisfactory response from you before that date.

Yours sincerely,

Geoffrey Leowerk

Complaint Department
Securities and Exchange Commission
Office of Investor Education and Assistance
450 Fifth St. NW
Washington, DC 20549

Re: Complaint against Merton Lyman Prentice:

On November 2, I sent a fax to my broker, Quentin Pimble, at MLP, placing a
buy order for 100 shares of International Flange. The price at that time was
20 1/4. The purchase was not made for more than 24 hours, during which
time the price of this stock had risen to 28 3/4 on news of the impending
merger with National Hinge.

When I complained to Mr. Pimble, he acknowledged by telephone that the fax
was received while International Flange was still at 20 1/4, but by the time he
got around to filling my order, the stock had already zoomed upward.

When I requested that the sum of $850 (100 times 8 1/2) be credited to my
account, Mr. Pimble denied the request, and pointed out that I did not specify
a maximum price for the purchase. That is true, but if my order had been
executed any time within six hours of receipt, I would have had the lower
price. Mr. Pimble pointed out that there are no time performance guarantees
in my agreement with MLP.

I find this response and behavior reprehensible and inappropriate, and beg
your assistance in setting this matter right, by crediting the $850 to my
account number 3746-273621.

Sincerely,

Geoffrey Loewerk

26. A credit report that's not a credit to the customer

A credit report that contain errors is a serious problem. This letter should be sent certified, with a return receipt requested. If you get the return receipt and have not yet heard from the recipient, you should certainly telephone for an explanation. Note the statement at the end of the first paragraph. The law is on your side!

John Parker
88 Buttercup Drive
Springfield, IL 62703
(217) 555-0987

July 7

Ms. Amanda T. Glaxon, Vice President, Customer Service
Accuport Credit Reporting Service
1422 Morganthal Road
Memphis, TN 38138

Dear Ms. Glaxon:

Your company's errors have been so harmful to me, I hardly know where to turn. I ask for your _immediate_ assistance in setting things right. Under the Fair Credit Reporting Act you have a legal obligation to make these corrections!

The problem should be such a simple one. There is another man here in Springfield with exactly the same name as mine, but he clearly has some major financial problems. The current Accuport credit report attributes several of this other person's credit problems to me and, as a result, I have been unable to obtain a car loan, and look forward to even worse problems when I go house-hunting next week.

Please have someone print out a copy of my report right now, and follow along, as I identify the errors:

Line 16: Two bankruptcies. That is the other man, not me. I have never declared bankruptcy. Never!

Line 24: Slow payments to the Arbuthnot Department Store. I have never shopped there, and do not have a credit card.

Line 31: Checking account at First National Bank frequently overdrawn. While I do have my account there, it has been overdrawn once, for only a few dollars, in the past nine years.

Please, please, please take care of these problems at once. Keep in mind the fact that I will be applying for a preapproved home loan next week. It is imperative that you deal with this immediately. Please telephone me to assure me that the problems have been taken care of.

Thank you,

John Parker

27. Demanding payment for moving damages

The better your back-up, the more likely that the offender will decide that giving you what you want is the easiest course of action. Whenever there have been previous communications—whether in person, by phone, or other written correspondence—be sure to refer to them in the letter.

Loretta Modern
3677 Marquette Way
Louisville, KY 40205
Phone/fax (556) 555-8723

June 1

Arnold Kornell
Bluegrass Moving Company
6754 Derby Road
Louisville, KY 40205

Dear Mr. Kornell:

As we discussed this morning, I am extremely displeased with the treatment I received from the Bluegrass company. The damages to my furniture, recently moved to my new home by your company on May 20, have made me question your company's commitment to quality. I reiterate the damages below, and ask for your immediate response, and a timely payment for the damages incurred.

1. Deep scratches in the surface of my antique armoire (see enclosed photo). These scratches are clearly new.
2. Small drawer missing from a family heirloom desk (see enclosed photo). This desk was recently appraised; if necessary, I can provide the appraisal papers, showing that the drawer was, in fact, in place at that time.
3. Light-colored sofa was not properly protected, resulting in stains on the back and arms. I have had a professional cleaner examine the sofa, and he says that these stains will not come out.

As I told you on the phone this morning, cleaning and repairing these items will cost about $10,000 (see attached estimates from antique restoration firm). Please send me whatever paperwork I need to fill out in order to be reimbursed. This is a matter of great concern to me, and I would like to receive the paperwork by fax today; I will fax it back within one hour, and expect to receive a check within one week.

Thank you for your attention to this matter.

Sincerely,

Loretta Modern

28. A vacationer who won't settle for heartbreak hotel

While you can return a defective product, poor service is sometimes more difficult to quantify. Take pictures, get signed statements or second opinions, or whatever level of documentation seems appropriate. Remember, the company wants repeat business and doesn't want to get a bad reputation. Calmly remind them of this.

———

Gerald Cotton
234 Calendar Court
Montgomery, AL 36120
(334) 555-2387

August 4

Amanda Cliffs
Pleasant Family Holidays
4455 Travel Plaza
Chicago, IL 60611

Dear Ms. Cliffs:

As a parent of three, I have used your service ever since I saw it recommended in the annual Family Vacation Guidebook, and have recommended you to friends on a number of occasions. Unfortunately, I recently had an unpleasant and rather costly experience with one of your package tours.

My family and I decided to splurge on your Tahitian Adventure Package, as a treat for the kids. When we arrived, however, we were shocked at the conditions we found. The Happy Hotel was rundown, and our rooms lacked air-conditioning and were infested with insects. The promised pool was closed for repairs, and the manager could not tell us when it would be available. He also would not move us to better rooms. After one night in these conditions, I decided to move us to a better location, at my own cost.

Please refund both the cost of the Happy Hotel, which we prepaid for seven days ($1,400), as well as the six days I paid for at the far superior Lagoon Hotel ($1,200), for a total of $2,600.

I enclose photos of the conditions at the first hotel, as well as of our pleasant rooms at the second, and credit card receipts for both stays.

I reiterate that this was my first bad experience with your agency, and I hope it was just a fluke. I am writing to the Guidebook to suggest that they investigate the Happy Hotel, and suggest that you do the same. I look forward to receiving a check for $2,600, and to a continued pleasant relationship with your company.

Sincerely,

Gerry Cotton

29. Broken walkways mean concrete plan of attack

It's okay to offer options to someone who's wronged you—just make it clear that at least one of the options must be taken. When a lot of money is at stake, and the provider has really messed up, a stern, businesslike tone is best. Note the not-so-gentle hint at the letter's end—no one wants to be sued, after all.

Louis Condon
Shaloware Court Apartments
1163 Shawnee Avenue
Bellevue, WA 99833
(360) 555-4399

March 16

Matthew Broylston
Concrete Ideas
6789 Calloway Street
Bellevue, WA 99804

Dear Mr. Broylston:

Your company recently replaced the concrete walkways at the apartment building I own, at a cost of $3,000. Last week, I noticed cracks appearing in the surface (see enclosed photos). I decided to spot-check the pavement's thickness, and discovered that it ranges from 2 to 3 inches throughout the complex. The attached contract clearly show that it was to be 4 inches throughout, and this discrepancy is not acceptable.

This can be addressed one of two ways:
1. Your firm can remove the substandard walkways, and replace them according to the original specifications, or
2. You can refund the $3,000 in full.

Please call me by week's end to let me know of your decision, so the we can proceed to a mutually agreeable resolution, and avoid any further complications.

Sincerely,

Louis Condon

30. Fare compensation is a fair request

Clever writing draws the reader into this letter, but it is the straigthforward approach and effective organization of facts, details, and demands that makes it a winner.

———

J. D. Sanchez
2776 23rd St.
Portland, OR 97200

March 19

Mr. Christopher Kay
General Manager
Municipal Transit Company
1422 Argus Lane
Portland, OR 97222

Dear Mr. Kay:

Thirty-five minutes. That's how long I stood on the corner of 18th and Church Streets yesterday morning, March 18th, starting at 8 am, waiting for a 41 bus to arrive. The schedule says there are 15 minutes between buses at that hour.

$7.80. That's how much I spent on a taxi, because I could not afford to be late for work.

$6.55. That's the amount that Municipal Transit owes me (the difference between the taxi charge and what the bus fare would have been) for your miserable performance.

March 31st. That's the day by which I expect to have your check in hand.

A pit bull. That's what my friends call me when I have been wronged. Once I get my teeth into something, I don't let go. Please don't think you can ignore me, just because the amount is so small. I know my options, and I assure you I will not rest.

Improved service. That's what the MTC should be giving us, and then there would be no need to write letters like this one.

Sincerely,

Jake Sanchez

31. Airport runaround grounds flight plans

The writer introduces the letter with a situation that anyone could relate to—a great way to get the attention and empathy of the reader. The idea of writing the complaint letter on the stationery of another airline is a great idea—it not-so-subtly reinforces the notion that some other company could get this customer's business.

Andrea Bellamy
246 W. Seaview Rd.
Bolinas, CA 95373

October 15

Kathryn Golden, Chairman of the Board
Trans-Global Airlines
1422 Sikorsky Blvd.
St. Louis, MO 63101

Dear Ms. Golden:

How would you like it if you arrived on time for a doctor's appointment, and then had to sit in the waiting room for two hours, with no information whatsoever about when the doctor could see you, or even if he was in his office.

Well, that is exactly how I felt when I attempted to fly Trans-Global between San Francisco and Pittsburgh earlier today. The problem was not that the flight was endlessly delayed, and finally canceled entirely. These things happen, I know. The problem was that none of us passengers were told what was going on. We did not know if it was a repair problem, a weather problem, a staff problem, or what.

My fellow passengers and I felt as if we were being jerked around by Trans-Global. No matter what the situation was, we should have been kept in the loop. When the flight was finally canceled, we were offered the option of a later flight on Trans-Global.

You will notice that I am writing this letter on the in-flight stationery of United Airlines, en-route to Pittsburgh.

To make up for my lost time, and my annoyance, may I suggest that a discount on my next Trans-Global flight would go a long way toward calming me down.

Yours sincerely,

Andrea Bellamy

32. Refuse to lose in airline overbooking game

Writing a bare-bones, straightforward letter such as this may actually get it looked at by somebody with greater authority. A longer story would probably just get re-routed to the giant pile of "bumped-from-flight—customer grumpy" letters in some office where they just churn out form letters in response.

C. L. Matheson
5 Arden Trail
Charlotte, NC 28226

September 10

Mr. Harold Hughes, CEO
South Central Airlines
Box 27272
Charlotte, NC 28226

Dear Mr. Hughes:

You're busy. I'm busy. Let's make this short and simple.

1. I had a confirmed ticket on SCA flight 14, Charlotte to Miami on September 9.

2. I arrived at the gate with 15 minutes to spare.

3. The plane was oversold, and I was bumped.

4. I was put on another flight three hours later, and reached Miami so late that I missed the first three-quarters of the Dolphins game.

5. To compensate me for this experience, I would like you to issue me a complimentary round-trip business-class ticket between Charlotte and Miami, and to reimburse me for the missed football game (copy of my ticket purchase invoice enclosed).

6. Please let me hear from you, or one of your staff, by October 1.

Thank you,

C. L. Matheson

33. When a collection correction is in order

Sometimes it takes breaking the rules to get attention. Instead of writing to the collection agency and sending a copy of the letter to the store, this customer chose to ignore standard business letter form in order to encourage faster action. This is a stern letter, with a legitimate threat at the end. You don't have to bring in the consumer advocates early, but when things are dragging on, and your credit rating is at risk, it's worth a little research to figure out where you can get help.

Alice Nguyen
1422 Crocker Plaza, Apt. 373
Shaker Heights, OH 43756

May 9

James L. Dunmore, President   June McLachlan, Manager
Dunmore Collection Agency   Save-Mart Department Store
1422 Hollister St.   Westfield Mall
Cleveland, OH 43434   Cleveland, OH 43422

Dear Mr. Dunmore and Ms. McLachlan:

I am writing to you at the same time, since both of you are involved in a situation that is threatening to damage my credit history. It is my hope that either one or both of you will now get involved in making things right for me.

Three months ago, on February 9, I purchased a sofa at Save-Mart, for $610, which I paid for with my personal check, number 1422. When the sofa was delivered the next day, it was clear to me that it was too large for my living room, and the color, when seen in the light of my living room, simply did not go with either my carpet or drapes. I had your men put it right back on the truck and take it away. And I immediately telephoned my bank to stop payment on the check.

Ms. McLachlan, your accounting department noticed the stopped check, but I cannot get through to them that the sofa was never accepted. You wrote to me twice demanding payment, and then turned the matter over to the collection agency. Mr. Dunmore, you cannot and will not collect for something that I do not owe.

Will you two please talk to each other, and straighten this out? And then, will one or both of you write to me, to let me know the matter has been settled, and that you have not made any adverse reports to any credit information agency.

Please let me hear from you by June 1, or I assure you, I shall notify the American Collectors Association in Minneapolis, and the Consumer Protection Unit in the state Attorney General's office.

Sincerely,

Alice Nguyen

34. Lost luggage is a case for complaint

One of the most likely causes of complaint among frequent travelers is lost luggage. Although most airlines have policies that compensate customers for such inconvenience, the terms are often not communicated. In the case that lost luggage results in expenses to replace items lost, it pays to complain.

M. Pierce
International Public Relations Syndicate
1 Rockefeller Center
New York, NY 10009
(212) 555-9000

June 3

Mr. Adam Lovecraft, President
Beta Airlines
Los Angeles International Airport
Los Angeles, CA 90011

Dear Mr. Lovecraft:

Your airline lost my luggage, gave me misleading information, and ruined my business trip to Dallas. The damage has already been done, but now I expect you to help make things better. Here are the details:

What happened
I flew on Beta flight 363 from Boston to Dallas on June 1. The flight arrived on time, but my luggage either was not on board, or was stolen from your baggage claim area.

How I was misled
First, your agent virtually promised me that the bag would be found and brought to my hotel. Second, he did not tell me what my rights are in this sort of situation. Your agent could have authorized me to purchase replacement clothing and toiletries, but he did not mention that possibility. Furthermore, the agent's name badge was covered by some promotional badge he was wearing. He only told me his name was Tom.

Why this was a big problem
I was headed for a very important three-day business conference. I was forced to wear my rumpled suit on arrival day. Then, when it became clear my bag was not going to arrive at the hotel, I had to scurry around to try to find some decent ready-to-wear clothing. Mr. Lovecraft, have you ever gone to an important meeting in an off-the-rack suit bought after midnight at Wal-Mart?

What I want you to do
At the very least, I expect you to reimburse me for the clothing that I had to purchase. Copies of my invoices are enclosed. If my suitcase does not turn up in three days, I shall assume it was stolen from your baggage claim area, where luggage tags are not checked. In that event, I shall expect payment in full for the current value of the contents of the bag. A complete list, along with prices, is also enclosed.

May I please hear from you by June 15th at the latest? Thank you for your prompt attention.

Sincerely,

Mildred Pierce

Enclosures: copies of all receipts

35. Chronic cable complaints lead to strong treatment

In short order, the writer manages to convey the monumental impact that just a few minutes of poor service can cause. He builds a solid case for a reasonable demand, and also communicates the consequences if the poor services continues—or his requests are ignored.

Vincent Galatano
872 College Court
Minneapolis, MN 55409
(612) 442-4759
Account Number: 13900-872

October 24

Alison Pride, President
VLS Cable Company
1422 Lakeshore Drive
Minneapolis, MN 55545

Dear Ms. Pride:

The score is tied with three minutes left in the game. The Crusaders have the ball on the 30 yard line. Sonny Crenshaw fades back to pass. He spots a receiver downfield. The crowd goes wild as...

...as once again, VLS Cable service conks out at exactly the wrong moment, causing me (and presumably many, many others) to miss the dramatic conclusion.

Since I figure I am paying you about five cents an hour for my service, it is not going to do any good whatsoever to credit me with a nickel for this miserable experience (and as you well know, this wasn't the first time). And, because you are a monopoly, I cannot switch to another cable company (although I must say, those little satellite dishes are looking better and better for someone in my situation).

To make me a happy (or at least happier) customer, I respectfully request these two things:

1. That you spend more time and effort in your technical department, so that this sort of situation does not happen quite so often.
2. That you give me one month of credit on my basis bill, to recompense me for your unreliable service.

Thank you for your kind attention to these two requests. I look forward to hearing from VLS by November 5.

Sincerely,

Vincent Galatano

36. Damming the junk-mail flood

Unsolicited information pours into our homes—and it's difficult to put a stop to it. Especially troublesome is the fact that your name may be sold and resold to other companies, so even if you manage to stop the flow from some companies, more catalogs and mail are trickling in from other sources.

One step you can take is to write to the Direct Mail and Marketing Association, 6 East 43rd St., New York, NY 10017, and request that your name be blocked from all direct mailing lists they service (which is several hundred). The other course of action is to write to specific catalog companies and direct marketers and request that they stop mailing to you.

The following letter is a good template. Just insert the appropriate company name and send it off. And good luck.

Marjorie Toynbee
2776 Easter Way
Springfield, MD 28374

January 3

Harvey's Guns and Ammo
Catalog List Manager
30 Highway One
Helena, MT 59620

RE: Removal of my name from your list

I do not wish to receive further catalogs from your company.

Please remove my name from your mailing list.

Please do not sell my name to any other company that sells products by mail.

I thank you for your prompt attention to this matter.

Sincerely,

Marjorie Toynbee

37. Just say no to negative-option marketing

Many book and music clubs have finally caught on to the fact that people are avoiding them because of the dreaded "send this back or we'll send you something you don't want" factor. But there are still enough out there that this letter is a public service. Don't take what you don't want and didn't order!

James Randolph Burgeron
1422 Naipaul Lane
Evergreen, WA 97878

October 8

Mr. Ambrose Pierce, Chairman of the Board
Carberry Book Club
42 Eveningwood Rd.
Scarsdale, NY 11223

Dear Mr. Pierce,

Please forgive me for writing to you at home (I got your address from your listing in Who's Who in Business and Industry), and for enclosing the copy of Great Railroads of South America, but I think it is the only way I can get the attention of your company.

Something seems to have gone haywire with your system, and I can't get anyone's attention. For the last three months, my monthly newsletter, with that dreaded postcard that must be returned within 10 days, has come so late that there was no time to stave off the sending of an unwanted monthly selection.

I dutifully returned the unwanted books (and, thank heavens, I wasn't charged for them), but my accompanying messages have been ignored or overlooked. And, of course, I have had to pay the postage to return the books.

So, when you get to your office tomorrow, would you please have someone make sure that my newsletters are sent out on time. If you cannot guarantee this, then please cancel my membership.

Yours sincerely,

James Randolph Burgeron

P.S. Instead of reimbursing me for the postage I have had to use to return unwanted books (copies of receipts enclosed), if you'd like to send me the new Stephen King novel, I wouldn't be disappointed.

Enc.

38. When cupid misses the mark

It's hard to quantify value when dealing with a dating service. How can you measure "getting your money's worth"? The writer of this letter does a good job in illustrating how his expectations were not met as he cites the promises made by the service.

Ronald H. Hyde
3 The Towers
Boston, MA 01125

February 15

Mrs. Audrey Kroninger, General Manager
Bluebirds of Happiness Computer Dating Service
P. O. Box 1422
Middlesex, MA 01237

Dear Mrs. Kroninger:

Well you can't refund my wasted time, and you can't refund my miserable evening, but you can darn well refund my $60 membership fee, and the $45.77 that it cost me to have one of the worst evenings of my life.

Your sales literature promises "sophisticated computer matching, so that you and your date will share the same interests, the same values, and the same tastes in food, music, and romance."

Bullfeathers! Any court in the land would agree that matching a liberal Democrat (the lovely Alexa, my date) with a conservative Republican (that's me) is already clear evidence of a mismatch. The fact that she had no interest in my three Bs of having a good time (bowling, be-bop, and barbecue) simply compounded the problem.

Yes, I am aware that my contract covers three introductions. With this letter, I am informing you that I have no wish to meet any more of your Bluebirds of Happiness, and you can jolly well make good for the one you <u>did</u> provide. My receipts for the disastrous dinner at Pete's Bar-B-Q Shack (she's a vegetarian), one line of bowling (not even completed—she complained the bowling shoes didn't match her outfit) at the Avenue Bowl, and two admissions to the Pot-O-Gold Ballroom (where after one dance she insisted I take her home), are enclosed. They total $45.77. That plus my membership fee comes to $105.77.

You can take off $5.77 for your administrative costs, and I shall expect your check in the mail for exactly $100.

Ronald H. Hyde

39. An alterations service can mend a relationship

Some situations really are hopeless. If a dry cleaner or alterations place has lost a garment, all the complaining in the world won't get it back. The writer of this letter recognizes this, and offers alternative solutions.

Tracy Podolsky
1101 Daffodil Lane, No. 202
Wilberforce, OH 43952

June 8

Karl Kamenetz, Owner
Ace Alterations and Custom Clothing
1422 Sampson Avenue
Wilberforce, OH 43952

Dear Mr. Kamenetz:

You could buy me one.

You could rent me one.

You could make me one.

But if you don't get me a decent dress to wear to the prom on June 12, then Bob Trimble will never ask me out again, and we'll never get married, and we'll never have children, and our son will never invent the cure for cancer. And it will be all your fault!

I brought my one-and-only prom dress in to be taken in and shortened on June 1. It was promised for June 6, two days ago. When I came by to get it, the friendly lady at your front counter could not find it. She couldn't even find any record of it. She shrugged her shoulders, and said maybe it will come in tomorrow.

Well yesterday was tomorrow, and it didn't. And today is today and it didn't.

I simply cannot afford to buy another dress. I don't know anyone who is my size and my taste, from whom I could borrow one. So it's up to you, Ace Alterations. You caused the problem, you solve it. And pronto.

Here is exactly what I want from you:
1. My own dress. That is my first choice. But if you don't find it:
2. A $50 credit at Laverne's Party Rentals, where there are three formals available for rent that would meet my needs.
3. A new dress, of my choice, from Sudbury's, up to $150. I will wear it once, then give it back to you. You can keep it, return it, or pour ketchup on it and eat it for lunch; I don't care.

But whatever you do, you must do it immediately. The prom is four days away. That's why I brought this letter in personally. Please phone me at 555-3635 anytime until midnight, or early tomorrow morning. Thank you.

Sincerely,

Tracy Podolsky

40. Housecleaning service should clean up its act

It's good to document problems even when they don't seem like a super big deal. After all, even minor annoyances add up. In this situation, the irritations mentioned are little, "oh, it's not worth complaining about" situations that end up causing the non-complainer to switch to a new service provider. So, by complaining, you're actually doing the company a favor by helping it to keep a customer. Note the documentation and the relatively gentle tone—the writer doesn't want the offenders fired or punished, he just wants the job done right.

———

Robert Browne
998 Minna Street
Cavern Falls, ID 88657

Susan Randall
Tidy Team Housecleaners
5546 Sparkling Way
Cavern Falls, ID 88654

December 13

Dear Ms. Randall,

Re: Problems with housecleaning service

Over the past month, I've become increasingly disappointed with the service I've received from Tidy Team. This is surprising to me, as you've always done a great job in the past. I realize that with the holiday season upon us you're probably very busy. Still, I do pay for a service and expect to receive it. In the past month:

- Most importantly, on December 6, no one showed up at all to clean. This is obviously a major problem, and I expect that my next bill will reflect one less charge than usual. In the future, if there are scheduling problems, I urge you to call me advance, and I'm sure we can work something out.
- On several visits, the cleaner did not vacuum under tables or behind furniture (see attached photos.) This may not seem like a big deal, but one of the reasons I hired a cleaning service is to do a better job than I would do myself.
- This week, the cleaner was obviously in a hurry, and left cleaner and water splashed on the bathroom floor (see attached photo). Again, not a super big deal, but not something I want to pay $50 a week for, either.

Please have a talk with your staff, and let them know that customers really do appreciate a good, thorough job. Also, of course, please make sure that I am not billed for the missed visit. Thank you, and I look forward to many more happy years with the Tidy Team.

Sincerely,

Robert Browne

41. A bad haircut leaves customer scissor-shy

People develop ongoing relationships with service workers such as hairdressers, personal trainers, childcare professionals, etc. But when the complaint includes a request for a refund or for some kind of reimbursement, it's best to have things down in writing.

Louise Kazinsky
29 Overlook Drive
Fargo Heights, ND 72626
(701) 555-6789

July 23

Marie Rigrutsky
Marie's House of Charm
1422 Cypress Street
Fargo, ND 72626

Dear Marie,

Of course I could come in and talk again in person, but I wanted to put this in writing, to carefully explain my feelings. I've been pleased with your cuts and style recommendations over the past five years, and I've referred a number of my friends—so I know we both value our relationship.

When I came to you last Tuesday, July 13, for my usual cut and styling, you recommended a slightly shorter cut for summer, and I agreed. But the end result was not at all to my liking. I am not the Liza Minelli type, and I frankly am quite embarrassed by how I look. You assured me that I look great, but I simply do not agree. From the looks I have been getting from the people in my office, and at the bridge club, it is clear to me that they also do not agree.

I know you will be distressed to hear of my unhappiness, and I'm sure, once my hair grows back a little, we'll both be relieved that I'll be able to return to my old style. But I honestly think it would be appropriate for you to reimburse me for the cost of the summer hat that I have had to buy to cover up the cut. My invoice is enclosed. I will be happy to give you the hat once my hair is presentable again.

You can reach me at my home number after 4:30 most afternoons, if you'd like to talk this over. I hope to hear from you soon.

Sincerely,

Louise Kazinsky

42. Alerting a newspaper to fraudulent advertising

When you have complaints about information that appears in the media, be sure to establish your own credibility—why should the publication listen to you? Explain why. And make your case as widely applicable as possible.

Brazleton State University
College Park
Remington, OH 40273
Department of Education—Alan Toroni, Ed.D.

December 1

Josie Bass, Advertising Director
The Washington Examiner
123 Main Street
Arlington, VA 19283

Dear Ms. Bass:

I am a professor at Brazleton State University, and I have been a reader of your newspaper for more than five years.

While I always appreciate your news and editorial material, even when I disagree with it, I have been growing more and more concerned with some of the advertisements you have been running lately.

Specifically, I am referring to those advertisements that purport to offer accredited university degrees in a matter of weeks.

I have been involved in higher education for many years, and I am very familiar with the rise of fraudulent credentials in America. There is no legitimate or legal way to earn a graduate degree in four weeks.

I fear that many of your readers are being taken in and are wasting their money on these frauds, and when they suffer serious consequences, they may well hold you partially responsible.

You may say that you cannot possibly check out or prescreen every advertiser. But I can assure you that most other responsible publications do just that.

You would not run ads selling solid gold Rolex watches for $5, or offering prescription drugs for sale. But in running the kind of ad I am referring to, you are doing much the same thing.

Please review the education section on your classified pages, and ask anyone in higher education about the damage you are doing. Please ask your corporate counsel to review those ads, since they are clearly promoting an illegal service.

Thank you most kindly for your attention. My colleagues and I look forward to seeing some positive changes in that part of your otherwise excellent publication.

Sincerely,

Alan Torroni, Ed.D.
cc: David Kerrigan, Publisher

43. Speaking out against stereotyping

A popular columnist or radio personality makes a disparaging remark about a segment of his or her audience. While the remark may simply be part of the script that makes up the individual's media image, your complaint letter may have some influence in making a change. For best results, respond in a rational and level-headed manner—if the recipient is indeed a dyed-in-the-wool bigot, you don't want to provide more ammunition that could end up in a column or on the air.

———

Richard Marks
6543 Lowland Avenue
Baltimore, MD 21201

March 23

Gerald Pullet, Columnist
c/o The Starling Morning Star
1 Newspaper Square
Baltimore, MD 21201

Dear Mr. Pullet:

I read your column every morning. I don't always agree with your views, but that's what makes it interesting. As a longtime reader, I can always count on being interested and entertained. Lately, though, I've noticed a few comments that bother me. In an item on the new development out by Flagstone Way, you joked that "At last, a little culture's coming to white-trash trailerland."

And then last week, you referred to a laid-off factory worker as "another cracker on the dole." I expect this sort of thing from Rush Limbaugh or Howard Stern, but you've always managed to poke fun at people and their foolishness without stereotyping or being mean. A lot of folks around here are blue-collar working men and women who flinch a little when terms like "white trash," "cracker," and the like are used. We don't all live in trailers, and even when we do, we deserve to be treated with the same dignity given any of the citizens of our community.

I invite you to come meet the fine folks at the Lowland Trailer Park, maybe even get an item out of it. I guarantee that you will come away with a new attitude about your less-affluent, but still loyal, readers. Call me any time, I'd love to set something up with you.

Sincerely,

Richard Marks

44. Company tunes in to customer preferences

Often, our dissatisfaction with a product or service isn't one that prompts us to immediate action ("...or I'll cancel my subscription," "...or I'll take my business elsewhere"). But often, a letter requesting improvements or changes could have more impact than you might imagine.

Gina Ashanti
9954 48th Street
Reno, NV 87632
(776) 555-1987

April 4

Quentin Smith, Director of Programming
Silver State Cable
P.O. Box 6543
Reno, NV 87652

Dear Mr. Smith:

As a long-time cable customer who has recently moved to the Reno area, I am very surprised at the lack of quality family programming on your service. I've come to count on cable to not just entertain but also give my children a learning experience.

With cable facing so much competition from direct satellite programming these days, it struck me that you might want to know what your customers want, and how to keep them from making the change to dish-based delivery systems. Might I hear back from you regarding any future plans you have to add:

The Learning Channel
The History Channel
Discovery

I would like to continue with your service, as it certainly is convenient and reasonably priced, but I would like to know that you have plans to expand your family offerings in the immediate future. Thank you.

Sincerely,

Gina Ashanti

45. Sunday school's "fire and brimstone" approach

When you're complaining about the performance or behavior of a techer or childcare professional, documentation of events will be valuable. Because the information in such a letter will most likely be shared with the individual, and possibly other community members, it is crucial that you be accurate, thorough, and impartial.

———

Pat and Hal Ryan
(and four other concerned families)
2524 Greenbelt Way
Dusty Plain, WY 80955

23 September

Father Joseph O'Leary
St. James Church
345 Valley View
Dusty Plain, WY 80955

Dear Father O'Leary:

This is a difficult letter to write but we, the undersigned parents, think it is an important one. We ask that you strongly reconsider having Sarah McCarthy teach Sunday School, as she has been doing for the past three months since Lucy Meyers moved away.

We are very concerned about her harsh way with the children, and her somewhat rigorous interpretations of Scripture. More than one of our children reports that Miss McCarthy has threatened that they will go to Hell. Our daughter Hannah came home crying because she was told she was a sinner when she lost her weekly charity donation. And we have personally overheard Miss McCarthy tell the children that if they get sick, it's because they've done something wrong. We feel that she is giving the children a view of our religion that is not in keeping with the gentle spirit of St. James.

Several children have been threatened with physical violence (as in "I'll take you over my knee if you speak up again"). Although this may be a mere figure of speech, they find it upsetting. And so do we.

The undersigned parents are seriously considering removing their children from Sunday School if Miss McCarthy remains. We have tried to discuss these concerns with her, but she seems unaware or unable to admit that there is a problem.

We love our church, and cherish the spiritual leadership you have provided. Might we meet with you to discuss a way around this problem, so that we won't be forced to choose between our spiritual lives and our concern for our children?

Sincerely,

Patricia Ryan   Richard Calista
Harold Ryan   Cynthia Ladd
Margaret Simmons   Jean Crew
Bartholemew Simmons   Leon Crew

46. Phone company policy disconnects customer

Many consumers are willing to sacrifice service, price, and quality when a company's politics are in conflict with their own. Of course, you don't have to, but you might be doing yourself, the company, and others a service by letting the company know why you've severed your relationship.

———

Salvatore Bernardi
987 Davenport Way, #7
Shreveport, LA 71106
(654) 555-0978

January 30

Tim C. Turnaround, CEO
Megabig Telephone Company
7894 Megabig Towers
Atlanta, GA 30367

Dear Mr. Turnaround:

I have just switched my long-distance carrier to ResourceCo, following a four-year stint with Megabig, because I very strongly disapprove of your corporate charity policy. I just read in my local paper that you have decided to stop giving a major endowment to the AIDS Foundation, as a result of pressure from anti-gay groups.

I understand that you have the right to give money to whomever you please, but I don't want you making these sorts of decisions with my money. I have already fielded several calls from your salespeople, asking what sort of deal it would take to get me to switch back to Megabig. They did not seem to understand that this was not about my rates (although I do make a large number of long-distance calls, as I work from home and have family in Europe).

My principles are more important than the per-minute rate I'm charged, and until I read or hear from you that you are no longer taking direction from the radical right, my money will be going to other services.

Sincerely,

Salvatore Bernardi

47. Who is your representative representing?

When writing to government representatives, be succinct. Your letter will almost certainly be read by an aide, not the elected official. If you are writing about a specific bill, cite it, and don't make it hard for the reader to figure out your position.

Barry Lopez
765 Blueberry Circle
Rockham, ME 01234

April 22

The Honorable Lois Langton
United States House of Representatives
Washington, DC 20515

Re: HR 8764

Dear Ms. Langton:

Please vote no on HR 8764, the veterans' rights bill. As a veteran of the conflict in Vietnam, I can assure you that your benefits are not excessive—indeed, I feel that, given the service we gave our country, they may even be insufficient.

I understand that there's a lot of talk about "cutting the fat" in government, but please don't cut off the men and women who have done so much for that government. Please vote no on HR 8764. Thank you.

Sincerely,

Barry Lopez

48. Writer protests insurance practices

It's no easy task to change the policies of large insurance companies, but a good letter that logically positions the writer's objections and announces plans to pull other "big guns" into the fight might have some impact.

Julia Washington
4458 Granite Blvd.
Chicago, IL 60045

January 5

Dr. Phyllis K. Pfeister
Friendly Insurance Company
1422 Guilford Tower
Rowayton, CT 06345

Dear Dr. Pfeister:

Your company, which should be helping my friends and me, has a policy that could very well send us to our early graves. And we must tell you, we are annoyed. We are so annoyed, we are holding a letter-writing "party" next month, to write and send letters to our elected officials, to the state insurance regulatory board, and to all the daily newspapers in the state.

I refer to the matter of withholding health insurance payments for preventive medicine, most especially for mammograms. What is going through your minds at F.I.C. when you establish these policies? Do any of you really believe that it is not a good idea for us to have mammograms? Would you really rather pay for our cancer treatments later on than our tests now? We just can't understand this.

Do you have any plans in mind to reverse your outdated policies, and take the position that health insurance can, should, and must cover preventive medical procedures? We certainly hope so, since that will save us the considerable amount of time we are planning to spend lobbying our politicians and contacting the media.

Maybe there are some good reasons against preventive care, which we have not thought of. We're willing to listen.

Either way, we'd really like to hear from you before our group meets again on the 14th. Thank you.

Sincerely,

Julia Washington

49. Changing the world one letter at a time

Another example of a situation in which corporate politics may negatively influence a consumer. The reader takes a compassionate stance, which is also conveyed in his approach with the recipient.

George W. Miller
27 Arlington Vista
Danville, VA 23226

March 22

Mr. Sam Argonaut, Vice President, Purchasing
SaveMart Department Stores
National Headquarters
1422 Main St.
Harrisburg, PA 17110

Dear Mr. Argonaut:

Last Sunday, a small group of Tibetan monks came to our church, where they uplifted everyone's spirits with their songs, their broad smiles, and their obvious joy of life and living.

Why am I telling you this?

Because the message that these wonderful men brought us is that their homeland is steadily and methodically being destroyed by the political and industrial growth of China. The photographs that they showed us nearly broke our hearts. Their beautiful land is being overrun with factories and military installations.

Why am I telling you this?

Because I have read that fully 30 percent of all the items sold at SaveMart are made in and purchased from China. I cannot tell you how to run your business. But I wish I could get you thinking about how much power you have to change the world, just a little bit. What if you looked for other vendors in other countries? What if you told your suppliers that you are cutting down on your order because you are uncomfortable with what's going on in Tibet?

Why am I telling you this?

Because, Mr. Argonaut, you and SaveMart are truly in a place where you could do just a little bit to make this a better world.

Thank you for listening.

George Miller

50. Neighbor raises a stink over refinery

This letter alerts a corporate executive to a situation in which his business is causing difficulty for its neighborhood. This is an angry letter, but the anger is well-controlled. The introduction is guaranteed to get the reader's attention.

Charles Dubonnet
27 Sonora Drive
Richmond, CA 94700

February 1

Mr. Arthur Strickland
Vice President, Consumer Affairs
Belchfire Oil Company
123 Main Street
Richmond, IN 40304

Dear Mr. Strickland:

You stink!

Well, not you personally, Mr. Strickland, but I hope I have gotten your attention.

I live about a mile from your Richmond Refinery. I've lived here for seven years, and I must tell you that the bad odors emanating from your plant have been getting worse each year. There is no longer even any respite on weekends.

Before I petition my neighbors, and send a formal complaint to the Air Pollution Control Board at 420 Ninth St. in Sacramento, perhaps you can tell me what steps Belchfire is planning to implement in order to alleviate this problem.

May I please hear from you by February 17? Thank you most kindly for your attention to this important matter.

Sincerely,

Charles Dubonnet

51. Resident alerts police to potential crime

Many people fear repercussions when reporting possible crime, so it's not surprising that such letters to the police are often anonymous. The effectiveness of an anonymous letter can still be strong, as long as the writer supports claims with documented events. The writer of this letter reports helpful details, such as location, time, and description of suspicious activity.

August 15

Chief Henry Lee
Helena Police Department
9876 Ardmore Street
Helena, MT 59620

Dear Chief Lee:

I am writing to inform you about a situation you may not be aware of in the Butte Park neighborhood. Drug dealers appear to have set up shop in the park, and I have not noticed any police response. In the past week:

- Three young men have been hanging around the pay phone near the children's play area, clearing doing business of some sort.
- Car traffic on Baskerville, normally a quiet street, has increased significantly.
- Graffiti has been spray-painted on several garage doors in the area.
- The suspicious activity usually occurs between 3 pm and 6 pm during school days.

Please have your officers investigate this situation. I hope that increased patrols will be enough to discourage these dealers.

Thank you.

Sincerely,

A concerned citizen

52. Taking the bite out of a complaint to a neighbor

It may be worrisome to confront a neighbor with a complaint; you'll want to do so with diplomacy to maintain friendly relations. But in a case where the problem is a threat to the safety of your family, a letter may be the best way to handle it. You avoid emotional confrontations, and you create a paper trail in case you need to involve others (animal control, or a homeowner association).

Ben Persons
455 Guerrero
Santa Fe, NM 87650
(445) 555-0098

June 29

Ray Lizardo
457 Guerrero
Santa Fe, NM 87650

Dear Ray:

We never seem to be home at the same time, and I'm really pretty concerned about the situation with Bruno jumping into our yard, so I thought it best to write you this letter.

I know you've told me Bruno wouldn't hurt a fly, and I'm sure that's true, but he barks so much and flings himself at the fence (he's actually jumped it a couple of times, as I'm sure you recall) so hard that our little Timmy is afraid to go outside when he's there.

I'm sure we can come up with a solution. Could Bruno maybe stay indoors or in the front yard while you're at work? Has he been through obedience training? Is there a local doggy daycare or other solution that would allow him to work off his energy?

I don't want to tell you how to handle your pit bull, but he's really starting to affect my quality of life, and scare my kid. Do give me a call tonight, or just drop by after 6, and I'm sure we can work something out.

See you,

Ben

53. Lessons in class don't add up to gender equality

Because of the risk of negative repercussions to their children, parents are often reluctant to complain about teachers. But a good letter will present concerns and document facts in a way that the criticism isn't personal. Be relatively concise: Just state the problem, give examples, and tell what you'd like done about it.

———

Thalia Bannerjee
4567 Raleigh Street
Dusty Mills, SC 29260

October 16

Sharon Smith, Principal
Emerson Middle School
9876 Softshell Parkway
Dusty Mills, SC 29260

Dear Ms. Smith:

I am concerned about the education my daughter Ajanta is receiving in her sixth-grade class, and would like to meet with you to discuss options. My strong feeling is that her teacher, Mr. Wayne Wood, is not the best instructor for her, and that she would do better in a different class. The following issues worry me:

- Ajanta has always been an A student and very active in class leadership, but her grades have suffered since entering Mr. Wood's class, and she shows no interest in daily classroom duties.
- When I asked her about this, she said that Mr. Wood never calls on her or any of the girls, and that only boys are encouraged to take on special science and math projects. While allowing for the natural tendency of any sixth-grader to exaggerate, I am still alarmed.
- I raised my concern to Mr. Wood at a parent-teacher conference, and he was unresponsive, saying that a lot of girls stop being interested in math and science around this age. I did not get the sense that he was interested in why this former A student had suddenly become disinterested in her classes.
- My son Raj had Mr. Wood for home room last year, and did well with him, which only underscores my concern that he simply isn't the right teacher for Ajanta.

Can we please meet to discuss this situation? I would prefer to meet without Mr. Wood initially, so that I may air all of my feelings without constraint, although I am certainly happy to talk with him, as well. I would like to hear from you within the week, as my daughter's education is of paramount concern to me. Thank you.

Sincerely,

Thalia Bannerjee

54. Doctor's bedside manner needs work

Often when we get shoddy treatment from authority figures—doctors, therapists, teachers—we don't feel that we have the right to complain. Ah, but we do! Everybody serves somebody, and doctors need to keep their "clients" satisfied, as well. If complaining to the offending doctor doesn't seem to get you anywhere, contact the HMO, an overseeing board, or professional organization. You deserve much better!

Julianne Barker
777 Gold Coast Way
Juneau, AK 99887

May 3

Dr. Emily Wolsey, Chairperson
HealthWave
4 Margolin Medical Complex
San Anselmo, CA 95670

Dear Dr. Wolsey:

I am writing to register my deep anger and dismay at the way I was treated by one of your member physicians. I recently started a new job and joined your HMO. I chose Dr. Henry Batard out of your directory to be my primary care physician, based on his convenient office location, and my belief that any doctor associated with your plan would be equally proficient. This was clearly a mistake.

Last month, I discovered a lump in my breast, and made an appointment to see Dr. Batard. He entered the examination room, and immediately commented on my weight. I am a large woman, but a perfectly healthy one, and I had come about an entirely different issue. I told him that my weight was not the problem, that I'd found a disturbing lump that needed to be examined. He continued to discuss weight loss options with me before finally examining me. He told me that the lump was probably benign, and left to order a biopsy. I heard him pass a nurse in the hallway, and say to her, "How could she even find a lump in all that fat?"

This is absolutely unacceptable. I did not come to see the doctor about my weight, nor was I looking for weight-loss advice. I have never felt so unwelcome or so dismissed. I could have had cancer! Does this mean nothing to this man?

I strongly suggest that you remove Dr. Batard from your HMO or, at the very least, ask him to enroll in sensitivity training. I expect to hear from you on this issue. If you do not discipline the doctor in some way, or otherwise address this issue, I will do everything I can to get my company to switch health providers, as I do not want my money going to support a company that treats people this way.

Sincerely,

Julianne Barker

55. When environment is hazardous to happiness

Being forced to endure the tortures of unneighborly neighbors or co-workers can make for a miserable situation. If you can't resolve the problems directly with the culprits, a letter to a higher power may be in order.

Marjorie Bow
4456 Lincoln Way, #475
Bayville, WI 53202
(567) 555-9834

July 7

Louis Zachary
677 Peralta
Bayville, WI 53202

Dear Mr. Zachary:

As a longtime tenant of your Lincolnwood Arms apartment building, I am writing to let you know of an unacceptable situation in the complex. Surely you must be aware that the family who recently moved into the apartment above mine, #575, has six young children living in the one-bedroom apartment.

I understand that times are tough all over and, believe me, I don't want to see this family out on the streets. However, the noise and commotion are unbelievable. The children run up and down the walkways unsupervised all day, screaming at the top of their lungs and at night jump up and down on the floor so hard that cracks are appearing in my ceiling.

I have spoken to other tenants, and we all agree that this situation must change. I've been looking into local law, and it does appear that cramming eight people into a one-bedroom apartment is not only unwise, but a zoning violation.

Perhaps you have a larger apartment in one of your other complexes that could accommodate this family? Perhaps one with yard access, so that the kids have something else to do besides damage your property? I don't want to have to go to the point of reporting this to the Zoning Commission, but believe me, when I lie awake listening to eight people yelling at each other over my head, it seems like the only answer.

Thank you for your prompt attention to this matter.

Sincerely,

Marjorie Bow

56. Discriminatory treatment warrants complaint

The management or owners of an establishment, whether a restaurant or retail store, will benefit from customer complaints about poor treatment from waiters or clerks. You're doing a service by alerting them to a problem that may be causing them to lose business—not to mention drawing lawsuits.

Jose Gonzales
9870 Channing Way
Grenville, AZ 85013

September 16

Melody Smithers, Owner
Nut Basket Restaurant
6572 Oak Grove Boulevard
Grenville, AZ 85013

Dear Ms. Smithers:

I've eaten at your restaurant for years, and am just "nuts" about your daily specials. However, a recent experience made me question my lifelong allegiance to the Nut Basket.

Last Tuesday, I went to the restaurant with three other members of the Grenville High Hispanic Achievers Club, a Latino pride and civic works club at our local high school. It took us a long time to get seated, with the waitress, Susan (according to her name tag), seating several other parties before us. When I pointed this out to her, she said in an exasperated tone, "Okay you kids, you can sit over there," pointing to an uncleared table near the kitchen.

The restaurant was not crowded (it was about 4 p.m.), but Susan took a long time to bring our menus, and then a long time again to take our order. When we ordered several expensive items, she said, "That's pretty expensive. Can you kids afford that?" She brought us the check with our food, not asking whether we might want any dessert, coffee, or anything else.

Normally, I wouldn't complain about something like this, but I had the strong sense that our age and maybe even our ethnic background had something to do with the treatment we received. I don't want to see the Nut Basket suffer as a result of bad service, nor do I want to spend my life without ever tasting your "Nuts Away Sundae" again.

I hope this was an isolated incident, due to one person having a bad day, but I thought you should know about it nonetheless. My friends and I hope to hear from you within the next week. We are ready to schedule our next club meeting, and hope to hear that we will be assured courteous treatment, so we don't have to hold our meeting at another restaurant.

Sincerely,

Jose Gonzales

57. When a good friend betrays a confidence

Is it appropriate to write a complaint letter to a friend? Sometimes it's the best way to handle an awkward situation. Writing a letter allows you to separate yourself from emotions and approach the situation calmly. This doesn't mean your letter shouldn't have a personal tone, however.

Although you won't be asking for a refund or a replacement, you should ask for some sort of response—whether it's simply an explanation or an apology. Be clear about what response you expect. Finally, a personal complaint letter can be very short. You may not want to go into details in writing, but just open the door to resolving the problem.

May 2, 1999

Dear Dana,

I spoke with you about my confusion about my job and relationship in strictest confidence because I felt you are my closest friend. Can you imagine how I felt when I met Susan on the street and she asked me when I was moving and what Bob thought about it? I feel really betrayed at a very difficult time. I need to hear from you, because I need to decide if my boss is likely to hear about this. It would make my job very difficult if he did. Please call me.

J.

58. A break in a friendship over damaged property

When writing to a friend, it might be acceptable to hand-write your complaint letter—especially if it is regarding an emotional or personal issue. A handwritten letter conveys intimacy, which may be appropriate. If your hand writing is poor, however, or the issue involves a lot of details or a complicated chronology, it might be best to use a computer. Still, remember that you are writing to a friend and avoid stiff, formal language.

September 3

Dear Mike,

You're hard to reach by phone, and I need to tell you this because I value our friendship. If I didn't, I wouldn't have loaned you my car for your job interview last Friday.

I appreciate that you didn't have time to put gas in the car before returning it, and thanks for the $10 you left. But you know it's my first decent car and that I try to take good care of it. That was the reason, you said, that you wanted to borrow it—because it would make a good impression at the company where you were interviewing.

Here's why I'm writing: This morning I noticed that there's a crack in the bottom part of the front bumper, like you get when you ram into a curb. I can guarantee it wasn't there when I loaned the car to you, because I washed the car that morning before you picked it up. Maybe you didn't notice it, but I would appreciate it if you'd call me to work out some way to get an estimate for repairing it.

Sincerely,

Lily

59. Have your say before writing off a colleague

All personal complaint letters are a big deal. Generally the person writing the letter feels let down—even betrayed—by a friend or a colleague. If you know the person well, just ending the letter formally, with "sincerely" rather than something more friendly, can underline the message that you're feeling as if you weren't treated right and an apology is in order.

Sometimes the person you need to write to isn't a friend, but a business acquaintance. In that case, a typed letter will probably be better—and you can fiddle around with the wording on screen to get it right.

Jan Polus
Newsletter Central
2540 State Blvd.
Sacramento, CA 95700

October 5

Mark Lineman
FineLine Graphics
55 Ridge Road
Napa CA 96801

Dear Mark,

We've worked together for many years, and you know I've admired your graphic work in the past. That's why, when an associate asked me to recommend someone to help with the graphics for a marketing campaign, you came to mind. Your work on the CompuneX launch was outstanding and I still see those mouse pads you designed in people's offices.

When I phoned you last July, you said you had some time available and were grateful for the recommendation. After I'd connected you with Sam Parker, I assumed you two would just take it from there.

It was very distressing to run into Sam at a party last Saturday and hear that things really didn't work out. "Disaster" is the word he used. Sam reported a long list of missed deadlines, unreturned calls, and unsatisfactory product that, he says, you were unwilling to change to fit their specifications.

I know there are always two sides to every story, so I'd appreciate hearing your side at your earliest convenience. As you know, the printing world is a small one in some ways, and a job gone wrong has a bad impact on all the people connected to it. I feel that my recommendation was a small part of the disaster and I need to talk to you about it.

Sincerely,

Jan

60. Ski trip causes downhill slide in friendship

Personal complaint letters can be the hardest to write. Especially when writing to friends, be careful to avoid attacking the individual. Instead of comments such as "How could you be so thoughtless?" use statements such as, "It upset me deeply that you..." or, "I feel hurt that...." Note that the first paragraph of this letter could be the opener for a number of personal complaint letters.

June 6

Dear Vivian,

Over the past few years I've come to think of you as one of my best friends, and that's why I'm writing this letter. It's hard to write, but I don't want to let things come between us so that we just drift apart.

When I invited you for dinner last night, you knew how important the evening was to me. My sister is in town for such a short time and I wanted her to meet the good friends I've been telling her about. That it was also her birthday, made it even more of a celebration.

I know you love skiing, and the chance to get a free ride up with a fun group for the long weekend must have been irresistible. But when I heard your message on my answering machine, I was very disappointed. My party had been planned for over two weeks, and I was counting on your being there.

Ordinarily I'd just phone you to say this, but you're gone for the next two days and I wanted to tell you this morning, while I'm still feeling the hurt, that your absence was very much noticed and you were missed.

Yours truly,

Sydney

61. Show me the money—or I'll sue!

Most complaints can be resolved without resorting to threats of lawsuits. But sometimes it's necessary to pull out the big guns. Another alternative might be to have the letter come from your lawyer.

———

Lucille Wilco
678 Judson Boulevard
Santa Teresita, CA 90034
(765) 555-9847

June 28

Percy Garland
5493 Indiana Street
Orangeville, CA 90126

Dear Mr. Garland:

As you know, I moved out of the house I had been renting from you at 764 Wilcox Way four months ago, on March 1. Since then, I have tried repeatedly to have my $6,200 deposit returned to me with interest, as is required by law. I have left numerous messages on your voice mail, and sent letters, including my last, registered, letter, which your wife apparently signed for on June 14. Mr. Garland, I am running out of patience.

I have photos that I took of the apartment when I moved out. While there was some normal wear and tear, certainly nothing in those photos warrants your keeping my entire deposit, particularly as you have given me no accounting of why you are holding my deposit, or what costs it may have been applied to.

If I don't hear from you by next Monday, the 5th of July, I will have no recourse but to consult my lawyer as to what legal action I can pursue to recoup my money and, at this point, some additional damages. My time is worth a good deal of money, and I have spent more than I care to on what should have been a simple administrative matter. I will look into compensation for my time, and for mental pain and suffering as well.

Neither of us wants to go to this time and expense, Mr. Garfield. Please just return my deposit.

Sincerely,

Lucille Wilco

62. Defective freezer gets writer hot

The threat of a class action suit has been known to make a company suddenly develop a genuine interest in a complaint. Even though all lawsuits are costly and time-consuming, the class action suit generally starts out with the judge on your side. That the complainant has already found somebody who has a complaint against the company is another strong element in his favor.

The letter is wisely addressed to the company's lawyer. You can telephone the corporate headquarters and ask for the name. It may also be listed on the company's Web site, or in one of the corporate directories mentioned in previous chapters.

The next letter that goes out, if you still don't get satisfaction from the company, will come from your lawyer. The really smart move in this letter, however, is the promise that if nothing is done to resolve the complaint, the consumer is not going to be alone when he knocks on the door next.

How do you find other disgruntled consumers who share your bad experience with a company? You might run an ad in the most likely place you can think of, asking people who have had similar problems with the company to get in touch with you.

John A. Dikranian
45 Moose Run
Jefferson City, MO 65102
(406) 555-8989

March 23

Mr. Artemus Wardlow, General Counsel
The Coldspot Company
444 Industrial Parkway
Mobile, AL 36609

Dear Mr. Wardlow:

Here's why I am writing directly to you, instead of your consumer affairs department or to company president Arnold Joss.

Three words: Class Action Lawsuit.

During the time my 16 cubic-foot Coldpoint Deluxe refrigerator, model 1422-A, was under warranty, both the freezer and the ice-cube-making mechanism were repaired at least five times. After the expiration of the warranty last January, the problems reoccurred, but your company was both unwilling and, it seems, unable to make things right.

As it happens, my dental hygienist, Mary Lee Hamilton, has the identical model, and has had the identical problems. And she tells me that she knows three other people in the same situation.

I have now spoken to an attorney who specializes in class action lawsuits. Her advice is to make one final request to Coldpoint to make things right, and that is the purpose of this letter.

Will you please take any necessary actions to properly repair or to replace, my model 1422-A. I have scheduled an appointment with this attorney for October 9, which I would be happy to cancel if all is made well.

Yours sincerely

John A. Dikranian

Chapter 7

When You Can't Get Satisfaction

John purchased a dozen bottles of mineral water a major supermarket. At the checkout counter, the automatic bar code reader decided that some of the bottles would cost 65¢ while others would cost 72¢. The clerk said she could not change what the bar code reader said. John asked for the manager. An assistant manager arrived and said that there was nothing he could do. John asked for his name. Bob. Last name? "We're not allowed to give that out," Bob said.

John didn't plan to make a federal case over 56¢, so he paid the amount. But he was really annoyed, and decided to take things a step or two further. He wrote a letter to the supermarket headquarters, explaining what Assistant Manager Bob had said. He signed it "Customer John." And, significantly, he added "Copy to: State Bureau of Weights and Measures" (the agency that regulates bar code readers).

Headquarters promptly mailed John a letter, offering him the refund *plus* three free bottles of the mineral water. And when he read, a few months later, that the state had launched an investigation of supermarket bar code readers, he could only smile.

In a perfect world, there would be no need for complaining. And in a nearly perfect world, if you did need to complain, your complaint would be dealt with promptly and fairly.

This just in: The world is neither perfect nor *nearly* perfect. And so even though a genuine complaint, made correctly and sincerely, will often be treated with respect and produce satisfaction, there are more than a few times when the initial complaint is either ignored entirely, or handled in a way that is simply not satisfactory.

Although we strongly advocate that an initial complaint be gentle and non-threatening, it may well be necessary to take more emphatic or dramatic action in order to achieve satisfaction.

In this chapter, we shall assume that you have taken all the recommended steps to resolve your complaint—and you are still dissatisfied and ready to take the next step.

This chapter discusses effective actions that you may wish to consider. Which one (or ones) you choose are, of course, entirely up to you, and will depend on your personality and style, your available time and finances, and how severe the complaint.

1. Take it up with the company

So you complained to the salesperson, manager, store, branch, or whatever—and you did not get your money refunded, free replacement, compensation—or even an apology? If you are not happy with the resolution (or lack thereof), it may well be worth trying one more time, in one of the following ways.

First, if you haven't gone to the top to resolve the problem, continue to climb the corporate ladder until you reach the highest rung. Especially if you've experienced resistance, you may wonder how to find out who's running the show. Two valuable resources are *Standard & Poor's Register of Corporations, Directors, and Executives* and the *Dun & Bradstreet Million Dollar Directory.* These directories of corporate listings will give you names of key executives, and the means to get in touch with them. An Internet source for this information is at www.hoover's.com.

Earlier chapters offered some creative ideas for grabbing the attentions of corporate leaders. (You'll recall the dissatisfied customer who called the wife of the CEO to register a complaint.) But whether you employ this strategy or simply send a letter, it's a good idea to make every effort to reach a person who has the power to resolve your complaint—if that doesn't work, here are some more ideas:

Return the product

Whether a ballpoint pen or a washing machine, a product that doesn't work is a valid source of complaint. One option is simply to send that product to the president of the company, with a short letter asking for either a repair or a new one.

John had a large and expensive boom box that failed, out of warranty, and the factory repair center refused to repair it for free. John argued that he expected more of a $400 item that was only a couple of years old. "Sorry," they said, "There is nothing we can do."

Wrong. John packed up the boom box and shipped it to the president of Panasonic, with a polite note explaining how unhappy he was. By return mail came a letter from the assistant to the president, apologizing, and offering the Panasonic product of John's choice at half-off. John was satisfied.

In recent years, we have also returned a small appliance to Sears and a $300 watch to Casio, each time getting a prompt replacement. We've read stories of people who have actually had their cars crated up and returned to the factory—but clearly this is a very last resort.

Write to the company's PR firm

Most large corporations—and many small and medium-sized companies—employ a public relations firm to assure positive community and media relations and create a healthy image for the company. These agencies, then, are particularly concerned about dissatisfied customers who might take their message to the media. And they might be concerned enough to resolve your complaint swiftly and satisfactorily.

Again, refer to *Standard & Poor's* or *Dun & Bradstreet* corporate listings, which might indicate the name of the public relations firm— or whether the company has an in-house PR department.

Write to many, many people in the organization

From the *Standard & Poor's* or *Dun & Bradstreet* directories or the Hoover's Internet site, get the names and titles of people within the organization. With a basic mail-merge program, you ought to be able to craft one powerful letter and address it to dozens of employees.

John did this once with a credit card company that had messed up his account and ignored polite letters. Replies were bouncing around like balls in a pinball machine, but the problem was solved in less than a week.

Contact the company's dealers or distributors

A man unhappy with his Land Rover, getting no satisfaction from the company, wrote letters to 50 dealers saying, in effect, "Please help me, because otherwise I'm going to do everything I can to keep people from coming into your dealership." When the dealers complained to headquarters, that got their attention.

This approach can be time-consuming and won't always work, but it can be very satisfying when it does. Dealer and distributor information can often be found in literature provided by the company, ranging from the warranty literature to sales brochures.

Have a lawyer write a letter on your behalf

Never underestimate the power of a lawyer's letterhead when trying to resolve a complaint. Often, when your letters have gone unanswered, a brief note from an attorney will result in immediate response. Many lawyers are willing to write a letter on your behalf for a reasonably minimal fee.

Debra was frustrated that her landlord had not repaid her house deposit months after she'd moved out. Letters and phone calls went unanswered. She contacted an acquaintance who was a lawyer. He wrote a letter, stating the same facts that Debra had included in her letters—but this time with the magic of "legalese"—and concluded that if there was not a satisfactory response in a short time, the next step would involve legal action. The cost to Debra? About $30. The result? She got a check for the full amount of her deposit, plus interest, within a week.

Often, if you write a draft letter outlining the details of the situation and give it to the attorney, this will cut down on the time—and the cost. If you don't have a lawyer, there are public-interest law offices that offer such services. Check the law association listings, typically found at the start of the yellow pages listings for "lawyers" or "attorneys."

Another tactic is to present your complaint in as "official" a format as possible. While we warn against trying to pass yourself off as a lawyer, there's nothing improper about using the same sort of "legal-ese" that lawyers use, in order to make the recipient of your letter stand up and take notice. So starting your letter out with something like, "In the matter of James Wilde vs. Industromat Corporation," may garner a little more attention.

2. Make use of third-party advocates

Ever since the Israelites asked Moses to help them complain about longer work hours, people with complaints have turned to third parties for help. Nowadays, we have a wide array of options, public and private, government and industry, helpful and unhelpful. Some do little more than send out form letters full of platitudes, while a few will (on occasion) marshal the troops and launch an all-out assault on your behalf. But the main finding in numerous research studies regarding the effect of third parties can be summarized in these four words: Don't expect a lot.

For many people, the main value of a third-party agency is being able to put "cc" or "copy to" at the bottom of your complaint letter. The simple fact that you know enough to drop such a name identifies you as a more knowledgeable and perhaps more persistent and effective complainer. There are five basic categories to consider:

Industry organizations and ombudsmen

Many companies and service providers, from car manufacturers to lawyers to banks to moving companies, belong to industry associations that can help resolve problems between members and consumers. Many such associations are listed in Appendix D; others can be found through library or Internet research.

Generally, there are three types of programs that try to resolve complaints: arbitration, conciliation, and mediation. Usually, the decisions of the arbitrators are binding and must be accepted by both the customer and the business. In conciliation, sometimes only the business is required to accept the decision; the customer can either accept it or continue complaining. Mediation is not binding on either party, but is a formal effort to try to work things out.

Although the companies are paying, it is not uncommon for these organizations to come down on the side of the complainer, or at least to work out some sort of compromise. Some industries agree to abide by the decision of such organizations, while others simply take their recommendations under advisement.

Media "help lines"

Many radio and television stations have consumer affairs departments, and offer the free service of helping people with their complaints. There is a national "call for action" organization that works with dozens of stations, and others do this on their own, often staffed by volunteers. In addition, quite a few newspapers and some national magazines have a regular "help" column, where reader complaints are addressed.

Realize, however, that there are no guarantees here, even that a given station or paper will even take on your problem, much less be able to resolve it. Indeed, a study by consumer advocate Laura Nader found that many of these services are quite selective in the complaints they take on, often taking pains not to offend advertisers and important people. Some really can be helpful, but others offer little more than routine and sometimes unhelpful referrals to government or private agencies.

The Better Business Bureau

Consumers turn to the Better Business Bureau (BBB) more than any other agency, registering more than 10 million information requests each year. BBB offices (each one is an independent affiliate of the national organization) have done a lot of good in resolving complaints. The BBB provides a lot of useful information, both in its publications, and through its Web site (http://www.bbb.org).

But it is important to remember that the BBB is a membership organization supported by local businesses, often the very ones that people complain about. Indeed, while many BBB offices claim to settle upward of 90 percent of complaints, "settle" doesn't necessarily mean the person with the complaint ends up satisfied.

It is simply important for complainers to realize that the BBB is not the be-all and end-all of consumer advocate agencies, and if one does not get satisfaction there, it does not signal the end of the complaining road.

National consumer organizations

Some excellent and worthy consumer organizations do a lot of good work—but they may not be the best places to file complaints. These agencies are more concerned with the "big-picture" issues that cause many people to complain (about telemarketing or junk mail or bank charges or HMO problems, etc.), but they do not take action on behalf of individual complainers.

Nonetheless, these may be excellent names to "drop" in a letter, since it shows that you are a knowledgeable consumer. When you mention that you are copying the Major Appliance Consumer Action, for example, that may get your reader's attention. The major national organizations are listed in Appendix D.

Arbitration

Industry-sponsored arbitration has already been discussed, and can be a viable alternative. But there may also be situations in which there is no industry-provided service, or the wronged party wishes a truly independent arbitrator. This process can be expensive—arbitrators are often attorneys, earning attorney's hourly fees—and so it should be reserved for more serious cases, as well as those in which the complainer has high confidence that he or she will prevail.

In some situations, the parties agree to share the cost; in others, it is agreed that the losing party will pay. Some arbitrators are listed in the yellow pages; further information is available from the American Arbitration Association, 140 West 51st Street, New York, NY 10020-1203, Toll free: 1-800-778-7879, Web site: www.adr.org.

3. Go public with the problem

Many organizations are uncomfortable with the idea of bad publicity. They realize that one negative story on the evening news could undo months of positive advertising and public relations. So, before you actually *go* public, often the mere threat of doing so—whether directly to the company or its PR firm—will hasten some response to your complaint. If you don't get the desired result, here are some ideas about how to take your story to the people:

Write a letter to the press

A pointed letter that appears in your small-town paper may just get the action you want. But your options are much broader and extend far beyond the editorial column in your local paper. First, there are other local media: Radio and TV stations, for example, are often scratching for public-interest stories that might capture ratings. And, depending upon the scope of your problem, you might even consider contacting national media. Who knows? Your complaint might even be featured on "60 Minutes."

But, we remind you, the purpose of complaining is *not* to parlay your problems into 15 minutes of fame, but rather to get your complaint resolved the way you want it to be resolved.

So, here's our advice: Write letters to whichever media source (or sources) you deem most effective—but don't send the letters *yet*. First, send copies of the letters to the offending organization, giving them one last chance for responding. Make it clear that if you don't hear from them within whatever time frame you propose, the letters will be mailed. They don't know how serious you are, or how the media will respond, and that uncertainty may bring about a settlement.

Picket the perpetrating organization

Bill invested $21,000 in a new car from his local dealer. It was a real lemon. The dealer kept trying to repair the car under warranty, but never fixed the problem. Bill asked for his full payment back, plus a bit more for his own expenses and irritation. The dealer refused. Soon after, the six-foot lemon was born.

On a Saturday afternoon, busiest time of the week for a car dealer, Bill dressed up in a bright yellow shirt and pants and yellow hard hat with green plastic leaves affixed. He walked back and forth in front the dealership. He wisely refrained from verbally attacking either the dealer or the car company, but simply carried a sign saying that before anyone bought from this dealer, they might wish to hear his story.

Bill was in the catbird seat because the dealer had no idea how long this street theater would continue: an hour, a day, a month, forever? Only Bill knew, and he wasn't talking. By the end of the weekend, the dealer offered a settlement: He would buy the car back for $22,000—$1,000 more than Bill had paid, if only he would pack up his lemon suit and go home. The deal was done.

The fun of picketing is that it is *so* public and *so* immediate and *so* annoying to the offending store or business. And the beauty of picketing as a tactic is that the business has no way of knowing how long it will last. You may be there for a half-hour, or you may have taken early retirement so you can stay there for the next 20 years.

Stores and businesses are fond of claiming that picketing is illegal, but in almost every situation, it isn't, as long as you follow certain guidelines. Here are some common ones: (Please be advised that we are writers and not lawyers, so if you do consider this strategy for solving your complaint, we also advise that you verify that your actions are in accordance with your local ordinances.)

1. The picketer must have a genuine dispute, and actions the picketer is seeking must be lawful.
2. Any messages on signage must be truthful.
3. Abusive language or violence is prohibited.
4. The picketer must not block customers from the store or business.
5. Picketing of a private residence or a nonbusiness site is prohibited.

Complain through advertising

Some people take their complaints to the public through advertising, in hopes the company will cave in and resolve the matter. Broadway producer David Merrick ran a series of ads attacking Chrysler when he couldn't get his car repaired properly. Of course, such a strategy can get expensive, but there are ways to keep the costs down while reaching a mass market.

Californian Jeremy Dorosin was just an ordinary guy who felt he was treated badly by Starbucks Coffee when he attempted to return an unsatisfactory espresso machine. He has spent thousands of dollars of his own money buying ads in *The Wall Street Journal* and elsewhere, urging people not to patronize Starbucks Coffee. He even created a Web site dedicated to the situation. Those acts propelled him onto all the major morning television talk shows. And, of course, the Internet makes it much easier and cheaper to get your complaint out in front of thousands or millions of people.

Complain on the Internet

While the Internet makes it easy and inexpensive to get your complaint out in public, where it can be viewed by millions of people, it is often ineffective simply because your message is just one of many millions posted every day. There are numerous "complaining" sites that come and go, and that seem to serve the purpose of enabling people to get things off their chests, rather than achieve results. One of the larger sites is www.opencomplaint.com.

The Internet can be much more helpful when there is a specific newsgroup or chat room devoted to a topic, rather than a general all-purpose "complain here" site. Whether the topic is computer printers or headache medicine, you are more likely to reach just the right audience when you take your complaint to a narrowly focused site.

For example, a woman discovered that the correspondence school she was dealing with was not properly accredited. The school refused to refund her fees. By searching the list of more than 60,000 newsgroups, readily available through Netscape, Internet Explorer, AOL, or any major internet service, she discovered a newsgroup called alt.education.distance, in which large numbers of people share their experiences with home study. Soon after her first "warning!" posting, the school, which obviously monitored the news group, approached her to settle, which she happily did.

Complain as a part of a group

When Coca-Cola introduced the "new Coke" in the 1980s, the company was taken aback by the number of complaints about the product's taste, and promptly dropped the formula. This, of course, isn't always the case. NBC ignored more than a million complaint letters after canceling "Star Trek."

As part of his Ph.D. research at Michigan State University, John contacted more than 100 major companies, as well as dozens of politicians and all the major networks, to learn more about how they deal with group complaints through letter writing campaigns and petitions. The findings were clear: In most cases, one or a few sincere letters are likely to be more effective than an organized campaign. When 10 or 50 or 1,000 copies of the same letter arrive, even with different handwriting and minor changes in wording, none of them is likely to have any influence at all. But a single letter, from the heart, can have a dramatic result.

A local television station ran an ad for its own newspaper with the slogan "We're smaller, but we're yours." It had a "cute"

cartoon of dwarves running around with cameras and TV equipment, occasionally running into big buys with big recording equipment, falling over, and getting up. The station got one letter from a local teenager who was a little person. He explained that he felt the TV ad mocked his condition. The station took heed, scrapped the cartoon, and substituted a series with puppies and other small animals in amusing settings.

To be sure, some companies and many politicians love photo opportunities with great stacks of mail, but only if it supports something they have done, or a position they have taken. But when the mail or the petitions oppose them, it often has no effect. As one senator put it, "A ton of mail isn't going to have an ounce of effect. If they wanted me to weigh my mail, they should have elected a butcher."

The best advice, then, is that if you are part of a group, all with the same complaint, members should be urged to write on their own, and not from a form letter provided.

4. Lawsuits

There are situations in which it seems a lawsuit (or, as discussed earlier, the threat of a lawsuit) is the only way to get the attention of the party who has caused your complaint. Many people avoid even thinking about lawsuits, because they fear they may either be complicated or expensive or both. Indeed, they often are not only expensive, but so emotionally draining, that they are almost always best to avoid.

If the other strategies in this book are followed, in almost every case there should be no need for a suit—with the possible exception of the one judicial venue that serves many people with complaints quite nicely:

Small claims court

Typically, small claims cases involve individuals who, without legal knowledge or a lawyer's involvement, are able to bring forth grievances to be handled *relatively* quickly and with little cost.

Every state has its small claims courts, but the rules and regulations in each state are different: the amount you can sue for (the range is from under $2,000 to $15,000), the kinds of issues you can sue about (just cash losses; other financial losses, evictions, breach of contract, etc.), whether you and the other party can have a lawyer present, and how long it will take before your case is heard (with a range of a few weeks to many months).

While the concept of small claims is basically simple, the reality is often more complex. For example, there *are* costs, forms that have to be filed, procedures that must be followed. And even if you do win your case, you may still have problems in collecting payment from the other party—the court doesn't force them to pay up at the time of the verdict.

Although most of the courts have useful information on their procedures, we strongly recommend "seeking a second opinion" by consulting one of the many books on this topic, some of them specific to a given state (including the necessary forms), and others more general. Two are:

- *Winning in Small Claims Court: A Step-by-Step Guide for Trying Your Own Small Claims Cases* by Judge William E. Brewer (Career Press, 1998)
- *The E-Z Legal Guide to Small Claims Court* (E-Z Legal Forms, 1995).

Here's a simple and free technique that has worked for a lot of people: Get the necessary forms from the local small claims court. Fill them out, but don't file them. Instead, send a copy of the filled-out forms to the person or organization against which you have the complaint, with a cover letter saying that if they do not resolve the complaint by such-and-such a date, there are the very papers you will file. The recipient thus knows you are really serious, and may well offer to settle.

The class action lawsuit

When anywhere from a few people to thousands have the same complaint, a single suit may be filed on behalf of all of the victims— this is a class action suit.

A man who was extremely unhappy with the way his car was painted by a national chain of paint shops felt he could *not* be the only dissatisfied customer. He found a lawyer eager to explore a class action suit. Small classified ads uncovered more than 50 unhappy customers of the firm, and that was sufficient to go to court and get the necessary permission for a class action.

The three words most likely to strike fear in the heart of a corporate counsel are "class action lawsuit." Even if you do not follow through, the mere mention of those words can have immediate effect. The prospect of making good on one paint job is no big deal, but refunds to 50 or 5,000 or 5 million people is truly a big deal.

There are law firms that specialize in this approach. The topic, however, is too complex for this book. It is our hope that most of your complaints are simple enough to be resolved through the strategies set forth.

5. Seek creative vengeance—with caution

Ole and Lars, two brothers in a rural Minnesota town, applied for a business expansion loan at the only bank in town. They were turned down by the bank president not because they were unqualified, but, they were quite sure, because 20 years earlier, Lars had married a woman in whom the bank president also had a serious interest. The president lived on a large parcel of land, with rolling green hills, bordering the interstate just outside of town.

Time passed—and it appeared as if Ole and Lars forgot about the loan denial. Winter came and went—but with spring, the daffodils Ole and Lars had planted in late fall came into full bloom on the hillside by the highway, spelling out a very rude seven-letter word, plus an arrow pointing to the banker's home. The flowers didn't last long—but they lasted long enough for a photograph to be taken, and copies of that photo are still being passed around there in rural Minnesota.

When all else fails as you try to resolve your complaint, you may come to the point where you must "let it go." But, often, it's impossible for us to move on until we've at least relished some small, albeit childish, victory. (Remember the long-suffering wife who swished her obnoxious husband's toothbrush in the toilet each night?)

The best revenge, of course, is to tell all your friends not to give their business to the offending party (every business values the power of word-of-mouth advertising, both bad and good). But if that's too mundane, you may want to use your imagination for a more dramatic vengeance.

But....please do so with caution. After all your frustrations, the last thing you want is for your prank to backfire and result in costs, fines, or even jail. If you must consider something in this direction, please be gentle. Be creative. You can make your point without causing harm. Consider the family whose morning newspaper was regularly tossed into their fish pond. When complaints failed, they paid their bill with currency floating in a jar of water.

Chapter 8

When the Shoe Is on the Other Foot

An elderly woman had been a loyal and regular customer of a particular West Coast department store for years. She came into the store one day to return a vacuum cleaner she claimed was not working properly. Not surprising, since the vacuum cleaner was decades old. But, what's more, the appliance had not even been purchased at that store—the chain had never a housewares department!

Nevertheless, a smiling clerk gracefully accepted the vacuum cleaner and offered the woman the refund she asked for (of course, she didn't have a receipt). While some may believe the clerk's actions to be grounds for termination, she was merely following a store policy—a wise policy that recognizes the lifetime value of a good customer.

Now, some may question the wisdom of this policy. After all, the store lost money—nearly $100! But, what it retained was the goodwill and future business of a loyal customer who had spent thousands of dollars there. In that light, it seems like a very sound strategy.

We all serve someone. And, try as we may, it is unlikely that we'll retire without ever having to face a complaint. Whether you're an employee or a business owner, on the front line or behind the scenes, one thing is certain: You *will* receive complaints. Your goal should not be to avoid them—that's impossible. But rather your objective should be to deal with them in such a way that you successfully resolve the problem and actually *strengthen* your relationship with that customer. It's not so difficult.

Remember, whether you're a clerk at a discount store or the owner of your own company, a doctor, a lawyer—or even an errant friend, many of these hints apply. Almost everyone has customers, almost every customer has the potential to complain, and almost every one of those complaints can be handled well, with just a little preparation.

Don't forget that complaints can be great market research. If 30 customers a week complain that the sweater doesn't come in red—hey, maybe you should order it in red! And if the baked octopus gets more bad feedback than any other dish, it may be time to eliminate an entree from the menu. In short, corny as it sounds, a complaint can be a gift from a customer. Use it wisely.

Close your eyes and hope it goes away?

For years, the smiling face of Art Linkletter, on television and in people's mailboxes, was instrumental in selling hundreds of thousands of Craftmatic electric folding beds, mostly to senior citizens who were visited by aggressive salespeople representing independent distributors, making unproven health claims, and pushing $6,000 beds.

For years, the company ignored the complaints, blaming its independent distributors for the problems. But after some complainers brought lawsuits or sought the aid of state consumer protection agencies, it became clear that most people initially wrote or called the main office at the urging of Mr. Linkletter. Even though Linkletter was not personally responsible for the problems, he felt the blame was shared, and urged the company to change its selling tactics, and, most importantly, to deal appropriately with complaints.

Craftmatic finally got a toll-free complaint phone line (located in the corporate lawyer's office!) and agreed to binding arbitration for any complaints that could not be otherwise settled. Although the company eventually addressed the complaints, the delay resulted in dramatic costs—both in terms of revenues, expenses, and the company's reputation.

Classic Motor Carriages was a large Florida manufacturer of elaborate kits that enabled people to build replicas of famous sports cars onto the chassis of inexpensive and reliable American cars.

A flood of complaints raged forth from people who found the kits took months to arrive, were missing up to half the parts, and required a level of skill far beyond that of the weekend tinkerer. The company ignored the complaints for years. Finally, state regulators stepped in, demanding compliance with consumer laws. But it was too late. As the former editor of *Kit Car Illustrated* wrote, "They had it all. But when consumers started complaining, it was a clarion call. They didn't act to solve the problems. If they had acted properly, they would have risen even higher." Instead they sank lower and lower, finally disappearing in a wake of anger, hostility, and unsettled claims.

One thing's for certain. "Ignore them and maybe they'll go away," is indeed a successful strategy for dealing with customer complaints. If you ignore the complaints, your customers *will* go away.

On the other hand, a good customer-complaint policy is perhaps one of the best marketing tools your business could employ. Studies show that, often, when a complaint is successfully resolved, you actually strengthen the customer-vendor relationship, creating a greater sense of loyalty than from customers who are merely mildly satisfied with your service or product.

Of course we don't advise that you deliberately disappoint your customers so you can rebound as a hero. Instead, we suggest that you heighten your sensitivity to potential problems, *ask* your customers for feedback, respond quickly when you receive a complaint, and take the *extra* steps to reassure your customers that you care about them and their satisfaction.

Legendary customer service

Good complaint resolution, of course, starts with good customer service philosophies. We've all heard that the customer is always right, and we've all been confronted with individuals who are so unreasonable, rude, or offensive, that we question whether we really want their business. But the wise business person realizes that the issue isn't this one encounter or sale, but rather the lifetime value of that customer.

Hey, maybe one of the Kit Car customers lied, or lost the parts, or whatever. That's not the point. Good customer service is about creating an overall feeling that you are a good company that is willing to be fair to your customers. Will people take advantage of you? Some will. But chances are it will be a small tradeoff for retaining the loyalty of honest consumers who will return to your business, and tell others to patronize your business. Let's see how others have accomplished their great customer-service reputations.

Stew Leonard's in Connecticut is one of the largest dairy stores in the country. Engraved in a six-ton boulder at the entrance is: "Rule 1: The customer is always right. Rule 2: If the customer is ever wrong, reread Rule 1." The policy was put to the test when a woman came in with her Thanksgiving turkey, which she'd roasted all night at high temperature. It was shriveled and leathery. She complained that it was too dry. Without having to seek approval from some higher-up, the clerk offered this sincere if misguided complainer her choice of a new turkey or a $20 refund. (Wisely, the woman chose the money.)

L. L. Bean is legendary for its customer service policies. Complaining customers are asked, "What will satisfy you?" Whatever it is, the company will do it, unless it is completely outrageous. And even then, only a director of the company can say no to a customer. The system was well-taxed by the caller who ordered a jacket that happened to be out of stock. That was totally unacceptable to the caller; she had a friend who was going into the hospital the next day, and absolutely had to present said friend with that very jacket.

The Bean employee went into the mailing division, and searched through hundreds of customer returns. Against all odds, he found the jacket in the right size and color. He hired a local taxi to drive the parcel from Maine to the Boston airport, where it was put on an express flight to New York, which was met by a hired limousine, and delivered to the customer in the nick of time.

Now, you may not have the resources to go quite that far beyond the call of duty. But you can certainly be inspired by the story.

Avoiding customer complaints

While it's true we said at the beginning of this chapter that you can't avoid complaints, you can certainly do your best to reduce their potential. We don't have to tell you that if you follow ethical business practices and require high performance levels of yourself and others in your organization, this will go a long way in eliminating complaints.

But another important tool to combat complaints is to establish realistic expectations, and the best way to do that is to communicate clearly what your company can and will do for customers.

For example: Your menu, the sign on your restaurant, the ad in the yellow pages, and your radio commercial all advertise the fact that you offer the best sweet-potato french fries in the state. But on a regular basis your waitstaff is forced to tell customers that you're out of sweet-potato french fries.

Congratulations, my friend—you have just created the perfect recipe for stimulating customer complaints! Why? You've created an expectation among your diners that they have the opportunity to enjoy the best sweet-potato fries in the state—and then you take it away from them. If these special fries are indeed so rare, then don't advertise them as part and parcel of your menu.

Similarly, don't advertise fast delivery if it typically takes two weeks to get your product to your customer. Don't promote "budget rates" if your service is on the higher end of the price scale. And don't offer personalized attention if your floor sales force is skeletal.

Establishing customer complaint policies

It is absolutely essential that a business establish clear and customer-friendly complaint policies, that are shared with and communicated to all employees. Anticipate problems that might arise and determine how to address them. Include in the policies the proper steps that must be taken to resolve the complaint, as well as the decision-making authority.

Make sure all employees know the policies thoroughly, so that they can knowledgeably deal with customers. No representative of your busines should ever tell a customer, "You'll have to talk to...about that," or "I don't know anything about return policies." Post policies clearly, so that both employees and customers may have access to them.

Empower employees to make customers happy. Because it is usually the front-line clerk who is confronted with complaints, it doesn't make sense to require a high-level manager to step in when a complaint could be resolved with a $5 refund.

Make it part of your policy to go one step beyond what the customer asks for. The individual may only have asked for a refund for a defective product, but if you know the customer had to drive 20 miles to return it, a discount coupon on future purchases will go a long way in capturing this customer's loyalty.

Adopt a policy that the customer is always right—within reason. If an individual attempts to return a sweater without a receipt, don't give her a hard time if it's clearly a sweater you sell. Take the darn thing back! As we said earlier, better to lose the immediate profit in order to win long-term business.

Make it a policy to follow up on a complaint. Have employees call a week or so after the complaint was resolved, to ask if everything was done to the customer's satisfaction. Send a postcard or letter from a senior executive expressing regret about the problem and asking for feedback.

Dealing with a customer complaint

While many of us are not in a position to implement great customer complaint policies, we can certainly have a positive impact on the process, both by communicating with people within our company and by taking some initiative as an enlightened complainer.

Within your organization, pay especially close attention to the customers and how they are being treated. Whether you are a mail room envelope-stuffer or the head of one of the world's largest corporations, your customers pay your salary. The chairman of Avis Car Rental, Robert Townsend, used to require all his top management to "work the counters" at airports for two weeks of every year—the better to learn what made customers happy and what caused them to complain.

Here are a dozen "light bulbs" (or guidelines) to keep in mind, when one of your customers—one of those people who pay your salary—has a complaint.

- Be polite. Apologize immediately, and say you'll deal with it right away.
- Do so! Even if you can't resolve the problem immediately, at least take the first steps immediately. A friend became a Lands' End customer for life when the telephone order clerk said, "I can tell you're anxious to have this, so let me go out to the warehouse and make absolutely certain it is in stock."
- Be empathetic. Acknowledge the customer's distress. ("I can see this is very upsetting to you."Or, "I'm so sorry you had to drive all the way back here after you discovered the problem.")
- Don't ever put someone on hold without assuring them that it won't be for more than half a minute. And if you can't find help in that period, come back on, and offer to call back, even if it's to a cellular phone in Timbuktu.
- Get all of the facts. It will help your organization get to the bottom of the situation, and it will reassure the customer that you really care. ("When did you purchase this?" " Do you have the receipt?" "Can you remember which mechanic worked on your car?" "What did the waiter look like?")
- Don't ever utter an insincere, or flippant, response, like, "Sorry about that." That's probably even worse than saying nothing at all.
- "Sorry, that's not my job." "Sorry, that's not my table." Strike these phrases from your speech! If there is truly no one else who can possibly help at this moment, your only recourse is to apologize profusely (and sincerely!), tell the customer exactly when something will happen, and then see that it does, even if you have to call or write or tell him or her, yet again, that you have been unable to find help (yet).

- Help the customer identify what response he or she wants. Sometimes customers are so frustrated, they're not communicating effectively. It may be your job to probe. A refund? Store credit? The car fixed again? Some extra compensation? A public apology?

- When the customer appears to be wrong, be firm but gentle, and allow for the possibility of error on your part. ("I'm very sorry, but our records show that your car was never serviced at this garage. If we have made a mistake in this, perhaps due to a misspelling of your name, or incorrect license plate data, please accept our apologies. As soon as you find the paperwork, please bring it back in, and we'll do everything we can to resolve this situation.")

- Treat all customer complaints with equal attention and concern. That mildly annoying man who has sent the soup back to the kitchen twice might come back next week to book your banquet room for a luxury staff party of 200 people.

- The customer may not always be right, but the customer is always the customer and, like it or not, he or she is paying your salary.

With these guidelines in mind, you should have a relatively complaint-free company. Of course, if you've read the rest of this book, you can fill up that free time you've gained by complaining to everyone else, to make them as wonderful as you. Enjoy!

Four Words to Remember

As we leave you, we'd like to reemphasize what we think is the single most important idea in this book—a notion that is so obvious, nearly everyone nods their head and says, "Oh, yes, of course." And yet nearly everyone either overlooks it or ignores it, which is the main reason at least nine out of every 10 people who have been wronged never complain. But then, at least nine out of 10 people will never read this book. So the fact that you've gotten this far is a good sign. Now, if you will just remember these four words: You pay their salaries.

You pay the salary of the president of the company that made your car and the manager of your bank and the waitress at the restaurant and the clerk at the post office and the bureaucrat at the government office.

If their products or services are not to your liking, you must never think, "Oh, it must be my fault," or "I don't want to bother them." They wouldn't have a job if it weren't for you, and it is their *job* to make things right for you.

We hope we've been helpful, in both inspirational and practical ways. And we'd really like to hear from you, with suggestions, ideas, complaints (if you must!), and, most of all, stories. If you've had a grand success as a complainer, or an annoying failure, please tell us the story. We can't promise to respond to everyone, but we will read everything. After all, you're paying our salaries, too.

Thank you.

John and Mariah Bear

P. O. Box 7070

Berkeley, CA 94707

john@ursa.net

mariah@ursa.net

Consumer Complaint Agencies by State

Every state but Alaska has an office that deals with consumer complaints. Such offices typically mediate complaints, conduct investigations, prosecute offenders of consumer laws, promote consumer protection legislation, provide educational materials, advocate in the consumer interest, and, in some cases, license and regulate a variety of professionals.

Some states also have specialized offices dealing with auto problems, insurance problems, and so on. And there are many city and county consumer offices, as well. A complete listing would be very long indeed. The state offices should be able to refer you to another office, if appropriate.

It is often efficient to telephone an office before sending a written complaint to make sure the agency deals with the kind of complaint you have, and if there are special forms or procedures to use.

Alabama

Consumer Affairs Section,
Office of the Attorney General
  11 South Union Street
  Montgomery, AL 36130
  334-242-7334
  Toll free in AL: 1-800-392-5658
  Fax: 334-242-2433
  Web site:
  e-pages.com/aag/cuspro.html

Alaska

The Consumer Protection Section
in the office of the Attorney
General has been closed.

Arizona

Consumer Protection,
Office of the Attorney General
  1275 West Washington Street,
  Room 259
  Phoenix, AZ 85007
  602-542-5763
  Toll free in AZ:
  1-800-352-8431
  TDD: 602-542-5002
  Fax: 602-542-4377

Arkansas

Consumer Protection Division,
Office of Attorney General
  200 Catlett Prien
  323 Center Street
  Little Rock, AR 72201
  501-682-2341
  TDD toll free in AR:
  1-800-482-8982
  Web site: www.ag-state.ar.us

California

Department of Consumer Affairs
  400 R Street, Suite 3000
  Sacramento, CA 95814
  916-445-4465
  Toll free in CA: 1-800-952-5210
  TDD: 916-322-1700
  510-785-7554

Colorado

Consumer Protection Division,
Office of Attorney General
  1525 Sherman Street, 5th Floor
  Denver, CO 80203-1760
  303-866-5189
  Toll free: 1-800-332-2071
  Fax: 303-866-5691

Connecticut

Department of Consumer
Protection
  165 Capitol Avenue
  Hartford, CT 06106
  860-566-2534
  Toll free in CT: 1-800-842-2649
  Fax: 860-566-1531
  Web site: www.state.ct.us/dcp/
  compform.html

Delaware

Consumer Protection Unit,
Department of Justice
  820 North French Street,
  6th Floor
  Wilmington, DE 19801
  302-577-8600
  Fax: 302-577-6499

District of Columbia

Department of Consumer and
Regulatory Affairs
  614 H Street, NW, Room 1120
  Washington, DC 20001
  202-727-7120
  TDD/TTY: 202-727-7842
  Fax: 202-727-8073

Florida

Division of Consumer Services
  407 South Calhoun Street
  Mayo Building, 2nd Floor
  Tallahassee, FL 32399-0800
  Outside FL 850-488-2221
  Toll free in FL: 1-800-435-7352
  Fax: 850-487-4177
  Web site: www.fl-ag.com

Georgia

Governor's Office of Consumer Affairs
  2 Martin Luther King, Jr. Dr., SE
  Suite 356
  Atlanta, GA 30334
  404-656-3790
  Toll free in GA (outside Atlanta area):
  1-800-869-1123
  Fax: 404-651-9018

Hawaii

Office of Consumer Protection
  235 S. Beretania Street (96813)
  Room 801
  P.O. Box 3767
  Honolulu, HI 96812-3767
  808-586-2636
  Fax: 808-586-2640

Idaho

Office of the Attorney General, Consumer Protection Unit
  650 West State Street
  Boise, ID 83720-0010
  208-334-2424
  Toll free in ID:
  1-800-432-3545
  TDD/TTY: 208-334-2424
  Fax: 208-334-2830
  Web site: www.state.id.us/ag/
  middle\consumer\consumer.htm

Illinois

Consumer Protection Division
Office of Attorney General
  100 West Randolph, 12th Floor
  Chicago, IL 60601
  312-814-3000
  TDD: 312-793-2852
  Fax: 312-814-2593

Indiana

Consumer Protection Division, Office of Attorney General
  Indiana Government Center South
  402 West Washington Street, 5th Floor
  Indianapolis, IN 46204
  317-232-6330
  Toll free in IN:
  1-800-382-5516
  Fax: 317-233-4393
  E-mail: INATTGN@ATG.IN.US
  Web site:
  www.al.org/hoosieradvocate

Iowa

Assistant Attorney General, Consumer Protection Division
  Office of the Attorney General
  1300 East Walnut Street, 2nd Floor
  Des Moines, IA 50319
  515-281-5926
  Fax: 515-281-6771
  E-mail:
  consumer@max.state.ia.us
  Web site: www.state.ia.us/
  government/ag/consumer.html

Kansas

Deputy Attorney General
Consumer Protection Division
  Office of Attorney General
  301 West 10th
  Kansas Judicial Center
  Topeka, KS 66612-1597
  785-296-3751
  Toll free in KS:
  1-800-432-2310
  Fax: 785-291-3699

Kentucky

Consumer Protection Division,
Office of the Attorney General
  1024 Capital Center Drive
  Frankfort, KY 40601-8204
  502-696-5389
  Toll free in KY: 1-888-432-9257
  Fax: 502-573-8317
  Web site: www.law.state.ky.us/
  cp/default.htm
  E-mail:
  webmaster@mail.law.state.ky.us

Louisiana

Consumer Protection Section,
Office of the Attorney General
  1 America Place
  P.O. Box 94095
  Baton Rouge, LA 70804-9095
  504-342-9639
  Toll free nationwide:
  1-800-351-4889
  Fax: 504-342-9637
  Web site: www.laag.com

Maine

Office of Consumer Credit
Regulation
  35 State House Station
  Augusta, ME 04333-0035
  207-624-8527
  Toll free in ME: 1-800-332-8529
  Fax: 207-582-7699

Maryland

Consumer Protection Division
  200 Saint Paul Place, 16th Floor
  Baltimore, MD 21202-2021
  410-528-8662 (consumer
  complaint hotline)
  TDD: 410-576-6372 (MD only)
  Fax: 410-576-6566 and
  410-576-7040
  E-mail:
  consumer@oag.state.md.us
  Web site: www.oag.state.md.us

Massachusetts

Consumer Protection and
Antitrust Division, Department of
the Attorney General
  One Ashburton Place
  Boston, MA 02108-1698
  617-727-8400
  Fax: 617-727-5765

Michigan

Consumer Protection Division,
Office of the Attorney General
  P.O. Box 30212
  Lansing, MI 48909
  517-373-1140 (complaint
  information)
  517-373-1110
  Fax: 517-335-1935

Minnesota

Consumer Services Division,
Attorney General's Office
  1400 NCL Tower
  445 Minnesota Street
  St. Paul, MN 55101
  651-296-3353
  Toll free: 1-800-657-3787
  TDD/TTY toll free:
  1-800-366-4812
  Fax: 651-282-5801
  Web site:
  www.ag.state.mn.us/consumer
  E-mail: consumer.ag@state.mn.us

Mississippi

Consumer Protection Division
  802 North State Street,
  3rd Floor
  P.O. Box 22947
  Jackson, MS 39225-2947
  601-359-4230
  Toll free in MS:
  1-800-281-4418
  Fax: 601-359-4231
  Web site: www.ago.state.ms.us/
  consprot.htm

Missouri

Consumer Complaint Unit,
Office of the Attorney General
  P.O. Box 899
  Jefferson City, MO 65102
  573-751-3321
  Toll free in MO:
  1-800-392-8222
  TDD/TTY toll free in MO:
  1-800-729-8668
  Fax: 314-751-7948

Montana

Consumer Affairs Unit,
Department of Commerce
  1424 Ninth Avenue
  Box 200501
  Helena, MT 59620-0501
  406-444-4312
  Fax: 406-444-2903

Nebraska

Department of Justice
  2115 State Capitol
  P.O. Box 98920
  Lincoln, NE 68509
  402-471-2682
  Fax: 402-471-3297

Nevada

Consumer Affairs Division,
Department of Business and
Industry
  4600 Kietzke Lane, Bldg. B,
  Suite 113
  Reno, NV 89502
  702-688-1800
  Toll free in NV:
  1-800-326-5202
  TDD: 702-486-7901
  Fax: 702-688-1803

New Hampshire

Consumer Protection/Antitrust
Bureau, Attorney General's Office
  33 Capitol Street
  Concord, NH 03301-6397
  603-271-3641
  TDD toll free: 1-800-735-2964
  Fax: 603-271-2110
  Web site:
  www.state.nh.us/oag/cpb.htm

New Jersey

Consumer Affairs Division
  124 Halsey Street
  Newark, NJ 07102
  973-504-6200
  Fax: 973-648-3538
  TDD: 973-504-6588
  E-mail: askconsumeraffairs@
  oag.lps.state.nj.us
  Web site: www.state.nj.us/lps/ca/
  home.htm

New Mexico

Consumer Protection Division,
Office of Attorney General
  P.O. Drawer 1508
  Santa Fe, NM 87504
  505-827-6060
  Toll free in NM: 1-800-678-1508

New York

Bureau of Consumer Frauds and
Protection,
  Office of Attorney General
  State Capitol
  Albany, NY 12224
  518-474-5481
  Toll free in NY: 1-800-771-7755
  TDD toll free: 1-800-788-9898
  Fax: 518-474-3618
  Web site: www.oag.state.ny.us

North Carolina

Consumer Protection Section,
Office of Attorney General
  P.O. Box 629
  Raleigh, NC 27602
  919-716-6000
  Fax: 919-716-6050
  Web site: www.jus.state.nc.us/
  justice/cpsmain

North Dakota

Consumer Protection and Antitrust
Division,Office of the
Attorney General
  600 East Boulevard Avenue
  Bismarck, ND 58505-0040
  701-328-2811
  Toll free in ND: 1-800-472-2600
  TDD: 701-328-3409
  Fax: 701-328-3535
  Web site:
  www.state.nd.us/cpat/cpat.html

Ohio

Consumer Protection Section,
Office of the Attorney General
  State Office Tower, 25th Floor
  30 East Broad Street
  Columbus, OH 43215-3428
  614-466-4986 (complaints)
  Toll free in OH:
  1-800-282-0515
  TDD: 614-466-1393
  E-mail: consumer@ag.ohio.gov

Oklahoma

Office of Attorney General,
Consumer Protection Unit
  4545 N. Lincoln Blvd.,
  Suite 260
  Oklahoma City, OK 73105
  405-521-2029 (consumer
  hotline)
  Fax: 405-528-1867

Oregon

Financial Fraud Section,
Department of Justice
  1162 Court St. NE
  Salem, OR 97310
  503-378-4732
  503-378-4320 (hotline)
  503-229-5576 (in Portland only)
  Fax: 503-378-5017
  E-mail: boj@state.or.us
  Web site: www.doj.state.or.us/
  FinFraud/
  welcome3.html

Pennsylvania

Bureau of Consumer Protection,
Office of the Attorney General
  Strawberry Square, 14th Floor
  Harrisburg, PA 17120
  717-787-9707
  Toll free in PA: 1-800-441-2555
  Fax: 717-787-1190
  Web site:
  www.attorneygeneral.gov
  E-mail:
  info@attorneygeneral.gov

Puerto Rico

Department of Consumer Affairs
  Minillas Station, P.O. Box 41059
  Santurce, PR 00940-1059
  787-721-0940
  Fax: 787-726-6570
  E-mail: Jalicea@Caribe.net

Rhode Island

Consumer Unit, Department of
the Attorney General
  72 Pine Street
  Providence, RI 02903
  401-274-4400
  Toll free in RI: 1-800-852-7776
  TDD: 401-453-0410
  Fax: 401-277-1331

South Carolina

Department of Consumer Affairs
  2801 Devine Street
  P.O. Box 5757
  Columbia, SC 29250-5757
  803-734-9452
  Toll free in SC: 1-800-922-1594
  Fax: 803-734-9365
  E-mail: scdca@infoave.net
  Web site:
  www.state.sc.us/consumer

South Dakota

Consumer Affairs,
Office of the Attorney General
  500 East Capitol
  State Capitol Building
  Pierre, SD 57501-5070
  605-773-4400
  Toll free in SD: 1-800-300-1986
  TDD: 605-773-6585
  Fax: 605-773-4106

Tennessee

Division of Consumer Affairs
  500 James Robertson Parkway,
  5th floor
  Nashville, TN 37243-0600
  615-741-4737
  Toll free in TN: 1-800-342-8385
  Fax: 615-532-4994
  E-mail:
  mwilliams2@mail.state.tn.us
  Web site:
  www.state.tn.us/consumer

Texas

Consumer Protection Division,
Office of Attorney General
  P.O. Box 12548
  Austin, TX 78711-2548
  512-463-2070
  Fax: 512-463-8301

Utah

Division of Consumer Protection,
Department of Commerce
  160 East 300 South
  Box 146704
  Salt Lake City, UT 84114-6704
  801-530-6601
  Toll free in UT: 1-800-721-7233
  Fax: 801-530-6001

Vermont

Public Protection Division,
Office of the Attorney General
  109 State Street
  Montpelier, VT 05609-1001
  802-828-5507
  Fax: 802-828-2154
  E-mail:
  jhasen@ag10.atg.state.vt.us

Virginia

Office of Consumer Affairs,
Department of Agriculture and
Consumer Services
  Washington Building, Suite 100
  P.O. Box 1163
  Richmond, VA 23219
  804-786-2042
  Toll free in VA: 1-800-552-9963
  TDD: 804-371-6344
  Fax: 804-371-7479

Washington

Consumer Protection Division,
Office of the Attorney General
  P.O. Box 40118
  Olympia, WA 98504-0118
  360-753-1808 / 360-753-6210
  Toll free in WA: 1-800-551-4636
  TDD: 206-464-7293
  TDD toll free in WA:
  1-800-276-9883

West Virginia

Consumer Protection Division,
Office of the Attorney General
  812 Quarrier Street, 6th Floor
P.O. Box 1789
Charleston, WV 25326-1789
304-558-8986
Toll free in WV: 1-800-368-8808
Fax: 304-558-0184

Wisconsin

Division of Trade and
ConsumerProtection
Department of Agriculture,
Trade and Consumer Protection
  2811 Agriculture Dr.,
P.O. Box 8911
Madison, WI 53708
608-224-4976
Toll free in WI: 1-800-422-7128
Fax: 608-224-4939

Wyoming

Office of the Attorney General
  123 State Capitol Building
Cheyenne, WY 82002
307-777-7874
Fax: 307-777-6869

Virgin Islands

Department of Licensing and
Consumer Affairs
  Property and Procurement
  Building, Subbase #1, Room 205
St. Thomas, VI 00802
340-774-3130
Fax: 340-776-0605

Federal Complaint Agencies

Many federal agencies have enforcement and/or complaint-handling duties for products and services used by the general public. Others act for the benefit of the public, but do not resolve individual consumer problems.

Agencies also have fact sheets, booklets, and other information that might be helpful in making purchase decisions and dealing with consumer problems. The Web sites and/or e-mail addresses are listed for a number of federal agencies. TDD numbers for text telephones are also listed for individuals with speech or hearing impairments. To find the nearest local office, look in your telephone directory under "U.S. Government," usually in the blue pages.

If you need help in deciding what agency to contact with your consumer problem, call the Federal Information Center (FIC), 1-800-688-9889. Or contact the Consumer Information Center, Pueblo, CO 81009, 719-948-4000, Web site www.pueblo.gsa.gov.

Advertising claims

Federal Trade Commission
  Consumer Response Center
  6th Street & Pennsylvania Ave.,
  NW
  Room 240
  Washington, DC 20580
  202 -326-2222
  TDD/TTY: 202-326-2502
  Web site: www.consumer.gov
  Fax: 202-326-2050

Agriculture hotline

Inspector General's Hotline
Office of the Inspector General
Department of Agriculture
  P.O. Box 23399
  Washington, DC 20026
  202-690-1622
  Toll free: 1-800-424-9121

Airline Service Complaints:

Federal Aviation Administration
Aviation Consumer Protection
Division
  Washington, DC 20590
  202-366-2220

Banks
(Not members of Federal Reserve)

Compliance and Consumer
Affairs Division
Federal Deposit Insurance
Corporation
  550 17th St., NW
  Washington, DC 20429
  Toll free: 1-800-934-3342
  TDD: 1-800-925-4618
  E-mail: consumer@fdic.gov
  Web site: www.fdic.gov

Banks
(Members of Federal Reserve)

Board of Governors of the Federal
Reserve System
Division of Consumer and
Community Affairs
  20th & C Street, NW
  Washington, DC 20551
  202-452-2412
  TDD: 202-452-3544

Cable system complaints

Federal Communications
Commission
  2033 M Street, NW
  Washington, DC 20036
  202-418-7096

Census problems

Office of Consumer Affairs
Department of Commerce
  Room 5718
  Washington, DC 20230
  202-482-5001
  Fax: 202-482-6007
  E-mail: Caffairs@doc.gov

Civil rights

Commission on Civil Rights
  624 9 Street, NW
  Washington, DC 20425
  202-376-8513
  (complaint referral in DC)
  Toll free: 1-800-552-6843
  (complaint referral outside DC)
  TDD nationwide:
  202-376-8116
  (complaint referral)

Drugs and drug labeling

Consumer Affairs and
Information Staff
  Food and Drug Administration
  (HFE-88)
  Department of Health an
  Human Services
  5600 Fishers Lane, Room 1675
  Rockville, MD 20857
  301-827-4420
  Toll free: 1-888-463-6332 (drugs
  and labeling)

Environmental complaints

Inspector General's Fraud,
Waste and Abuse Hotline
  Environmental Protection
  Agency
  401 M Street, SW,
  Mail Code 2441
  202-260-4977
  Fax: 202-260-6976
  Web site: www.epa.gov/

FBI

Federal Bureau of Investigation
  935 Pennsylvania Avenue, NW
  Washington, DC 20535
  202-324-3000
  Fax: 202-324-4705

Food safety and nutrition hotline

Food and Drug Administration
  Center for Food Safety and
  Applied Nutrition
  202-205-4314 (noon to 4:00
  p.m. ET)
  Toll free: 1-800-332-4010
  (noon to 4:00 p.m.)
  Web site: www.fda.gov

Handicapped barriers

Architectural and Transportation
Barriers Compliance Board
  1331 F Street, NW, Suite 1000
  Washington, DC 20004-1111
  202-272-5434
  Toll free: 1-800-872-2253
  Fax: 202-272-5447
  TDD: 202-272-5449
  TDD/TTY toll free:
  1-800-993-2822
  E-mail: info@access-board.gov
  Web site:
  www.access-board.gov

Internal Revenue Service complaints

Internal Revenue Service (IRS)
  Toll free: 1-800-829-1040
  (information and problem
  resolution)
  Web site: www.irs.ustreas.gov

Mobile or manufactured home complaints

Manufactured Housing &
Standards Division
Office of Consumer & Regulatory
Affairs
Department of Housing and
Urban Development
  451 Seventh Street, SW,
  Room 9156
  Washington, DC 20410
  202-708-6409
  Toll free: 1-800-927-2891
  Fax: 202-708-4213
  E-mail: mbs@hud.gov
  HUD works with 36 states to
  respond to consumer complaints.

Meat and poultry Hotline

Department of Agriculture
  1400 Independence Avenue, SW
  Room 2925 S
  Washington, DC 20250
  202-690-1622
  TDD: 202-720-3333
  TDD toll free outside DC:
  1-800-535-4555
  Web site: www.usda.gov/fsis

Product safety

Consumer Product Safety
Commission (CPSC)
  Washington, DC 20207
  Toll free:
  1-800-638-CPSC (2772)
  Fax on demand: 301-504-0051
  TDD toll free: 1-800-638-8270
  (Product Safety Hotline)
  E-mail: info@cpsc.gov
  Web site: www.cpsc.gov
  Call the Product Safety Hotline to report a hazardous product or product-related injury weekdays from 8:30 a.m. to 5:00 p.m. (Injuries are apparently not permitted on evenings or weekends.)

Real estate loan transactions and borrowers rights

Real Estate Settlement
Procedures Act Division,
Department of Housing and
Urban Development
  451 Seventh Street, SW, Room 9146
  Washington, DC 20410
  202-708-4560
  Toll free: 1-800-217-6970
  (Home Buyer Assistance)
  E-mail: hsg-respa@hud.gov
  Web site: www.hud.gov
  Handles complaints and provides information under the Real Estate Settlement Procedures Act (RESPA)

Savings and loans

Office of Thrift Supervision
Division of Consumer and Civil
Rights
  1700 G Street, NW
  Washington, DC 20552
  202-906-6000
  Toll free: 1-800-842-6929
  Web site: www.ots.treas.gov/
  Handles complaints about Federal savings and loans and Federal savings banks.

Stockbrokers

Securities and Exchange
Commission (SEC)
Office of Investor Education and
Assistance
  450 Fifth Street, NW,
  Mail Stop 11-2
  Washington, DC 20549
  202-942-7040 (information and complaints)
  Fax: 202-942-9634 (information and complaints)
  TDD: 202-628-9039
  E-mail: help@sec.gov
  Web site: www.sec.gov

Telephone systems complaints

Common Carrier Bureau
Consumer Protection Division
Federal Communications
Commission
  2025 M Street, NW, Room 6202
  Washington, DC 20554
  202-632-7553

Television or radio complaints

Mass Media Bureau
Enforcement Division
Federal Communications
Commission
  2025 M Street, NW
  Washington, DC 20554
  202-418-1430

Workplace health and safety

Occupational Safety and Health
Administration
  Office of Information and
  Consumer Affairs
  Department of Labor
  200 Constitution Avenue, NW
  Washington, DC 20210
  202-761-8518
  Web site: www.osha.gov

U.S. Postal Service

Consumer Affairs
  475 L'Enfant Plaza
  Washington, DC 20260
  202-268-2284
  Fax: 202-268-4365
  Web site: www.usps.gov
  *In addition, all post offices and
  letter carriers have postage-free
  Consumer Service Cards
  available for reporting mail
  problems and submitting
  comments and suggestions.*

Directory
of
Corporations

Even if you decide to go directly back to a store or dealer, it can't hurt to let the consumer affairs department of the company know about your complaint. This section lists more than 600 major companies. If you do not find the name of the company you are looking for in this section, check the product label or warranty for the name and address of the manufacturer. If it isn't there, once again it is time for either the public library or the Internet. The *Standard & Poor's Register of Corporations, Directors and Executives; Trade Names Directory; Standard Directory of Advertisers;* and *Dun & Bradstreet Directory* are four sources that list information about most firms.

If you do not know the name of the manufacturer, directories such as *Brands and Their Companies*, and the *Thomas Register of American Manufacturers* index companies by their brand names. We don't list the names of the presidents or other officers; that list is impossible to keep up to date. But if you do write directly to an officer, by name, you can learn it through simple research, the simplest of which is a phone call to the company itself.

A

AAMCO Transmissions
One Presidential Blvd.
Bala Cynwyd, PA
19004-1034
610-668-2900
Toll free: 1-800-523-0401
Fax: 610-664-5897

ABC
77 West 66th Street
New York, NY 10023
212-456-7477
E-mail: abcaudr@abc.com

Ace Hardware
2200 Kensington Court
Oak Brook, IL 60523
630-990-6600
Fax: 630-990-6856
Web site: www.acehardware.com

Acura
1919 Torrance Blvd.
Torrance, CA 90501-2746
Toll free: 1-800-382-2238
Fax: 310-783-3535
Web site: www.acura.com

Admiral-Maytag Appliances.
240 Edwards Street
Cleveland, TN 37311
Toll free: 1-800-688-9920
TDD toll free:1-800-688-2080

Adobe Systems
345 Park Avenue
San Jose, CA 95110
408-536-6000
206-470-7000
Toll free: 1-800-685-3507
Web site: www.adobe.com

AETNA
151 Farmington Avenue
Hartford, CT 06156
860-273-0123
Toll free outside CT:
1-800-US-AETNA
Fax: 860-273-9806
TDD/TTY: 860-273-3081
Web site: www.aetna.com

Alamo Rent A Car
P.O. Box 22776
Ft. Lauderdale, FL 33335
954-522-0000
Toll free: 1-800-445-5664
Web site: www.goalamo.com

Alaska Airlines
P.O. Box 68900
Seattle, WA 98168
206-431-7286
Fax: 206-439-4477

Alberto Culver
2525 Armitage Avenue
Melrose Park, IL 60160
708-450-3163
Fax: 708-450-3435
Web site: www.alberto.com

Alfa-Romeo
6220 W. Orange Blossom Trail
Suite 606
Orlando, FL 32809
407-856-5000
Fax: 407-438-0804

Allied Van Lines
P.O. Box 4403
Chicago, IL 60680
630-717-3590
Toll free: 1-800-470-2851
Fax: 630-717-3123
Web site: www.alliedvan.com

Allstate Insurance

2775 Sanders Road
Northbrook, IL 60062
847-402-5448
Fax: 847-402-0169
Web site: www.allstate.com

Aloha Airlines

P.O. Box 30028
Honolulu, HI 96820
808-836-4115
Toll free: 1-800-803-9454
Fax: 808-836-4206
E-mail: aloha@alohaair.com

Amana Appliances

2800 220th Trail
Amana, IA 52204
Toll free: 1-800-843-0304
Web site: www.amana.com

America West Airlines

4000 East Sky Harbor Blvd.
Phoenix, AZ 85034
602-693-0800
Toll free: 1-800-235-9292
Fax: 602-693-3707
Web site: www.americawest.com

American Airlines

P.O. Box 619612 MD 2400
DFW International Airport, TX
75261-9612
817-967-2000

American Automobile Association

Mail space 61
1000 AAA Drive
Heathrow, FL 32746
(written complaints only)

American Express

777 American Express Way
Fort Lauderdale, FL 33337
Toll free: 1-800-528-4800

American Greetings

One American Road
Cleveland, OH 44144
216-252-7300, ext. 1281
Toll free: 1-800-777-4891

American Home Products

5 Giralda Farms
Madison, NJ 07940
973-660-5000
Toll free: 1-800-322-3129
Web site: www.ahp.com

American Standard

P.O. Box 6820
Piscataway, NJ 08855-6820
Toll free: 1-800-223-0068
Fax: 732-980-6170

American Stores

P.O. Box 27447
Salt Lake City, UT 84127-0447
801-539-0112
Toll free: 1-800-541-2863
Fax: 801-531-0768

Ameritech

225 West Randolph Street,
Room 30-D
Chicago, IL 60606
312-722-9411
Toll free: 1-800-244-4444
Web site: www.ameritech.com

Amoco Oil

200 East Randolph Drive
Chicago, IL 60601
Toll free: 1-800-333-3991
Fax: 312-616-0889

Amtrak

Washington Union Station
60 Massachusetts Avenue, NE
Washington, DC 20002
202-906-2121
Fax: 202-906-2211
Web site: www.amtrak.com

Amway

7575 East Fulton Road
Ada, MI 49355
616-787-6000
Fax: 616-787-4369
TDD toll free:
1-800-548-3878
Web site: www.Amway.com

Anheuser-Busch

One Busch Place
St. Louis, MO 63118-1852
314-577-2000
Toll free: 1-800-DIAL BUD
Fax: 1-800-FAX-2ABI
Web site: www.budweiser.com

Apple Computer

20525 Mariani Avenue
Cupertino, CA 95014
Toll free: 1-800-776-2333
Web site: www.info.apple.com

Armour Swift Eckrich

2001 Butterfield Road
Downers Grove, IL 60515
630-512-1000
Toll free: 1-800-325-7424
Fax: 630-512-1124

Armstrong World Industries

P.O. Box 3001
Lancaster, PA 17604
717-396-4780
Toll free: 1-800-233-3823
Fax: 717-396-4270

AT&T

295 North Maple Avenue
Basking Ridge, NJ 07920
908-221-2000
Fax: 908-221-1211

Atlantic Richfield, ARCO Products

P.O. Box 5077
Buena Park, CA 90622-5077
213-486-3511
Toll free: 1-800-322-2726
Web site: www.arco.com

Atlas Van Lines

P.O. Box 509
Evansville, IN 47703-0509
812-424-2222
Toll free: 1-800-252-8885
Fax: 812-421-7129
Web site:
www.atlasvanlines.com

Audi

3800 Hamlin Road
Auburn Hills, MI 48326
Toll free: 1-800-822-2834
Fax: 248-340-4660
Web site: www.audiusa.com

Avis Rent-A-Car

4500 S. 129th East Avenue
Tulsa, OK 74134-3802
Toll free: 1-800-352-7900
Fax: 918-621-4819
E-mail: custserv@avis.com
Web site: www.avis.com

Avon Products

1251 Avenue of the Americas
New York, NY 10020
212-282-7571
Toll free: 1-800-367-2866
Web site: www.avon.com

B

Bacardi-Martini

2100 Biscayne Blvd.
Miami, FL 33137
305-573-8511
Toll free: 1-800-BACARDI
Fax: 305-573-2730
Web site: www.Bacardi.com

Bali

3330 Healy Drive
Winston-Salem, NC 27103
910-519-6053
Toll free: 1-800-225-4872
Web site: www.balinet.com

Bally Entertainment

8700 West Bryn Mawr
Chicago, IL 60631
773-399-1300

Bank of America

Box 37000
San Francisco, CA 94137
415-622-6081

Bank of New York

48 Wall Street, 16th Floor
New York, NY 10286
212-495-1784
Fax: 212-495-1398
Web site: www.bankofny.com

Bausch and Lomb

1400 North Goodman Street
Rochester, NY 14692
716-338-6000
Toll free: 1-800-553-5340
Fax: 716-338-0495
E-mail: bausch@aol.com
Web site: www.bausch.com

Bayer

36 Columbia Road
Morristown, NJ 07962-1910
973-331-4536
Toll free: 1-800-331-4536
Fax: 973-408-8000

Bell Atlantic

1095 Avenue of the Americas
New York, NY 10036
212-395-2121
1-800-621-9900
TTY toll free: 1-800-974-6006
Web site: www.bellatlantic.com

BellSouth Telecommunications

37D57 BellSouth Center
675 West Peachtree Street, NE
Atlanta, GA 30375
404-927-7400
Toll free: 1-800-346-9000
Fax: 404-584-6545
TTY toll free:
1-800-251-5325
E-mail: Hq.Appeals@bridge.
bellsouth.com
Web site: www.bellsouth.com

Benihana of Tokyo

8685 NW 53rd Terrace
Miami, FL 33166
305-593-0770
Toll free: 1-800-327-3369
Fax: 305-592-6371

Best Western International

P.O. Box 42007
Phoenix, AZ 85080-2007
602-780-6181
Toll free: 1-800-528-1238
Fax: 602-780-6199
Web site: www.bestwestern.com

BIC

500 Bic Drive
Milford, CT 06460
203-783-2000
Web site: www.bicworld.com

Black and Decker

6 Armstrong Road
Shelton, CT 06484
Toll free: 1-800-231-9786
Fax: 203-926-3057

Blockbuster

1201 Elm Street
Dallas, TX 75270
214-854-3000
Toll free: 1-800-667-6767

Bloomingdale's by Mail, Ltd.

475 Knotter Drive
P.O. Box 593
Cheshire, CT 06410-0593
203-271-1313
Toll free: 1-800-777-0000
Fax: 203-271-5321
TDD/TTY toll free:
1-800-838-2892
E-mail: bloomiessh@aol.com

Blue Cross and Blue Shield

1310 G Street, NW, 12th Floor,
Washington, DC 20005
202-626-4780
Fax: 202-626-4833
Web site: www.bluecares.com

BMW

300 Chestnut Ridge Rd.
Woodcliff Lake, NJ 07675
Toll free: 1-800-831-1117 (BMW
Customer Service Center)
Web site: www.bmwusa.com

Bob Evans Farms

3776 South High Street
Columbus, OH 43207
614-491-2225
Toll free outside OH:
1-800-272-7675
Toll free: 1-800-939-2338
Fax: 614-497-4330
E-mail:
tammy.myers@bobevans.com

Bojangles

P.O. Box 240239
Charlotte, NC 28224
704-527-2675, ext. 3226
Toll free: 1-800-366-9921
Fax: 704-522-8677
Web site: www.bojangles.com

Borden

180 East Broad Street
Columbus, OH 43215
614-225-4511
Toll free: 1-800-426-7336
Fax: 614-225-7680

Bridgestone/Firestone

P.O. Box 7988
Chicago, IL 60680-9534
Toll free: 1-800-367-3872
Fax: 1-800-760-7859
E-mail:
firestone_consumer_affairs
@faneuil.com

Bristol-Myers Squibb

P.O. Box 4000
Princeton, NJ 08543-4000
609-252-4000
Toll free: 1-800-332-2056
Web site: www.bms.com

British Airways

7520 Astoria Blvd.
Jackson Heights, NY 11370
718-397-4000
Toll free: 1-800-247-9297
Fax: 718-397-4395
Web site:
www.british-airways.com

Brown-Forman Beverages Worldwide

P.O. Box 1080
Louisville, KY 40201
502-585-1100
Toll free: 1-800-753-4567

Budget Rent-A-Car

P.O. Box 111580
Carrollton, TX 75011-1580
Toll free: 1-800-621-2844
Fax: 972-404-7869

Buick

902 East Hamilton Avenue
Flint, MI 48550
Toll free: 1-800-521-7300
TDD toll free: 1-800-832-8425
Web site: www.buick.com

Bulova Watch

26-15 Brooklyn Queens
Expressway
Woodside, NY 11377
718-204-3300

Burlington Coat Factory

1830 Route 130 North
Burlington, NJ 08016
609-387-7800
Fax: 609-387-7071

Burlington Industries

3330 West Friendly Avenue
Greensboro, NC 27420
336-379-2472
Fax: 336-379-4504

C

C & R Clothiers

8660 Hayden Place
Culver City, CA 90232
310-559-8200
Fax: 310-839-7480

C.F. Hathaway

10 Water Street
Waterville, ME 04901
207-873-4241
Toll free: 1-800-341-1003
Fax: 207-873-8390

Cabela's

One Cabela Drive
Sidney, NE 69160
308-254-5505
Toll free: 1-800-237-8888
Fax: 308-254-6669
TDD/TTY toll free:1-800-695-5000
Web site: www.cabelas.com

Cadillac

P.O. Box 436004
Pontiac, MI 48343-6004
Toll free: 1-800-458-8006
TDD toll free: 1-800-TDD-CMCC
Web site: www.cadillac.com

Calvin Klein

205 West 39th Street,
10th Floor
New York, NY 10018
212-719-2600

Campbell Soup

Campbell Place
P.O. Box 26B
Camden, NJ 08103-1799
609-342-3714
Toll free: 1-800-257-8443
Fax: 609-342-6449
Web site:
www.campbellsoup.com

Canandaigua Wine

116 Buffalo Street
Canandaigua, NY 14424
716-394-7900
Toll free: 1-888-659-7900
Fax: 716-393-6950

Canon Computer Systems

15955 Alton Parkway
Irvine, CA 92618
714-753-4000
Toll free: 1-800-423-2366
Fax: 714-753-4239
Web site: www.ccsi.canon.com

Canon USA

One Canon Plaza, Bldg. C
Lake Success, NY 11042
516-488-6700
Toll free: 1-800-828-4040

Carl's Jr.

1200 North Harbor Blvd.
P.O. Box 4349
Anaheim, CA 92803
714-774-5796
Toll free: 1-800-758-2275
Fax: 714-490-3695
Web site: www.ckr.com

Carnival Cruise Lines

3655 Northwest 87th Avenue
Miami, FL 33178-2428
305-599-2600
Toll free: 1-800-438-6744
Fax: 305-406-4718
E-mail: grelations@carnival.com
Web site: www.carnival.com

Carrier Air Conditioning

P.O. Box 4808
Syracuse, NY 13221
315-432-7885
Toll free: 1-800-227-7437
1-800-428-4326
Fax: 315-432-6620

Carter-Wallace

1345 Avenue of the Americas
New York, NY 10105
212-339-5000
Toll free: 1-800-833-9532
Fax: 212-339-5100

Carvel

20 Batterson Park Road
Farmington, CT 06032-2502
Toll free: 1-800-322-4848

Casio

570 Mt. Pleasant Avenue
Dover, NJ 07801
973-361-5400
Toll free: 1-800-962-2746
Fax: 973-361-3819
Web site: www.casio.com

CBS

Audience Services
524 West 57th Street
New York, NY 10019
212-975-3247
E-mail: audsvcs@cbs.com
Web site: www.cbs.com

Chanel

9 West 57th Street,
44th Floor
New York, NY 10019-2790
212-688-5055
Fax: 212-752-1851

Chase Manhattan Bank

270 Park Avenue
New York, NY 10017
212-270-9300
Fax: 212-270-1882

Chesebrough-Pond's

800 Sylvan Avenue
Englewood Cliffs, NJ 07632
201-871-3143
Toll free: 1-800-243-5804
Web site: www.unilever.com

Chevrolet/GeoChevrolet/Geo Motor Division

General Motors Corp.
P.O. Box 7047
Troy, MI 48007-7047
Toll free: 1-800-222-1020
TDD toll free:
1-800-TDD-CHEV
Web site: www.chevrolet.com

Chevron

P.O. Box H
Concord, CA 94524
Toll free: 1-800-962-1223
Fax: 510-827-6820
Web site: www.chevron.com

Chi-Chi's

10200 Linn Station Road
Louisville, KY 40223
502-426-3900
Toll free: 1-800-436-6006
Fax: 502-429-6243

Chicken of the Sea

4510 Executive Drive, Suite 300
San Diego, CA 92121
619-558-9662
Fax: 619-597-4566
Chrysler Corporation
P.O. Box 21-8004
Auburn Hills, MI 48321-8004
Toll free: 1-800-992-1997
Web site: www.chryslercorp.com

CIBA Vision

11460 Johns Creek Parkway
Duluth, GA 30097
770-418-5117
Toll free: 1-800-875-3001
Web site: www.cibavision.com

CIGNA Property and Casualty

1601 Chestnut Street
Philadelphia, PA 19192
215-761-4555
215-761-2489

Circuit City

9950 Mayland Drive
Richmond, VA 23233
804-527-4000
Toll free: 1-800-627-2274
Fax: 804-342-6481

Citicorp/Citibank

1 Court Square
Long Island City, NY 11120
1-800-234-6377
Fax: 718-248-0512

Citizen Watch

8506 Osage Avenue
Los Angeles, CA 90045
Toll free: 1-800-321-1023

Clorox

1221 Broadway
Oakland, CA 94612-1888
510-271-7000
Toll free: 1-800-292-2200

Club Med

40 West 57th Street
New York, NY 10019
212-977-2100
Fax: 212-315-5392
Web site: www.clubmed.com

Coca-Cola

P.O. Drawer 1734
Atlanta, GA 30301
404-676-2121
Toll free: 1-800-438-2653
Fax: 404-676-4903
TDD toll free: 1-800-262-2653

Colgate/Palmolive

300 Park Avenue
New York, NY 10022
212-310-2000
Toll free: 1-800-228-7408
Web site: www.colgate.com

Colonial Penn

399 Market Street, 5th Floor
Philadelphia, PA 19181
215-928-8000
Toll free: 1-800-523-9100

Columbia House

1221 Avenue of the Americas
New York, NY 10020-1090
Toll free: 1-800-457-0500
Web site:
www.columbiahouse.com

Compaq Computer

P.O. Box 692000
Houston, TX 77269
281-370-0670
Toll free: 1-800-852-6672
Fax: 970-282-9225
Web site: www.compaq.com

Congoleum

3705 Quakerbridge Road,
Suite 211
Mercerville, NJ 08619
609-584-3610
Toll free: 1-800-274-3266
Web site: www.congoleum.com

Continental Airlines

3663 North Sam Houston
Suite 500
Houston, TX 77032
281-987-6500
Toll free: 1-800-932-2732
E-mail: custo@coair.com

Continental/General Tire

1800 Continental Blvd.
Charlotte, NC 28273
704-583-8895
Toll free: 1-800-847-3349
Fax: 1-888-TIREFAX
(847-3329)
Web site: www.contigentire.com

Converse

One Fordham Road
North Reading, MA 01864-2680
508-664-1100
Toll free: 1-800-428-2667
Fax: 508-664-7440
Web site: www.converse.com

Coors Brewing

NH475
Golden, CO 80401
Toll free: 1-800-642-6116
Fax: 303-277-5415

Corel

1600 Carling Avenue
Ottawa, ON K1Z 8R7
Canada
613-728-1990
613-728-8200
Toll free: 1-800-772-6735
Fax: 613-761-9176
E-mail: custserv@corel.com

Corning

1300 Hopeman Parkway
Waynesboro, VA 22980
Toll free: 1-800-999-3436

CPC International

International Plaza
Box 8000
Englewood Cliffs, NJ
07632-9976
201-894-4000
Toll free: 1-800-338-8831
Fax: 201-894-2126

Craftmatic

2500 Interplex Drive
Trevose, PA 19053-6998
215-639-1310
Toll free: 1-800-828-1033
Fax: 215-639-9941

Crown Books
3300 75th Avenue
Landover, MD 20785
Toll free: 1-800-831-7400
Web site: www.crownbooks.com

Cuisinart
One Cummings Point Road
Stamford, CT 06904
203-975-4600
Toll free 1-800-726-0190
Fax: 203-975-4660
E-mail: cuisinart@conair
Web site: www.cuisinart.com

Culligan
One Culligan Parkway
Northbrook, IL 60062
847-205-6000
E-mail: drudolph@culligan.com
Web site: www.culligan.com

Cunard Line
555 Fifth Avenue
New York, NY 10017-2416
Toll free: 1-800-528-6273

D

Daihatsu
4422 Corporate Center Drive
Los Alamitos, CA 90720
714-761-7000
Toll free: 1-800-777-7070

Dairy Queen
P.O. Box 39286
7505 Metro Blvd.
Minneapolis, MN 55439-0286
612-830-0200
Fax: 612-830-0480
Web site: www.dairyqueen.com

Dannon
P. O. Box 1102
Maple Plain, MN 55592
Toll free: 1-800-321-2174

Danskin
P.O. Box 15016
York, PA 17405-7016
717-840-5817
Toll free: 1-800-288-6749
Fax: 717-840-5855

Dayton's, Hudson's, Marshall Field's
Box 1197
700 Nicollet Mall
Minneapolis, MN 55402
612-375-3382
Fax: 612-375-2402

Deere & Company
8601 John Deere Road
Moline, IL 61265-8098
309-765-8000
Web site: www.deere.com

Del Monte Foods
P.O. Box 193575
San Francisco, CA 94119-3575
415-247-3000
Toll free: 1-800-543-3090
Fax: 415-247-3080

Delta Air Lines
Hartsfield Atlanta International
Airport
Atlanta, GA 30320
404-715-1450
Fax: 1-888-286-3163
Web site: www.delta-air.com

Delta Faucets
P.O. Box 40980
Indianapolis, IN 46280
317-848-1812

Denny's

203 East Main Street
Spartanburg, SC 29319
864-597-8000
Toll free: 1-800-7DENNYS

DeVry

1 Tower Lane
Oakbrook Terrace, IL 60181
630-571-7700
Toll free: 1-800-225-8000
Fax: 630-574-1693

Dial

15101 N. Scottsdale Road
Scottsdale, AZ 85254
Toll free: 1-800-528-0849

Digital Equipment

111 Powder Mill Road
Maynard, MA 01754
978-493-5111
Toll free: 1-800-344-4825
Web site: www.digital.com

Diners Club International

183 Inverness Drive West
Englewood, CO 80112
303-799-9000
Toll free: 1-800-234-6377
Fax: 303-649-2891
TDD: 303-643-2155
Web site: www.dinersclub.com

Dole Food

5795 Lindero Canyon Road
Westlake Village, CA 91362-4013
818-874-4000
Toll free: 1-800-232-8888
Fax: 818-874-4997
Web site: www.dole.com

Domino's Pizza

P.O. Box 997
Ann Arbor, MI 41806-0997
734-930-3030

Doubleday Book & Music Clubs

401 Franklin Avenue
Garden City, NY 11530-5806
516-873-4628

DowBrands

P.O. Box 68511
Indianapolis, IN 46268-0511
317-873-7000
Toll free: 1-800-428-4795
Fax: 317-873-8564
Web site: www.dowclean.com or
www.ziploc.com

Dr Pepper/Seven Up

5301 Legacy Drive
Plano, TX 75024
972-673-7000
Toll free: 1-800-527-7096
Fax: 972-673-7867
E-mail:
Philippa_Dworkin@dpsu.com
Web site: www.drpepper.com or
www.7up.com

Drug Emporium

155 Hidden Ravines Drive
Powell, OH 43065
614-548-7080, ext. 104
Fax: 614-548-6651
Web site:
www.drugemporium.com

Dunkin Donuts/ Baskin Robbins

P.O. Box 317
Randolph, MA 02368
781-961-4000

Dunlop Tire

P.O. Box 1109
Buffalo, NY 14240-1109
716-639-5439
Toll free: 1-800-828-7428
Fax: 1-800-253-6702
E-mail:
rpokrzyk@dunloptire.com
Web site: www.dunloptire.com

DuPont

Barley Mill Plaza
Reeves Mill Building
Wilmington, DE 19880-0010
302-774-1000
Toll free: 1-800-441-7515

Duracell

Duracell Drive
Bethel, CT 06801
203-796-4304
Toll free: 1-800-551-2355
Fax: 203-796-4565
TDD/TTY toll free:
1-800-341-0654
Web site: www.duracell.com

E

E-Machines

1211 Alderwood Avenue
Sunnyvale, CA 94089
408-541-1720

Kodak

343 State Street
Rochester, NY 14650-0811
716-724-9977
Toll free: 1-800-242-2424
Fax: 716-724-9261
TDD/TTY toll free:
1-800-755-6805
Web site: www.kodak.com

Eckerd Drug

8333 Bryan Dairy Road
P.O. Box 4689
Clearwater, FL 34618
813-395-6000
Toll free: 1-800-284-8212
Fax: 813-399-7063
TDD/TTY toll free:
1-800-760-4833
Web site: www.eckerd.com

Eddie Bauer

P.O. Box 9700
Redmond, WA 98073-9700
425-882-6100
Toll free: 1-800-426-6253
Fax: 425-882-6383
E-mail: eddiebauer@aol.com
Web site: www.eddiebauer.com

Edmund Scientific

101 East Gloucester Pike
Barrington, NJ 08007-1380
609-547-3488
Toll free: 1-800-728-6999
Fax: 609-547-3292

Electrolux

300 East Valley Drive
Bristol, VA 24201
Toll free: 1-800-243-9078
Fax: 540-645-2863

Eli Lilly

Lilly Corporate Center
Indianapolis, IN 46285
317-276-2000
Toll free: 1-800-545-5979
Web site: www.lilly.com

Emery Worldwide

One Lagoon Drive
Redwood City, CA 94065
650-596-9600
Toll free: 1-800-227-1981
Fax: 650-596-7983

Encyclopedia Britannica

310 South Michigan Avenue
Chicago, IL 60604-4293
312-347-7000
Toll free: 1-800-747-8503
Fax: 312-347-7399
Web site: www.eb.com

Epson

20770 Madrona Avenue
Torrance, CA 90503
310-796-6292
Fax: 310-782-0770
Web site: www.epson.com

Equifax

P.O. Box 105873
Atlanta, GA 30348
Toll free: 1-800-685-1111

Equitable

1290 Avenue of the Americas,
13th Floor
New York, NY 10104
212-554-1234

Esprit de Corps

900 Minnesota Street
San Francisco, CA 94107-3000
415-648-6900
Toll free: 1-800-4ESPRIT
Fax: 415-550-3960

Estee Lauder

767 Fifth Avenue
New York, NY 10153-0003
212-572-4200

Ethan Allen

Ethan Allan Drive
Danbury, CT 06813
203-743-8668
Fax: 203-743-8354
E-mail:
ethanadv@ethanallen.com
Web site: www.ethanallen.com

Eureka

1201 East Bell Street
Bloomington, IL 61701-6902
309-823-5735
Toll free: 1-800-282-2886

Experian

P.O. Box 949
Allen, TX 75013-0949
Toll free: 1-888-EXPERIAN
Web site: www.experian.com

Exxon

P.O. Box 4712
Houston, TX 77210-4712
713-680-7901
Toll free: 1-800-243-9966
Fax: 713-680-5047

F

Family Circle Magazine

375 Lexington Avenue
New York, NY 10017-5514
212-499-2000

Farallon Products, Netopia

2470 Mariner Square Loop
Alameda, CA 94501
510-814-5100
Fax: 510-814-5020
Web site: www.farallon.com

Federal Express

P.O. Box 727, Dept. 1845
Memphis, TN 38194-1845
901-395-4562
Toll free: 1-800-238-5355
Fax: 901-395-4511
E-mail: webmaster@fedex.com

Federated Department Stores

7 West Seventh Street
Cincinnati, OH 45202
513-579-7000
Fax: 513-579-7185
Web site:
www.federated-fds.com

Ferrari

250 Sylvan Avenue
Englewood Cliffs, NJ 07632
201-816-2652 (technical
department)

Fieldcrest Cannon

1 Lake Circle Drive
Kannapolis, NC 28081
Toll free: 1-800-343-6955
Fax: 704-939-2302

Finast

17000 Rockside Road
Cleveland, OH 44137-4390
216-587-7100
Fax: 216-475-4354

Fingerhut

11 McLeland Road
St. Cloud, MN 56395
320-259-2500
Fax: 320-654-4858

First Brands

83 Wooster Heights Road
Danbury, CT 06813-1911
203-731-2590
Toll free: 1-800-835-4523
E-mail: answers@stp.com

First Union National Bank

1525 West W.T. Harris Blvd.
Charlotte, NC 28212
Toll free: 1-800-733-3862
Web site: www.firstunion.com

Fisher-Price

636 Girard Avenue
East Aurora, NY 14052
716-687-3000
Toll free: 1-800-432-5437
Fax: 716-687-3494
TDD toll free: 1-800-382-7470
Web site: www.fisher-price.com

Florida Power and Light

P.O. Box 029100
Miami, FL 33102-9100
305-552-4645
Toll free: 1-800-397-6544
Fax: 305-552-3792
TDD toll free: 1-800-432-6554
Web site: www.fpl.com

FTD

3113 Woodcreek Drive
Downers Grove, IL 60515
630-719-7800
Toll free: 1-800-669-1000

Florsheim

200 North LaSalle
Chicago, IL 60601
312-458-2710
Toll free: 1-800-633-4988
Fax: 312-458-7470
E-mail: florsheim@aol.com

Forbes

60 Fifth Avenue
New York, NY 10011
212-620-2409
Fax: 212-206-5199
E-mail: syablon@forbes.com

Ford

300 Renaissance Center
P.O. Box 43360
Detroit, MI 48243
Toll free: 1-800-392-3673
TDD toll free: 1-800-232-5952
Web site: www.ford.com

Ford Dispute Settlement Board

P.O. Box 5120
Southfield, MI 48086-5120
Toll free: 1-800-392-3673

Franklin Mint

U.S. Route One
Franklin Center, PA 19091
610-459-6000
Toll free: 1-800-523-7622
Fax: 610-459-6040

Frigidaire

P.O. Box 7181
Dublin, OH 43017-0781
614-792-2153
Toll free: 1-800-451-7007
Fax: 614-792-4092
Web site: www.frigidaire.com

Friskies

P.O. Box 96384
Phoenix, AZ 85093
818-549-5998
Toll free: 1-800-555-3747
Fax: 818-549-6330

Fruit of the Loom

One Fruit of the Loom Drive
Bowling Green, KY 42102-9015
502-782-5400
Fax: 502-781-0903
Web site: www.fruit.com

Fuji Photo Film

400 Commerce Blvd.
Carlstadt, NJ 07072-3009
Toll free:
1-800-800-FUJI (3854)
Toll free:
1-800-659-3854, ext. 2564
Fax: 201-507-2591
Web site: www.fujifilm.com

Fujitsu Computer

2904 Orchard Parkway
San Jose, CA 95134
408-432-6333
Toll free: 1-800-626-4686
Fax: 408-894-1709
Web site: www.fcpa.com

Fuller Brush

Customer Resource Center
P.O. Box 1247
Great Bend, KS 67530-0729
316-792-1711
Toll free: 1-800-523-3794
Fax: 316-793-4523
Web site: www.fullerbrush.com

G

G.D. Searle

P.O. Box 5110
Chicago, IL 60680
847-982-7000
Toll free: 1-800-323-1603
Fax: 847-470-6633
Web site: www.monsanto.com

Gallo Winery

P.O. Box 1130
Modesto, CA 95353
209-341-3161
Fax: 209-341-6600

General Electric

General Host
P.O. Box 10045
Stamford, CT 06904
203-357-9900
Toll free: 1-800-626-2000
Fax: 203-357-0148

General Mills

P.O. Box 1113
Minneapolis, MN 55440-1113
612-540-2311
Toll free: 1-800-328-6787
(bakery products)
1-800-328-1144 (cereals)
1-800-222-6846 (Gorton's)
1-800-231-0308 (snacks)
Fax: 612-540-8330
Web site: www.genmills.com

General Motors Acceptance

3044 West Grand Blvd.,
Room AX348
Detroit, MI 48202
Toll free: 1-800-441-9234
TDD toll free:
1-800-TDD-GMAC
Web site: www.gmacfs.com

Genesee Brewing

445 St. Paul Street
Rochester, NY 14605
716-546-1030
Toll free: 1-800-SAY-GENNY
(729-4366)
Fax: 716-546-5011
Web site: www.highfalls.com

Georgia-Pacific

P.O. Box 105605
Atlanta, GA 30348-5605
404-652-4000

Gerber

445 State Street
Fremont, MI 49413-1056
616-928-2000
Toll free: 1-800-4-GERBER
Fax: 616-928-2723

Giant Food

P.O. Box 1804
Department 597
Washington, DC 20013
301-341-4365
Fax: 301-618-4968
TDD: 301-341-4327

Gillette

P.O. Box 61
Boston, MA 02199
617-421-7000
Toll free: 1-800-872-7202
Fax: 617-463-3410

Glaxo Wellcome

5 Moore Drive
Research Triangle Park, NC
27709
919-483-2100
Fax: 919-483-0751
Web site:
www.glaxowellcome.com

GMC Truck

P.O. Box 436008
Pontiac, MI 48343-6008
Toll free: 1-800-462-8782
TDD toll free: 1-800-462-8583

Golden Grain

4576 Willow Road
Pleasanton, CA 94588
Toll free: 1-800-421-2444

Goldstar

P.O. Box 6166
Huntsville, AL 35824
205-772-8860
Toll free: 1-800-243-0000
Fax: 1-800-448-4026

BF Goodrich Tires
P.O. Box 19001
Greensville, SC 29602-9001
864-458-5000
Fax: 864-458-6650
Toll Free: 1-800-521-9796
Web site: www.michelin.com

Goodyear Tire & Rubber
1144 East Market Street
Akron, OH 44316
330-796-20059
Toll free: 1-800-321-2136
Fax: 330-796-3753
TDD: 216-796-6055
Web site: www.goodyear.com

Greyhound Lines
P.O. Box 660362
Dallas, TX 75266-0362
214-849-8000

GTE
One Stamford Forum
Stamford, CT 06904
203-965-2000
Toll free: 1-800-643-0997
Fax: 203-965-2277
Web site: www.gte.com

Guess?
1444 South Alameda Street
Los Angeles, CA 90021
213-765-3100
Toll free: 1-800-394-8377
Fax: 213-744-0855

Guinness
Six Landmark Square
Stamford, CT 06901-2704
203-323-3311
Toll free: 1-800-521-1591
Fax: 203-359-7209

H

H&R Block
4410 Main Street
Kansas City, MO 64111-9986
816-753-6900
Toll free: 1-800-829-7733
Fax: 816-932-1800
Web site: www.hrblock.com

Hallmark Cards
P.O. Box 419034
Kansas City, MO 64141-6034
816-274-5111
Toll free: 1-800-425-6275
Toll free: 1-800-425-5627
Web site:
www.hallmark.com

Hanes Hosiery
5650 University Parkway
Winston-Salem, NC 27105
910-768-9540
Toll free: 1-800-342-7070
Web site:
www.onehanesplace.com

Hanover-Direct
340 Poplar Street
Hanover, PA 17333-9989
717-637-6000
Toll free: 1-800-447-3164
Fax: 717-633-3199
TDD/TTY toll free:
1-800-617-2381
E-mail:
allcats@hanoverdirect.com

Harry & David, Jackson & Perkins

2518 South Pacific Highway
P.O. Box 299
Medford, OR 97501
541-776-2400
Toll free: 1-800-345-5655
Fax: 541-776-2194
Web site:
www.harryanddavid.com

Hartz Mountain

400 Plaza Drive
Secaucus, NJ 07094
201-271-4800

Hasbro

P.O. Box 200
Pawtucket, RI 02860-0200
Toll free: 1-800-242-7276
Toll free: 1-800-255-5516

Hayes Microcomputer Products

5854 Peachtree Industrial Blvd.
Norcross, GA 30092
770-840-9200
Fax: 770-449-0087
Web site: www.hayes.com

Heath Kit/Heath Zenith

455 Riverview Drive
Benton Harbor, MI 49022
616-925-6000
Toll free: 1-800-530-0570
Fax: 616-925-2898
E-mail: heathkit@heathkit.com
Web site: www.heathkit.com

Heinz USA

P.O. Box 57
Pittsburgh, PA 15230
412-237-5740
Fax: 412-237-5922

Helene Curtis

325 North Wells Street
Chicago, IL 60610-4713
312-661-0222
Toll free: 1-800-682-8301
Toll free: 1-800-782-8301
Fax: 312-661-2787;
312-836-0125

Hershey Food

100 Crystal A Drive
Hershey, PA 17033
717-534-6799
Web site: www.hersheys.com

Hertz

225 Brae Blvd.
Park Ridge, NJ 07656
201-307-2000
Toll free: 1-800-654-3131
Fax: 201-307-2928
Web site: www.hertz.com

Hewlett-Packard

P. O. Box 10301
Palo Alto, CA 94303
650-857-1501
Fax: 650-813-3254
E-mail: francesca_rude@hp.com
Web site: www.hp.com

Hilton Hotels

9336 Civic Center Drive
Beverly Hills, CA 90210
310-278-4321
Fax: 310-205-4437
E-mail: billbrooks@hilton.com
Web site: www.hilton.com

Hitachi

3890 Steve Reynolds Blvd.
Norcross, GA 30093
770-279-5600
Toll free: 1-800-241-6558
Fax: 770-279-5699
Web site: www.hitachi.com

Holiday Inns
Three Ravenia Drive,
Suite 2900
Atlanta, GA 30346
1-800-465-4329
(1-800-HOLIDAY)

Home Depot
2727 Paces Ferry Road, NW
Atlanta, GA 30339
770-433-8211
Toll free: 1-800-553-3199
Fax: 770-384-2345
Web site: www.homedepot.com

Home Shopping Network
One HSN Drive
St. Petersburg, FL 33729
813-572-8585
Toll free: 1-800-284-3900
Fax: 813-572-8854

Honda
1919 Torrance Blvd.
Torrance, CA 90501-2746
310-783-2000
Toll free: 1-800-999-1009
Fax: 310-783-3785

Honeywell
Honeywell Plaza
P.O. Box 524
Minneapolis, MN 55440-0524
612-951-1000
Toll free: 1-800-468-1502

Hoover
101 East Maple
North Canton, OH 44720
330-499-9499
Toll free: 1-800-944-9200
Fax: 330-497-5065

Horchow Collection
111 Customer Way
Irving, TX 75039
972-401-6300
Toll free: 1-800-395-5397
Fax: 972-401-6740
TDD/TTY toll free:
1-800-533-1312

Hormel Foods
One Hormel Place
Austin, MN 55912-9989
507-437-5032
Toll free: 1-800-523-4635

Howard Johnson
3400 NW Grand Avenue
Phoenix, AZ 85017
602-264-9164
Fax: 602-264-7633

Huffy Bicycle
P.O. Box 1204
Dayton, OH 45401
Toll free: 1-800-872-2453
Fax: 937-865-2835

Humana
500 West Main Street
P.O. Box 1438
Louisville, KY 40201-1438
502-580-1000
Toll free: 1-800-664-4140
Web site: www.humana.com

Hunt-Wesson
P.O. Box 4800
Fullerton, CA 92834-4800
714-680-1431

Hyatt Hotels
200 West Madison Street,
39th Floor
Chicago, IL 60606
312-750-1234
Toll free: 1-800-228-3336
Fax: 312-609-8875

Hyundai

10550 Talbert Avenue
P.O. Box 20850
Fountain Valley, CA 92728-0850
714-965-3000
Toll free: 1-800-633-5151
Fax: 714-965-3837
E-mail: cmd@hma.service.com

Isuzu

2300 Pellisier Place
P.O. Box 995
Whittier, CA 90608
562-699-0500
Toll free: 1-800-255-6727
Fax: 562-908-9575
Web site: www.isuzu.com

I

IBM

1500 Riveredge Parkway
Atlanta, GA 30328
919-517-2480
770-858-5980
Toll free: 1-800-426-4968
Fax: 770-644-5530
Web site: www.ibm.com

Intel

1900 Prairie City Road
Folsom, CA 95630
916-356-8080
Toll free: 1-800-628-8686
Fax: 800-525-3019
Web site: www.intel.com

Iomega

1821 West Iomega Way
Roy, UT 90467
801-778-1000
Toll free: 1-800-450-5522
Toll free: 1-888-4-IOMEGA
(446-6342)
Fax: 801-779-5632
Web site: www.iomega.com

J

Jackson & Perkins

2518 South Pacific Highway
Medford, OR 97501
541-776-2400
Toll free: 1-800-872-7673
Fax: 800-242-0329

Jaguar

555 MacArthur Blvd.
Mahwah, NJ 07430-2327
201-818-8500
Toll free: 1-800-452-4827
Web site: www.jaguarcars.com

James River

P.O. Box 6000
Norwalk, CT 06856-6000
203-854-2458
Toll free: 1-800-243-5384

JCPenney Co.

P.O. Box 10001
Dallas, TX 75301-8212
972-431-1000
Fax: 214-431-8792
Web site: www.jcpenney.com

Jenn Air-Maytag Appliances

240 Edwards Street
Cleveland, TN 37311
Toll free: 1-800-688-1100
TDD toll free: 1-800-688-2080
Web site: www.jennair.com

Jenny Craig International

11355 North Terrey Pines Road
LaJolla, CA 92038
619-812-7000
Fax: 619-812-2700
Web site: www.jennycraig.com

Jockey International

2300 60th Street
P.O. Box 1417 (53141-1417)
Kenosha, WI 53140
414-658-8111
Fax: 414-658-1812
Web site: www.jockey.com

John Hancock Mutual Insurance

P.O. Box 111
Boston, MA 02117
617-572-6385
Toll free: 1-800-732-5543
Fax: 617-572-8707
TDD toll free: 1-800-832-5282
Web site: www.jhancock.com

Johnny Appleseed's

30 Tozar Road
Beverly, MA 01915
978-922-2040
Toll free: 1-800-767-6666
Fax: 1-800-755-7557

Johns-Manville

P.O. Box 5108
Denver, CO 80217-5108
303-978-2000
Toll free: 1-800-654-3103
Fax: 303-978-2318
Web site: www.jm.com

Johnson & Johnson

199 Grandview Road
Skillman, NJ 08558
908-874-1000

Johnson Publishing Co

820 South Michigan Avenue
Chicago, IL 60605
(written complaints only)

Jordache

1411 Broadway
New York, NY 10018
212-944-1330

JVC Company

107 Little Falls Road
Fairfield, NJ 07004
201-808-2100
Toll free: 1-800-252-5722
Fax: 201-808-3351
E-mail:
customerrelation@jvcamerica.com
Web site: www.jvc-america.com

K

Kmart

3100 West Big Beaver Road
Troy, MI 48084
810-643-1643
810-643-1000
Toll free: 1-800-635-6278
Fax: 810-614-1970

Karastan Rugmill Division of Mohawk Industries

P.O. Box 129
Eden, NC 27289
Toll free: 1-800-476-7113

Kawasaki Motor

P.O. Box 25252
Santa Ana, CA 92799-5252
714-770-0400
Fax: 714-460-5629
Web site: www.kawasaki.com

Keebler Co.

One Hollow Tree Lane
Elmhurst, IL 60126
630-833-2900
Fax: 630-833-9501

Kellogg's

P.O. Box CAMB
Battle Creek, MI 49016
Toll free: 1-800-962-1413
Web site: www.kelloggs.com

Kelly Springfield Tire

12501 Willow Brook Road, SE
Cumberland, MD 21502-2599
301-777-6635
Fax: 301-777-6225

Kemper Insurance

1 Kemper Drive, C-3
Long Grove, IL 60049-0001
708-320-2522
Toll free: 1-800-833-0355
E-mail:
Nbrebner@KemperInsurance.com
Web site:
www.kemperinsurance.com

Kenner Products

P.O. Box 200
Pawtucket, RI 02862-0200
401-431-8697
Toll free: 1-800-327-8264

Kensington Technology

2855 Campus Drive
San Mateo, CA 94403
650-572-2700
Toll free: 1-800-535-4242
Fax: 650-572-9675
Web site: www.kensington.com

Kimberly-Clark

P.O. Box 2020
Neenah, WI 54957
920-721-8000
Toll free: 1-800-544-1847
Fax: 920-721-4766
Web site: www.kimberly-
clark.com

KitchenAid

Sparks Administration Center
701 Main Street
St. Joseph, MI 49085
616-923-4600
Toll free: 1-800-422-1230
Web site: www.kitchenaid.com

Kohler

444 Highland Drive, Mail Stop
101, Kohler, WI 53044
920-457-4441
Fax: 920-459-1611

Kraft Foods

Consumer Response Center
1 Kraft Court
Glenview, IL 60025
Toll free: 1-800-323-0768
Fax: 847-646-7853
Web site: www.kraftfoods.com

Kroger

1014 Vine Street
Cincinnati, OH 45202
513-762-1589
Toll free: 1-800-632-6900

Krystal Company

One Union Square
Chattanooga, TN 37402
453-757-1550
615-757-1550

L

L'eggs Products

5660 University Parkway
Winston-Salem, NC 27105
336-519-3241
336-519-3342
Toll free: 1-800-234-5909

L'Oreal Cosmetics

P.O. Box 98
Westfield, NJ 07091-9987
Toll free: 1-800-332-2036
Fax: 732-499-2599

L.L. Bean

Casco Street
Freeport, ME 04033-0001
207-865-4761
Toll free: 1-800-341-4341
TDD toll free: 1-800-545-0090
E-mail: llbean@llbean.com
Web site: www.llbean.com

LA Gear

2850 Ocean Park Blvd.
Santa Monica, CA 90405
310-452-4327
Toll free: 1-800-786-7800

La-Z-Boy Chair

1284 North Telegraph Road
Monroe, MI 48162-3309
734-242-1444

Land O'Lakes

P.O. Box 64101
St. Paul, MN 55164-0101
612-481-2128
Toll free: 1-800-328-4155
Fax: 612-481-2959
Web site: www.landolakes.com

Lands' End

Two Land's End Lane
Dodgeville, WI 53595
608-935-9341
Toll free: 1-800-356-4444
Fax: 608-935-6254
TDD/TTY toll free:
1-800-541-3459
E-mail: myorder@landsend.com
Web site: www.landsend.com

Lane Furniture

701 Fifth Street
P.O. Box 151
Altavista, VA 24517
804-369-5641
Fax: 804-369-3677

Lee Apparel

9001 West 67th Street
Merriam, KS 66202
913-384-4000

Leichtung Workshops

5604 Alameda Place NE
Albuquerque, NM 87113
216-831-6191
Toll free: 1-800-321-6840
Fax: 505-821-7331

Lennox Industries

P.O. Box 799900
Dallas, TX 75379-9900
972-497-5000
Fax: 972-497-5299
Web site: www.davelennox.com

Lever Brothers Co.

920 Sylvan Avenue
Englewood Cliffs, NJ 07632
Toll free: 1-800-598-1223

Levi Strauss & Co.

1155 Battery Street
San Francisco, CA 94111
Toll free: 1-800-USA-LEVI
E-mail: www.levi.com

Levolor Home Fashion

4110 Premier Drive
High Point, NC 27265
910-812-8181
Toll free: 1-800-LEVOLOR

Lexmark International

740 New Circle Road
Bldg. 004-2
Lexington, KY 40550
606-232-3000
Fax: 606-232-2873
Web site: www.lexmark.com

Liberty Mutual Insurance

175 Berkeley Street
Boston, MA 02117-0140
617-357-9500
Fax: 617-574-6688
Toll free:
1-800-344-0197 ext. 41015
E-mail:
msmail.corporat@tsod.lmig.com
Web site:
www.libertymutual.com

Lillian Vernon

2600 International Parkway
Virginia Beach, VA 23452
757-430-1500
Toll free: 1-800-285-5555
Fax: 757-430-1010
TDD/TTY toll free:
1-800-285-5536
E-mail: LVCcustsrv@aol.com
Web site: www.lillianvernon.com

The Limited

Three Limited Parkway
Columbus, OH 43230
614-479-7000

Logitech

6505 Kaiser Drive
Freemont, CA 94555
510-795-6100
Toll free: 1-800-231-7717
Fax: 510-792-8901
Web site: www.logitech.com

Long John Silver's

315 South Broadway
P.O. Box 11988
Lexington, KY 40579-1988
606-388-6000
Web site: www.ljsilvers.com

Los Angeles Times

Times Mirror Square
Los Angeles, CA 90053
213-237-5000

Lotus Development

55 Cambridge Parkway
Cambridge, MA 02142
617-577-8500
Toll free: 1-800-346-3508
Web site: www.lotus.com

Lucky Stores

P.O. Box 5008
San Leandro, CA 94577
510-678-5444
Fax: 510-678-5410
E-mail: DECKER.J@amstr.com

M

M&M/Mars

High Street
Hackettstown, NJ 07840
908-852-1000

MAACO
381 Brooks Road
King of Prussia, PA 19406
610-337-6155
Toll free: 1-800-523-1180
Toll free: 1-800-521-6282
Fax: 610-337-6145

Macromedia
600 Townsend Street
San Francisco, CA 94103
415-252-2000
Toll free: 1-800-470-7211
Fax: 415-703-0924
Web site: www.macromedia.com

Macy's
151 West 34th Street
New York, NY 10001
212-695-4400
Toll free: 1-800-526-1202
Web site: www.macys.com

Marine Midland Bank, N.A.
One Marine Midland Center
Buffalo, NY 14203
716-841-1000
Fax: 716-841-2547

Marriott
One Marriott Drive
Washington, DC 20058
Toll free: 1-800-535-4028
Fax: 402-390-1698
Web site: www.marriott.com

Massachusetts Mutual Insurance
1295 State Street
Springfield, MA 01111
413-788-8411

MasterCard International
P.O. Box 28468-0968
St. Louis, MO 63146-0968
Toll free: 1-800-826-2181
Fax: 314-542-3724
Web site: www.mastercard.com

Matsushita
1 Panasonic Way
Secaucus, NJ 07094
201-348-7000
Toll free: 1-800-211-7262

Mattel Toys
333 Continental Blvd.
El Segundo, CA 90245-5012
310-252-2000
Toll free: 1-800-524-TOYS
(8697)
Fax: 310-252-4190
E-mail: carpenterg@mattel.com

Maxicare Health Plans
1149 South Broadway
Los Angeles, CA 90015
213-742-0900
Toll free: 1-800-234-6294
Fax: 213-365-3499
Web site: www.maxicare.com

Maxis
2121 North California Blvd., #600
Walnut Creek, CA 94596
510-933-5630
Toll free: 1-800-245-4525
Fax: 510-927-3736
Web site: www.maxis.com

May Department Stores Co.
611 Olive Street
St. Louis, MO 63101
314-342-6300
Fax: 314-342-3038
Web site:
www.maycompany.com

Maybelline
P.O. Box 1010
Clark, NJ 07066-1010
Toll free: 1-800-944-0730
Fax: 732-499-2599

Mayflower Transit
P.O. Box 26150
Fenton, MO 63026-1350
314 326-3100
Toll free: 1-800-428-1234

Maytag Appliance Sales Company
240 Edwards Street
Cleveland, TN 37311
Toll free: 1-800-688-9900
TDD toll free: 1-800-688-2080
Web site: www.maytag.com

McCormick & Co.
211 Schilling Circle
Hunt Valley, MD 21031
410-527-8753
Toll free: 1-800-632-5847
Fax: 410-527-6005
Web site: www.mccormick.com

Mazda
P.O. Box 19734
Irvine, CA 92713-9734
Toll free: 1-800-222-5500
Web site: www.mazdausa.com

McCrory Stores
2955 East Market Street
York, PA 17402
717-757-8181

McDonald's
Kroc Drive
Oak Brook, IL 60523
630-623-6198
Web site: www.McDonalds.com

McGraw-Hill
1221 Avenue of the Americas
New York, NY 10020
Toll free: 1-800-262-4729
Fax: 614-759-3641
Web site: www.books.mcgraw-hill.com

MCI Communications
1200 South Hayes Street
11th Floor
Arlington, VA 22202
Toll free: 1-800-677-6580
Web site: www.mci.com

Meineke Discount Muffler
P.O. Box 32401
Charlotte, NC 28232
704-377-3070
Toll free: 1-800-447-3070
Fax: 704-377-1490

Mellon Bank
One Mellon Bank Center, Room 5135
Pittsburgh, PA 15258-0001
412-234-8552
Fax: 412-236-1818

Mentholatum Co.
707 Sterling Drive
Orchard Park, NY 14127
716-882-7660

Mercedes Benz
Customer Assistance Center
1 Glenview Road
Montvale, NJ 07645
Toll free: 1-800-222-0100
Toll free: 1-800-367-6372 (800-FOR-MERC)

Merrill Lynch, Pierce, Fenner & Smith
P.O. Box 9084
Princeton, NJ 08543-9084
609-282-6920

Mervyn's

22301 Industrial Blvd., M02Q
Hayward, CA 94541
510-727-5208
Fax: 510-727-5027

Metropolitan Life Insurance

One Madison Avenue,
Area 12-A
New York, NY 10010-3690
212-578-2211
Fax: 212-685-8042
Web site: www.metlife.com

Michelin North America

P.O. Box 19001
Greenville, SC 29602
Toll free: 1-800-847-3435
Web site: www.michelin.com

Microsoft

One Microsoft Way
Redmond, WA 98052-6399
425-882-8080
Web site: www.microsoft.com

Midas International

225 North Michigan Avenue
Chicago, IL 60601
312-565-7500
Toll free: 1-800-621-8545
Fax: 312-565-7822
TDD/TTY toll free:
1-800-SAY-HEAR (729-4327)

Miles Kimball Co

41 West 8th Avenue
Oshkosh, WI 54906-0002
Fax: 920-231-6942
TDD: 920-231-5506

Milton Bradley Co.

443 Shaker Road
East Long Meadow, MA 01028
413-525-6411, ext. 2288
Fax: 413-525-1767
Web site: www.scrabble.com

Minolta

101 Williams Drive
Ramsey, NJ 07446
201-825-4000
Fax: 201-825-0282

Minwax/Sherwin Williams

10 Mountain View Road
Upper Saddle River, NJ 07458
Toll free: 1-800-526-0495
Fax: 201-818-7605
Web site: www.minwax.com

Mitsubishi Cars

6400 West Katella Avenue
Cypress, CA 90630-0064
Toll free: 1-800-222-0037
Toll free: 1-800-426-7038 (credit
information)
Toll free:
1-800-55MITSU (800-556-4878)

Mitsubishi Electronics

6100 Atlantic Blvd.
P.O. Box 5025
Norcross, GA 30071-1305
Toll free: 1-800-332-2119
Fax: 770-734-5486
Web site: www.mitsubishi.com

Mobil Oil

3225 Gallows Road
Fairfax, VA 22037
Toll free: 1-800-662-4592

Monsanto Co.

800 North Lindbergh Blvd.
St. Louis, MO 63167
314-694-1000
Web site: www.monsanto.com

Montgomery Ward

535 West Chicago Avenue
Chicago, IL 60610
312-467-2000
Toll free: 1-800-695-3553
Fax: 312-467-2175

Morgan Stanley, Dean Witter, Discover & Co.

2 World Trade Center,
66th Floor
New York, NY 10048
Toll free: 1-800-733-2307

Morton Salt

100 North Riverside Plaza
Chicago, IL 60606
312-807-2693
Fax: 312-807-2899
Web site: www.morton.com

Motorola

1303 East Algonquin Road
Schaumburg, IL 60196
847-576-2108
Fax: 847-576-7653
TDD: 847-538-7116
Web site: www.mot.com

Motts

P.O. Box 3800
Stamford, CT 06905
203-968-7500
Toll free: 1-800-426-4891
Web site: www.motts.com

Mutual Life Insurance of New York

1740 Broadway
New York, NY 10019
212-708-2000
Toll free: 1-800-487-6669
Web site: www.mony.com

Mutual of Omaha Insurance

Mutual of Omaha Plaza
Omaha, NE 68175
402-342-7600
Fax: 402-351-2194
Web site:
www.mutualofomaha.com

N

Nabisco Foods Group

100 DeForest Avenue
East Hanover, NJ 07936
973-503-2617
Toll free: 1-800-NABISCO
Fax: 973-503-2202
Web site: www.nabisco.com

Nationwide Insurance Enterprises

One Nationwide Plaza, 1-22-01
Columbus, OH 43215-2220
614-249-6985
Fax: 614-249-5544

NBC

30 Rockefeller Plaza
New York, NY 10112
212-664-2333

NEC Technologies

1250 Arlington Heights Road
Itasca, IL 60143
630-467-5000
Toll free: 1-800-388-8888
Fax: 630-467-5010

Neiman-Marcus

P.O. Box 729080
Dallas, TX 75372
214-761-2660
Toll free: 1-800-685-6695
Fax: 214-761-2650
Web site:
www.neimanmarcus.com

Nestle

P.O. Box 96383
Phoenix, AZ 85093
818-549-5998
Toll free: 1-800-225-2270
Fax: 818-549-6330

Neutrogena

5760 West 96th Street
Los Angeles, CA 90045
310-642-1150
Toll free: 1-800-421-6857
Fax: 310-337-5564

Nevada Bell

645 East Plumb Lane
Reno, NV 89520
702-333-4339
Fax: 702-333-2364
TDD toll free: 1-800-356-4040

New York Life Insurance Co.

51 Madison Avenue
New York, NY 10010
212-576-5081 ext. 8181
Fax: 212-447-4180

New York Magazine

444 Madison Avenue
New York, NY 10022
212-508-0700

New York Times Co

229 West 43rd Street
New York, NY 10036
212-556-7171

Newsweek

P.O. Box 59967
Boulder, CO 80322
Toll free: 1-800-631-1040
Fax: 201-335-5971

Nexxus Products

P.O. Box 1274
Santa Barbara, CA 93116-9976
805-968-6900
Toll free: 1-800-444-6399
Fax: 805-968-6540
Web site:
www.nexxusproducts.com

Niagara Mohawk Power

Dey's Centennial Plaza
401 South Salina Street
Syracuse, NY 13202
315-460-7015
Fax: 315-460-7009

Nike

Nike/World Campus
1 Bowerman Drive
Beaverton, OR 97005-6453
503-671-6453
Toll free: 1-800-344-6453
E-mail: www.nike.com

Nikon

19601 Hamilton Avenue
Torrance, CA 90502
310-523-5250
Toll free: 1-800-645-6678
Fax: 310-523-9852
Web site: www.nikonusa.com

Nintendo of America

4820 150th Avenue N.E.
P.O. Box 957 (98073)
Redmond, WA 98052
425-885-7529
Toll free: 1-800-255-3700
TDD toll free: 1-800-422-4281
E-mail: nintendo@nintendo.com
Web site: www.nintendo.com

Nissan

P.O. Box 191
Gardena, CA 90248-0191
Toll free: 1-800-647-7261
Fax: 310-771-2025

Norelco

1010 Washington Blvd.
P.O. Box 120015
Stamford, CT 06912-0015
Toll free: 1-800-243-7884
Fax: 203-975-1812

Northwest Airlines

C6590
5101 Northwest Drive
St. Paul, MN 55111-3034
612-726-2046
Toll free: 1-800-225-2525
Web site: www.nwa.com

Northwestern Mutual Life

720 East Wisconsin Avenue
Milwaukee, WI 53202
414-299-7179
Fax: 414-299-2463
Web site:
www.northwesternmutual.com

Norwegian Cruise Line

7665 Corporate Center Drive
Miami, FL 33126
305-436-4000
Toll free: 1-800-327-7030
Fax: 305-436-4108
Web site: www.ncl.com

Novell

1555 North Technology Way
Orem, UT 84097
Toll free: 1-800-638-9273
Fax: 801-228-5176

Nu Tone

Madison and Redbank Roads
Cincinnati, OH 45227
513-527-5231
Fax: 513-527-5122

NutraSweet/Equal Co.

P.O. Box 2986
Chicago, IL 60654-0986
Toll free:
1-800-321-7254 (NutraSweet)
Toll free: 1-800-323-5316
(Equal)
Web site: www.equal.com or
www.nutrasweet.com

Nutri/System Inc.

410 Horsham Road
Horsham, PA 10944
215-698-2799
Fax: 215-442-0299

O

Ocean Spray Cranberries

One Ocean Spray Drive
Lakeville/Middleboro, MA 02349
508-946-7407
Toll free: 1-800-662-3263
Fax: 508-947-9791

Okidata

Toll free: 1-800-OKIDATA
(654-3282)

Oldsmobile

P.O. Box 436006
Lansing, MI 48343-6006
Toll free: 1-800-442-6537
TDD toll free: 1-800-TDD-OLDS
Web site: www.oldsmobile.com

Olympus America

2 Corporate Center Drive
Melville, NY 11747
516-844-5000
Toll free: 1-800-622-6372
Fax: 516-844-5262

Oneida, Ltd.

The Telemarketing Center
Sherrill, NY 13461
315-361-3000
Toll free: 1-800-877-6667
Fax: 315-361-3475

Ore-Ida Foods

P.O. Box 10
Boise, ID 83707
Toll free: 1-800-892-2401
Web site: www.oreida.com

Orkin

2170 Piedmont Road, N.E.
Atlanta, GA 30324
404-329-7400
Toll free: 1-800-346-7546
Fax: 404-633-2315

Ortho, Roundup and Greensweep

P.O. Box 5006
San Ramon, CA 94583-0906
Toll free: 1-800-225-2883
Fax: 510-355-3535
Web site: www.ortho.com

Owens Corning

One Owens Corning Parkway
Toledo, OH 43659-0001
419-248-8000
Web site:
www.owenscorning.com

P

Pacific Bell

140 New Montgomery Street
San Francisco, CA 94015
Toll free in CA: 1-800-791-6661
Toll free: 1-800-697-6500

Packard Bell

8285 West 3500 South
Magna, UT 84044
801-579-1552
Toll free: 1-800-227-3360
Fax: 708-808-4468
Web site: www.packardbell.com

PaineWebber Inc.

1000 Harbor Blvd., 8th Floor
Weehawken, NJ 07087
201-902-4936
Toll free: 1-800-354-9103
Fax: 201-902-5795

Pathmark Stores

301 Blair Road
Woodbridge, NJ 07095
732-356-6091
Fax: 732-499-3072

Pennzoil

P.O. Box 2967
Houston, TX 77252-2967
713-546-4000
Toll free: 1-800-990-9811
Fax: 713-546-6639

Pepperidge Farm

595 Westport Avenue
Norwalk, CT 06851
203-846-7276
Fax: 203-846-7278

Pepsi-Cola

1 Pepsi Way
Somers, NY 10589-2201
Toll free: 1-800-433-2652
Fax: 914-767-6177
Web site: www.pepsico.com

Perdue Farms

P.O. Box 1537
Salisbury, MD 21802
410-543-3000
Toll free: 1-800-473-7383
Web site: www.perdue.com

Perrier

777 West Putnam Avenue
Greenwich, CT 06830
203-531-4100
Fax: 203-863-0256

Peugeot

150 Clove Road
Little Falls, NJ 07424
973-812-4444
Toll free: 1-800-345-5549
Web site: www.peugeot.com

Pfizer First Connect

235 East 42nd Street
New York, NY 10017
Toll free: 1-888-879-FIRST
Fax: 212-573-7851

Pharmacia and UpJohn

7000 Portage Road
Kalamazoo, MI 49001
Toll free: 1-800-253-8600
Web site: www.pnu.com

Philip Morris USA

120 Park Avenue
New York, NY 10017
212-880-5000
Toll free: 1-800-343-0975

Philips Lighting Co.

200 Franklin Square Drive
P.O. Box 6800
Somerset, NJ 08875-6800
732-563-3081

Phillips Petroleum Co.

16 Phillips Building
Bartlesville, OK 74004
918-661-6600
Fax: 918-662-2075

Phillips-Van Heusen

1001 Frontier Road, Suite 100
Bridgewater, NJ 08807
908-685-0050
Fax: 908-704-8045

Pillsbury Company

MS 2866
200 South 6th Street
Minneapolis, MN 55402
612-330-4966
Toll free: 1-800-325-7130
Fax: 612-330-4875
Web site: www.pillsbury.com

Pioneer Electronics

P.O. Box 1760
Long Beach, CA 90810
310-952-2561
Toll free: 1-800-421-1404
Fax: 301-952-2821
Web site:
www.pioneerelectronics.com

Pirelli Tire Corporation

500 Sargent Drive
New Haven, CT 06511
203-784-2200
Fax: 203-784-2408

Playskool

P.O. Box 200
Pawtucket, RI 02862-0200
401-431-8697
Toll free: 1-800-752-9755
Fax: 401-431-8082
Web site: www.hasbro.com

Playtex Apparel

P.O. Box 631
MS 1526
Dover, DE 19903-0631
302-674-6000
Toll free: 1-800-537-9955
Fax: 302-674-6022

Playtex Products

215 College Road
P.O. Box 728
Paramus, NJ 07652
201-265-8000, ext. 3376
Toll free: 1-800-624-0825
Fax: 201-265-0630

Polaroid

201 Burlington Road
Bedford, MA 01730
Toll free outside MA:
1-800-343-5000
Fax: 781-386-5605
Web site: www.polaroid.com

Polo/Ralph Lauren

4100 Beachwood Drive
Greensboro, NC 27410
Toll free: 1-800-775-7656
Fax: 910-632-9097

Pontiac

General Motors Corp.
Mail Code 483-631-730
P.O. Box 436008
Pontiac, MI 48343-6008
Toll free: 1-800-762-2737
TDD toll free: 1-800-TDD-PONT
Web site: www.pontiac.com

Porsche

100 West Liberty Street
P.O. Box 30911
Reno, NV 89520-3911
702-348-3000
Toll free: 1-800-545-8039
Web site: www.porsche.com

Procter & Gamble Co.

P.O. Box 599
Cincinnati, OH 45201-0599
513-945-8787
(Toll free number on label)
Web site: www.pg.com

Prudential Insurance

751 Broad Street, 24th floor
Newark, NJ 07102
201-802-6000
Toll free: 1-800-837-3645
Fax: 201-622-4729

Prudential Property

23 Main Street
P.O. Box 500
Holmdel, NJ 07733
908-946-6000
Toll free: 1-800-437-5556
Fax: 908-946-6245

Prudential Securities

One New York Plaza
New York, NY 10292
Toll free: 1-800-367-8701
Fax: 212-778-2899

Publishers Clearing House

382 Channel Drive
Port Washington, NY 11050
516-883-5432
Toll free: 1-800-645-9242
Fax: 1-800-453-0272
TDD toll free: 1-800-248-8670

Q

Quaker Oats Co.

P.O. Box 049003
Chicago, IL 60604-9003
Toll-free number on label
Web site: www.quakeroats.com

Quaker State

225 E. John Carpenter Freeway
16th Floor
Irving, TX 75062
972-868-0400
Toll free: 1-800-759-2525
Fax: 972-868-0493
E-mail: Blum@quakerstate.com
Web site: www.quakerstate.com

Quantum

525 SycamoreStreet
Milpitas, CA 95035
Toll free: 1-800-826-8022

R

Radius

215 Moffett Park Drive
Sunnyvale, CA 94089
408-541-5700

Ralston Purina

Checkerboard Square
St. Louis, MO 63164
Toll free: 1-800-778-7462
Fax: 314-982-4580
Web site: www.purina.com

Readers Digest Association

Pleasantville, NY 10570-7000
Toll free: 1-800-431-1246
Fax: 914-238-4559
TDD toll free: 1-800-735-4327

Remington Arms

870 Remington Drive
P.O. Box 700
Madison, NC 27025-0700
Toll free: 1-800-243-9700
Fax: 910-548-7801

Remington Products Co.

60 Main Street
Bridgeport, CT 06004
203-367-4400
Toll free: 1-800-736-4648
Web site: www.remington-products.com

Revlon

P.O. Box 6113
Oxford, NC 27565
Toll free: 1-800-473-8566
Fax: 919-603-2953
Web site: www.revlon.com

Reynolds Metals

6603 West Broad Street
Richmond, VA 23230
Toll free: 1-800-433-2244
Fax: 804-281-2041
Web site: www.rmc.com/wrap

Rodale Press

33 East Minor Street
Emmaus, PA 18098
Toll free: 1-800-848-4735
Fax: 610-967-8964

Rolex Watch

665 Fifth Avenue
5th Floor
New York, NY 10022
212-758-7700
Fax: 212-980-2166

Roto-Rooter

300 Ashworth Road
West Des Moines, IA 50265
515-223-1343
Toll free: 1-800-575-7737
Fax: 515-223-4420
E-mail: rrcwdm@aol.com

Royal Silk

800 31st Street
Union City, NJ 07087
Toll free: 1-800-962-6262

Rubbermaid

1147 Akron Road
Wooster, OH 44691-0800
330-264-6464, ext. 2619

Ryder Truck Rental

P.O. Box 020816
Miami, FL 33102-0816
Toll free: 1-800-327-7777
Fax: 305-593-4463

S

S.C. Johnson and Sons

1525 Howe Street
Racine, WI 53403
414-260-2000
Toll free: 1-800-558-5252
Fax: 414-260-4805
Web site:
www.scjohnsonwax.com

Saab

4405-A International Bend
Norcross, GA 30093
770-279-0100
Toll free: 1-800-955-9007
Web site: www.saabusa.com

Safeway

5918 Stoneridge Mall Road
Pleasanton, CA 94588-3229
510-467-3000
Web site: www.safeway.com

Samsonite Corporation

Toll free: 1-800-262-8282
(Samsonite, Lark, American
Tourister)

Samsung Electronics

1 Samsung Place
Ledgewood, NJ 07852
973-347-8004
Toll free: 1-800-446-0262

Sanyo Fisher Co.

1411 West 190th St., #700
Gardena, CA 90248
310-769-5832
Toll free: 1-800-421-5013
Fax: 310-243-6566
E-mail:
custreld@sanyoservice.com
Web site: www.sanyoservice.com

Sara Lee

Three First National Plaza
70 West Madison Street
Chicago, IL 60602-4260
312-726-2600
Toll free: 1-800-621-5235
Fax: 312-726-3712

Saturn

100 Saturn Parkway
Spring Hill, TN 37174
Toll free: 1-800-553-6000
TDD toll free: 1-800-TDD-6000
Web site: www.saturn.com

Schering-Plough HealthCare Products

3030 Jackson Avenue
Memphis, TN 38151-0001
901-320-2998
Toll free: 1-800-842-4090
Fax: 901-320-2954

Scotts Miracle-Gro

800 Port Washington Blvd.
Port Washington, NY 11050
516-883-6550
Toll free: 1-800-645-8166
Fax: 516-883-6563
Web site: www.miracle-gro.com

Scudder Kemper Investments

345 Park Avenue
New York, NY 10154
617-295-1200
Toll free: 1-800-225-2470

Seagate Technology

920 Disc Drive
Scotts Valley, CA 95066
650-438-1211
650-936-1200
Fax: 408-429-6356
Web site: www.seagate.com

Seagrams

800 3rd Avenue
New York, NY 10022
212-572-1282
Fax: 212-572-1264

Sealy Mattress
1228 Euclid Avenue, 10th Floor
Cleveland, OH 44115
440-891-8200
Fax: 216-522-1366

Sears
3333 Beverly Road
731-CR
Hoffman Estates, IL 60179
847-286-5188
Fax: 800-427-3049
Web site: www.sears.com

SEIKO
1111 MacArthur Blvd.
Mahwah, NJ 07430
201-529-5730
201-529-3316
Fax: 201-529-1548
E-mail:
custserv@scamahwah.com
Web site: www.seiko-corp.co.jp

Serta
325 Spring Lake Drive
Itasca, IL 60143
630-285-9300
Toll free: 1-800-426-0371
Fax: 630-285-9330
Web site: www.serta.com

Sharp Electronics
1300 Naperville Drive
Romeoville, IL 60446
Toll free: 1-800-237-4277
Web site: www.sharp-usa.com

The Sharper Image
650 Davis Street
San Francisco, CA 94111
Toll free: 1-800-344-5555
Fax: 415-391-1584
Web site:
www.sharperimage.com

Shell Oil
P.O. Box 2463, Dept. 210
Houston, TX 77252-2463
Toll free: 1-800-248-4257
Fax: 713-241-0581
Web site: www.shellus.com

Sherwin-Williams Co. Paint
101 Prospect Avenue, N.W.
Cleveland, OH 44115-1075
216-566-2151
Toll free: 1-800-4SHERWIN
(474-3794)
Fax: 216-566-1660

Shoney's
1717 Elm Hill Pike, Suite B3A
Nashville, TN 37210
615-391-5201
Toll free: 1-800-522-9200
Fax: 615-231-1604

Showtime Networks
1633 Broadway, 17th Floor
New York, NY 10019
212-708-1555
Fax: 212-708-1212

Simmons Co.
P.O. Box 2768
Norcross, GA 30091-2768
770-798-9660
Fax: 770-613-5539

Simon and Schuster
200 Old Tappan Road
Old Tappan, NJ 07675
201-767-5000
Fax: 201-767-4017

Singer Corporation
4500 Singer Road
Murfreesboro, TN 37129
Toll free: 1-800-877-7762
Web site:
www.singersewing.com

Slim-Fast Foods

West Tower, Suite 1400
777 South Flagler Drive
West Palm Beach, FL 33401
561-833-9920
Fax: 561-223-1248

Smith Barney

388 Greenwich Street,
20th Floor
New York, NY 10013
212-816-6000
Fax: 212-723-2184

Snapple Beverages

333 West Merrick Road
Valley Stream, NY 11580
Toll free: 1-800-Snapple (762-7753)

Sonesta International Hotels

200 Clarendon Street
Boston, MA 02116
617-421-5451
Toll free: 1-800-SONESTA
Fax: 617-927-7649
Web site: www.sonesta.com

Sony of America

1 Sony Drive
Park Ridge, NJ 07656
Toll free: 1-800-282-2848
E-mail: contact@sel.sony.com
Web site: www.sel.sony.com

Southland

P.O. Box 711
Dallas, TX 75221-0711
214-841-6585
Toll free: 1-800-255-0711
Fax: 214-828-7090
E-mail: jcamach@7-11.com
Web site: www.7-Eleven.com

Southwest Airlines

Love Field
P.O. Box 36647
Dallas, TX 75235-1647
214-792-4223
Fax: 214-792-5099
TDD toll free: 1-800-533-1305

Spalding /Top Flite

425 Meadow Street
P.O. Box 901
Chicopee, MA 01021-0901
413-536-1200
Toll free: 1-800-225-6601
Fax: 413-535-2673
Web site: www.topflite.com or
www.sports@spalding.com

Speigel

3500 Lacey Road
Downers Grove, IL 60515
630-986-8800
Toll free: 1-800-345-4500
Fax: 630-769-2062

Spencer Gifts

6826 Black Horse Pike
Egg Harbor Township, NJ 08234
609-645-3300
Toll free: 1-800-762-0419

Springmaid

787 7th Avenue
New York, NY 10019
212-903-2100
Toll free: 1-800-537-0115
Fax: 212-903-2115

Sprint

1603 LBJ Freeway, Suite 300
Dallas, TX 75324
972-405-6100
Toll free: 1-800-347-8988
Fax: 972-405-6114

Stanley Hardware

480 Myrtle Street
New Britain, CT 06050
203-225-5111
Toll free: 1-800-622-4393

State Farm

One State Farm Plaza
Bloomington, IL 61710
309-766-7870
Web site: www.statefarm.com

Stokley

1230 Corporate Center Drive
P.O. Box 248
Oconomowoc, WI 53066-0248
414-569-1800
Toll free: 1-800-872-1110
Fax: 414-569-3760

Stop & Shop Supermarket

P.O. Box 1942
Boston, MA 02105
617-770-6040
Toll free: 1-800-767-7772
Fax: 617-770-6033
Web site: www.virtual-valley.com/stopandshop

Subaru

P.O. Box 6000
Cherry Hill, NJ 08034-6000
Toll free: 1-800-782-2783
Web site: www.subaru.com

Sunbeam/Oster

P.O. Box 948389
Orlando, FL 32794-8389
Toll free: 1-800-597-5978
Fax: 800-478-6737
Web site: www.sunbeam.com

Suzuki

P.O. Box 1100
Brea, CA 92822-1100
714-996-7040, ext. 380
(motorcycles)
714-996-7040, ext. 396
(outboard)
Toll free: 1-800-934-0934
(automotive only)
Fax: 714-970-6005
Web site: www.suzuki.com

Swatch Watch USA

1817 William Penn Way
Lancaster, PA 17604
717-394-7161
Fax: 717-399-2211

Swiss Colony

1112 Seventh Avenue
Monroe, WI 53566
608-324-4000
Fax: 608-242-1001
E-mail:
102506.2422@compuserve.com
Web site: www.swisscolony.com

Symantec Corporation

10201 Torre Avenue
Cupertino, CA 95014
408-253-9600
Toll free: 1-800-441-7234
Fax: 541-984-8020
Web site: www.symantec.com

T

3M

3M Center
Building 225-3S-05
St. Paul, MN 55144-1000
612-737-6501
Toll free: 1-800-364-3577
(3M HELP)
Toll free: 1-800-713-6329 (Fax)
Fax: 612-737-7117
Web site: www.3m.com

Talbots

175 Beal Street
Hingham, MA 02043
781-749-7600
Toll free: 1-800-TALBOTS
Fax: 781-741-4136
TDD toll free: 1-800-624-9179

Tandy Corp./Radio Shack

600 One Tandy Center
Fort Worth, TX 76102
817-390-3240
Toll free: 1-800-843-7422
Fax: 817-390-3292
E-mail:
rs.customer.relations@tandy.com
Web site: www.tandy.com

Target Stores

33 South 6th Street
P.O. Box 1392
Minneapolis, MN 55440-1392
612-304-6000
Fax: 612-304-4996
TDD/TTY toll free:
1-800-347-5842
Web site: www.target.com

Teledyne Water Pik

1730 East Prospect Road
Fort Collins, CO 80553-0001
970-484-1352
Toll free: 1-800-525-2774
Fax: 970-221-8298
Web site: www.waterpik.com

Teleflora

11444 West Olympic, 4th Floor
Los Angeles, CA 90064
310-231-9199
Toll free: 1-800-421-2815
Fax: 1-800-232-3811

Tenneco

1275 King Street
Greenwich, CT 06831
203-863-1000
Fax: 203-862-1914
Web site: www.tenneco.com

Tetley

100 Commerce Drive
P.O. Box 856
Shelton, CT 06484-0856
203-929-9341
Toll free: 1-800-732-3027
Toll free: 1-800-732-0084
Fax: 203-926-0876

Texaco

330 Barker Cypress Road
Houston, TX 77094
281-754-1728
Toll free: 1-800-938-2267
Fax: 281-754-1702

Texas Instruments

P.O. Box 6118
Temple, TX 76503-6118
972-917-8324
Toll free: 1-800-842-2737
Fax: 972-917-0747
Web site: www.ti.com

Thompson Waterseal

10136 Magnolia Drive
P.O. Box 647
Olive Branch, MS 38654
601-890-3000
Fax: 601-890-3013
Toll free: 1-800-647-9365
Web site:
www.thompson.waterseal.com

Time Warner

75 Rockefeller Plaza
New York, NY 10019
212-484-8000
Web site: www.timewarner.com

Timex Corp.

P.O. Box 2740
Little Rock, AR 72203-2740
501-370-5781
Toll free: 1-800-448-4639
Fax: 501-370-5747
Web site: www.timex.com

Titleist

P.O. Box 965
Fairhaven, MA 02719
Toll free: 1-800-225-8500
Fax: 1-800-641-4301

T. J. Maxx

TJX Companies
770 Cochituate Road
Framingham, MA 01701
508-390-1000
Toll free: 1-800-926-6299

Toshiba

82 Totowa Road
Wayne, NJ 07470
201-628-1000
Toll free: 1-800-631-3811
E-mail: tacpsvc@aol.com

Toyota

Department A102
19001 South Western Avenue
Torrance, CA 90509-2991
Toll free: 1-800-331-4331
Fax: 310-618-7814
TDD toll free: 1-800-443-4999
Web site: www.toyota.com

Toys "R" Us

461 Farm Road
Paramus, NJ 07652
201-599-8090
Fax: 201-262-7800

Travelers Companies

One Tower Square 4GS
Hartford, CT 06183-9079
860-277-0111
860-277-4098
Fax: 203-954-3956
Web site: www.travelers.com/
complain/index.htm

True Value Hardware Stores

8600 West Bryn Mawr
Chicago, IL 60631-3505
773-695-5000

Tupperware

P.O. Box 2353
Orlando, FL 32802-2353
Toll free: 1-800-858-7221
Fax: 407-847-1897

Turtle Wax

5655 West 73rd Street
Chicago, IL 60638-6211
708-563-3600
Toll free: 1-800-323-9883
Fax: 708-563-4302

TV Guide
Four Radnor Corporate Center
Radnor, PA 19088
610-293-8500
Toll free: 1-800-866-1400
Fax: 610-687-6965

Tyson Foods
P.O. Box 2020
Springdale, AR 72765-2020
501-290-4714
Toll free: 1-800-233-6332
Fax: 501-290-7930
E-mail: barberw@tyson.com
Web site: www.tyson.com

TWA
1415 Olive Street
Suite 100
St. Louis, MO 63103
314-589-3600
Fax: 314-589-3626
TDD toll free: 1-800-421-8480

U

U-Haul International
P.O. Box 21502
Phoenix, AZ 85036-1502
602-263-6771
Toll free: 1-800-528-0463
Fax: 602-263-6984

Umax Technologies
3561 Gateway Blvd.
Freemont, CA 94538
Toll free: 1-800-468-8629

Uniroyal Tires
P.O. Box 19001
Greenville, SC 29602-9001
864-458-5000
Toll free: 1-800-521-9796
Fax: 864-458-6650
Web site: www.michelin.com

UNISYS Corp.
P.O. Box 500
Blue Bell, PA 19424-0001
215-986-4011
Toll free: 1-800-328-0440
Fax: 215-986-5669
Web site: www.unisys.com

United Airlines
P.O. Box 66100
Chicago, IL 60666
847-700-4000
Fax: 847-700-2214
Web site: www.ual.com

United Parcel Service
55 Glenlake Parkway
Atlanta, GA
770-828-4300
Fax: 404-828-6204
Web site: www.ups.com

United Van Lines
One United Drive
Fenton, MO 63026
314-326-3100
Toll free: 1-800-948-4885
Fax: 314-326-3111
Web site:
www.unitedvanlines.com

US Airways
P.O. Box 1502
Winston-Salem, NC 27102-1501
910-661-0061
Fax: 910-661-8031
TTY toll free: 1-800-245-2966
Web site: www.usairways.com

US WEST Communications
P.O. Box 428, Room 117
Cheyenne, WY 82003
Toll free: 1-800-255-6920
Toll free: 1-800-954-1211
TDD toll free: 1-800-955-5833
Web site: www.uswest.com/com

V

Viacom

1515 Broadway, 52nd Floor
New York, NY 10036
212-258-6346
Web site: www.viacom.com

Visa USA

P.O. Box 8999
San Francisco, CA 94128-8999
650-432-3200
Fax: 650-432-4153, 3074
TDD/TTY: 650-432-3200
Web site: www.visa.com

Volvo

P.O. Box 915
7 Volvo Drive, Building A
Rockleigh, NJ 07647-0915
Toll free: 1-800-458-1552
Fax: 201-767-4816
Web site: www.volvocars.com

Vons

P.O. Box 51338
Los Angeles, CA 90051
626-821-2525
Fax: 626-821-3654
Web site:
www.supermarkets.com

W

Wal-Mart Stores

702 S.W. Eighth Street
Bentonville, AR 72716-0117
501-273-4000
Toll free: 1-800-WAL-MART
Fax: 502-273-4894
E-mail: letters@wal-mart.com

Walgreen Co.

200 Wilmot Road
Deerfield, IL 60015
847-914-2500

Walter Drake

Drake Building
Colorado Springs, CO
80940-0001
719-596-3140
Toll free: 1-800-525-9291
Fax: 719-637-4984

Wamsutta Pacific/Springmaid

1285 Avenue of the Americas
34th Floor
New York, NY 10019
212-903-2000
Toll free: 1-800-537-0115
Fax: 803-286-2513

Wang Laboratories

600 Technology Park Drive
Billerca, MA 01821-4130
508-967-5000
Toll free: 1-800-639-9264
Fax: 508-967-0829

Warner-Lambert Co.

182 Tabor Road
Morris Plains, NJ 07950
973-540-2000
Toll free: 1-800-223-0182
TDD toll free: 1-800-343-7805
Web site:
www.warner-lambert.com

Weider Health and Fitness

21100 Erwin Street
Woodland Hills, CA 91367
818-884-6800
Fax: 818-704-5734

Weight Watchers International
175 Crossways Park West
Woodbury, NY 11797-2055
516-390-1478
516-390-1657
Toll free: 1-800-651-6000
Fax: 516-390-1632
Web site:
www.weight-watchers.com

Wells Fargo Bank
420 Montgomery Street,
12th Floor
San Francisco, CA 94104
415-396-3832
Toll free: 1-800-511-2265
TDD: 916-322-1700

Wendy's
P.O. Box 256
Dublin, OH 43017-0256
614-764-6800
Toll free: 1-800-443-7266
Fax: 614-764-6707
Web site: www.wendys.com

West Bend Company
400 Washington Street
West Bend, WI 53095
414-334-2311
Fax: 414-334-6800
Web site: www.westbend.com

Western Union
13022 Hollenberg Drive
Bridgeton, MO 63044
314-291-8000
Toll free: 1-800-634-1311
Fax: 314-291-5271
E-mail:
karen.walters@firstdatacorp.com
Web site:
www.firstdatacorp.com

Whirlpool Corp.
2303 Pipestone Road
Benton Harbor, MI 49022-2427
616-923-7700
Toll free: 1-800-253-1301
Fax: 616-923-7829
Web site: www.whirlpool.com

Whitehall-Robins Health Care
P.O. Box 26609
Richmond, VA 23261-6609
Toll free: 1-800-322-3129
Web site: healthfront.com

Williams-Sonoma
1000 Covington Cross Drive
Las Vegas, NV 89134
702-360-7000
Toll free: 1-800-541-1262
Fax: 702-360-7091

Winn Dixie Stores
Box B
Jacksonville, FL 32203
904-783-5000
Fax: 904-783-5294

Winnebago
P.O. Box 152
Forest City, IA 50436-0152
515-582-6939
Toll free: 1-800-537-1885
Fax: 515-582-6704
Web site:
www.winnebagoind.com

Wrigley
410 North Michigan Avenue
Chicago, IL 60611
312-644-2121
Fax: 312-644-0015
Web site: www.wrigley.com

Wrangler
P.O. Box 21488
Greensboro, NC 27420
336-332-3564
Fax: 336-332-3223

X

Xerox Corp.
100 Clinton Avenue South
Rochester, NY 14644
716-423-5090
1-800-832-6979
(1-800-TEAM XRX)
Fax: 716-423-5490
TDD/TTY toll free:
1-800-421-1220
Web site: www.xerox.com

Y

Yamaha Motor Corp.
6555 Katella Avenue
Cypress, CA 90630-5101
714-761-7439
Toll free: 1-800-962-7926
Fax: 714-761-7559
Web site:
www.yamaha-motor.com

Z

Zale Corp.
901 West Walnut Hill Lane
Irving, TX 75038-1003
972-580-5104
Fax: 972-580-5523
Web site: www.zales.com

Zenith Electronics
1000 Milwaukee Ave.
Glenview, IL 60025
847-391-8752
Toll free: 1-888-3 ZENITH
E-mail:
Customer.Service@zenith.com
Web site: www.zenith.com

Directory of Industry Associations

Companies that offer similar products and individuals practicing similar professions often join together to form an association. The primary purpose of these associations is to provide service to their members. Some, by no means all, have established dispute-resolution programs to help resolve problems between their member companies and consumers.

Such programs vary: Some simply help the parties work out their own voluntary solutions, while others offer more formal arbitration programs in which a decision is rendered by a third party. In arbitration, the decision may be binding on both parties, only on the business, or not binding on either party. It is reasonable to ask if a company with which you are having problems is a member of an association. Here are some major organizations:

Accountants

American Institute of Certified
Public Accountants
  Harborside Financial Center
  201 Plaza III
  Jersey City, NJ 07311-3881
  201-938-3175
  Fax: 201-938-3367
  E-mail:
  HFINKSTON@aicpa.org

Advertising, truth in

National Advertising Division
(NAD)
  A Division of the Council of
  Better Business Bureaus, Inc.
  845 Third Avenue, 17th Floor
  New York, NY 10022
  212-754-1320
  Fax: 212-832-1296
  *Handles consumer complaints
  about the truth and accuracy of
  national advertising.*

Apparel

American Apparel Manufacturers
Association
  2500 Wilson Blvd., Suite 301
  Arlington, VA 22201
  703-524-1864
  Toll free: 1-800-520-2262
  Fax: 703-522-6741

Attorneys

American Bar Association
  740 15th Street, NW
  Washington, DC 20005
  202-662-1680
  Fax: 202-662-1683
  E-mail: dispute@abanet.org
  Web site:
  www.abanet.org/dispute
  *They publish a directory of state
  and local alternative dispute
  resolution programs. Provides
  consumer information on
  request.*

Appliances, major

Major Appliance Consumer Action
Program
  20 North Wacker Drive,
  Suite 1231
  Chicago, IL 60606
  312-984-5858
  *Third-party dispute resolution
  program of the major appliance
  industry.*

Auto repair

National Institute for Automotive
Service Excellence (ASE)
  13505 Dulles Technology Drive,
  Suite 2
  Herndon, VA 20171
  703-713-3800
  Fax: 703-793-6544
  Web site: www.asecert.org
  E-mail: rwhite@asecert.org
  (Certifies more than 400,000
  auto repair professionals.)
  *ASE is an independent,
  national nonprofit organization
  founded in 1972 to help improve
  the quality of automotive
  service and repair through the
  voluntary testing and
  certification of automotive
  repair professionals. More than
  424,000 ASE-certified
  technicians work in dealerships,
  independent repair shops,
  service stations, auto parts
  stores, fleets and schools. ASE
  publishes several consumer
  publications about auto
  maintenance and repair.*

Automobile manufacturers

American Automobile
Manufacturers Association
  1401 H Street, NW
  Washington, DC 20005
  202-326-5500
  Fax: 202-326-5546

Banks

American Bankers Association
   1120 Connecticut Ave., NW
   Washington, DC 20036
   202-663-5000
   Fax: 202-663-7578
   Web site: www.aba.com

Boats

Boat Owners Association
of the United States
   880 South Pickett Street
   Alexandria, VA 22304-0730
   703-823-9550
   Web site: www.boat/us.com
   Mediator in disputes between boat owners and the marine industry.

Career schools

Accrediting Council for
Independent Schools and
Colleges
   750 First Street, NE,
   Suite 980
   Washington, DC 20002
   202-336-6780
   Fax: 202-842-2593
   E-mail: acics@acics.org

Career College Association
   750 First Street, NE,
   Suite 900
   Washington, DC 20002
   202-336-6700
   Fax: 202-336-6828
   E-mail: briann@career.org

Carpets and rugs

Carpet and Rug Institute
   Box 2048
   Dalton, GA 30722
   706-278-3176
   Toll free: 1-800-882-8846
   Fax: 706-278-8835
   Web site: www.carpet-rug.com

Cemeteries

Cemetery Consumer Service
Council
   P.O. Box 2028
   Reston, VA 20195-0028
   703-391-8407
   Fax: 703-391-8416

Collection agencies

American Collectors
Association
   P.O. Box 39106
   Minneapolis, MN 55439-0106
   612-926-6547
   Fax: 612-926-1624
   Web site: www.collector.com

Commodity trading

National Futures Association
(NFA)
   200 West Madison Street
   Chicago, IL 60606-3447
   312-781-1370
   Toll free: 1-800-621-3570
   (outside IL)
   Fax: 312-781-1467
   E-mail:
   loatney@nfa.futures
   Web site:
   www.nfa.futures.org

Consumer electronics

Consumer Electronics
Manufactures Association
(CEMA)
   Attn: Consumer Affairs
   2500 Wilson Blvd.
   Arlington, VA 22201-3834
   703-907-7600
   Fax: 703-907-7601
   Web site: www.cemacity.org

Credit unions

Credit Union National
Association
  5710 Mineral Point Road
  Madison, WI 53705
  608-231-4000
  Toll free: 1-800-356-9655
  Web site: www.cuna.org
  (for consumer information and
  information about credit unions)

Door-to-door and in-home selling

Direct Selling Association (DSA)
  1666 K Street, NW, Suite 1010
  Washington, DC 20006-2387
  202-293-5760
  Fax: 202-463-4569
  E-mail: info@dsa.org
  Web site: www.dsa.org

Employment agencies

National Association of
Personnel Services
  3133 Mt. Vernon Avenue
  Alexandria, VA 22305
  703-684-0180
  Fax: 703-684-0071
  Web site: www.napsweb.org

Fabrics for clothing, furniture

American Textile Manufacturers
Institute
  1130 Connecticut Avenue, NW
  Suite 1200
  Washington, DC 20006
  202-862-0550
  Web site: www.atmi.org

Financial planners

Certified Financial Planner
Board of Standards
  1700 Broadway, Suite 2100
  Denver, Colorado 80290-2101
  303-830-7500
  Fax: 303-860-7388
  Web site: www.CFP-Board.org

Funeral directors

National Association of
Funeral Directors
  P.O. Box 27641
  Milwaukee, WI 53227
  1-800-662-7666
  *Third-party dispute resolution
  program for complaints
  regarding funeral homes.*

Health care facilities

American Health Care
Association
  1201 L Street, NW
  Washington, DC 20005-4014
  202-842-4444
  Toll free: 1-800-321-0343
  (purchase publications only)
  Fax: 202-842-3860

Hearing professionals

Better Hearing Institute (BHI)
  P.O. Box 1840
  Washington, DC 20013
  703-642-0580
  Toll free: 1-800-EAR-WELL
  Fax: 703-750-9302
  Voice/TDD: 1-888-HEAR-HELP
  E-mail:
  MAIL@betterhearing.org
  Web site:
  www.betterhearing.org

Hearing aids

Hearing Industries Association
515 King Street, Suite 420
Alexandria, VA 22314
703-684-5744
Fax: 703-684-6048
E-mail: hiallears@aol.com

Home builders

National Association of Home Builders
1201 15th Street, NW
Washington, DC 20005
202-822-0409
Toll free: 1-800-368-5242

Home study courses

Distance Education and Training Council
1601 18th Street NW
Washington, DC 20009
202-234-5100
E-mail: detc@detc.org

Insurance, all kinds

National Association of Professional Insurance Agents
400 North Washington Street
Alexandria, VA 22314
703-836-9340
E-mail: TEBE@PIANET.ORG
Web site: www.PIANET.com

Insurance, life

American Council of Life Insurance
1001 Pennsylvania Avenue, NW
Suite 500 South
Washington, DC 20004-2599
202-624-2000
Toll free: 1-800-942-4242
Fax: 202-624-2319

Mail order advertising

Mail Order Action Line
Direct Marketing Association
1111 19th Street, NW
Suite 1100
Washington, DC 20036
202-955-5030
E-mail:
consumer@the-dma.org
Web site: www.the-dma.org
Handles written complaints against a DMA member or nonmember.

Mail Preference Service
P.O. Box 9008
Farmingdale, NY 11735-9008
Handles written requests for name removal from most national advertising mailing lists.

Monuments and tombstones

Monument Builders of North America
3158 South River Road
Suite 224
Des Plaines, IL 60018
847-803-8800
Fax: 847-803-8823

Mortgages

Mortgage Bankers Association of America
1125 15th Street, NW,
7th Floor
Washington, DC 20005
202-861-6565

Moving and storage

American Moving and Storage
Association
  1611 Duke Street
  Alexandria, VA 22314-3482
  703-683-7410
  Fax: 703-683-7527
  Web site: www.amconf.org
*Sponsors the Household Goods
Dispute Settlement Program,
an arbitration service for
disputed loss and damage claims
on interstate moves that is
administered by the American
Arbitration Association.*

Photo finishing

Photo Marketing Association
  3000 Picture Place
  Jackson, MI 49201
  517-788-8100
  Fax: 517-788-8371
  Web site: www.pmai.org

Realtors

National Association of
Realtors
  430 North Michigan Avenue
  Chicago, IL 60601
  312-329-8361
  Web site: www.realtor.com

Savings and loan

America's Community Bankers
(ACB)
  900 19th Street, NW,
  Suite 400
  Washington, DC 20006
  202-857-3103
  Fax: 202-296-8716
  E-mail: info@acbankers.org
  Web site: www.acbankers.org

Soap and detergent

The Soap and Detergent
Association
  475 Park Avenue South
  New York, NY 10016
  212-725-1262
  Fax: 212-213-0685
  Web site: www.sdahq.org

Stock brokers, Security dealers

National Association of Security
Dealers
  125 Broad Street, 36th Floor
  New York, NY 10004
  212-858-4400
  Fax: 212-858-4429
  Third-party dispute resolution
  for complaints about over-the-
  counter stocks and corporate
  bonds.

Telemarketing

Telephone Preference Service
  P.O. Box 9014
  Farmingdale, NY 11735-9014
  *Handles written requests for
  name and telephone number
  removal from most national
  telemarketing lists.*

Television advertising, Children

Children's Advertising Review
Unit, Council of Better Business
Bureaus, Inc.
  845 Third Avenue
  New York, NY 10022
  212-705-0124
  Fax: 212-308-4743
  Web site: www.bbb.org
  *Handles consumer complaints
  about truth and accuracy of
  advertising directed to children
  under 12 years of age.*

Tires

Tire Association of North America
  11921 Freedom Drive, Suite 550
  Reston, VA 20190
  703-736-8082
  Toll free: 1-800-876-8372

Tour operators

United States Tour Operators
Association (USTOA)
  342 Madison Avenue,
  Suite 1522
  New York, NY 10173
  212-599-6599
  Fax: 212-599-6744
  E-mail: USTOA@aol.com

Toys

Toy Manufacturers of America
  1115 Broadway, Suite 400
  New York, NY 10010
  212-675-1141
  Fax: 212-633-1429
  Web site: www.toy-tma.com

Travel agents

American Society of Travel
Agents
  1101 King Street, Suite 200
  Alexandria, VA 22314
  703-739-8739 (consumer hot
  line)
  Fax: 703-684-8319
  Web site: www.astanet.com

Index of Letters

Index